NH   23.95

D0627659

 Washtenaw Library for the Blind & Physically Disabled @ AADL

If you are only able to read large print, you may qualify for WLBPD @ AADL services, including receiving audio and large print books by mail at no charge.

For more information:

Email   • wlbpd@aadl.org
Phone   • (734) 327-4224
Website • wlbpd.aadl.org

APR 1 0 2006

WHISTLING LEAD

Eugene Cunningham

CHIVERS
THORNDIKE

Ypsilanti District Library
5577 Whittaker Road
Ypsilanti, MI 48197

This Large Print book is published by BBC Audiobooks Ltd, Bath, England and by Thorndike Press®, Waterville, Maine, USA.

Published in 2006 in the U.K. by arrangement with Golden West Literary Agency.

Published in 2006 in the U.S. by arrangement with Golden West Literary Agency.

U.K. Hardcover ISBN 1–4056–3547–9 (Chivers Large Print)
U.K. Softcover ISBN 1–4056–3548–7 (Camden Large Print)
U.S. Softcover ISBN 0–7862–8122–7 (British Favorites)

Copyright © 1936, by Eugene Cunningham.
Copyright © renewed 1964 by Mary Caroline Cunningham.

All rights reserved.

This is a work of fiction and all characters and events in the story are fictional, and any resemblance to real persons is purely coincidental.

The text of this Large Print edition is unabridged.
Other aspects of the book may vary from the original edition.

Set in 16 pt. New Times Roman.

Printed in Great Britain on acid-free paper.

British Library Cataloguing in Publication Data available

Library of Congress Cataloging-in-Publication Data

Cunningham, Eugene, 1896–1957.
    Whistling lead / by Eugene Cunningham.
       p.   cm.
    "Thorndike Press large print British favorites."—T.p. verso.
    ISBN 0–7862–8122–7 (lg. print : sc : alk. paper)
    1. Large type books. I. Title.
PS3505.U428W48 2005
813'.54—dc22   2005021524

1. *'I ride toward La Fe'*

Gavity watched the country ahead of him as Nubbins jogged along at an easy foxtrot. It was rolling land, arid, dotted with shiny clumps of greasewood, the feathery foliage of mesquite, spiky with cactus and ocatillo. Arroyos cut its vast width, watercourses that were dry, now, but which in the rainy days poured turgid yellow torrents into the Rio Grande miles below.

Somewhere ahead, but invisible as yet, was La Fe. And that was his goal. He shifted the enormous bulk which gave him the nickname of 'Big.' He worked the saddle-kinks out of his back. Nubbins was topping a rise, long legs flashing. Big Gavity settled again in the swellfork and fumbled in a shirt pocket for tobacco and brown papers. He began to sing:

'Come gather round me, cowboys,
I'll tell you-all a tale—
All about my troubles
On the old Chisholm Trail;
  Coma ti yi youpy,
  Youpy ya, youpy yaaaa!
  Coma ti yi youpy,
  Youpy yaaaaa!
Started up the trail
October twenty-third,

1

Left old Texas
With the 2U herd—'

From somewhere ahead, over the rise they breasted, the sound of shots came. Gavity turned his head a little and Nubbins, too, stared that way. At the walk—horse and rider seeming of one cautious mind—they came to the top of the ridge. Gavity pulled the black in and stared along a sandy trail that wound through yucca and greasewood toward the river.

The shots had ceased and there was nothing human to see, below. Gavity shook his tawny head and shrugged. A hunter, it might be. But whoever it was he had not made himself visible.

'Oh, foot in the stirrup,
Hand on the horn!
Best damned cowboy
Ever was born!
    Coma ti yi youpy,
    Youpy ya, youpy yaaaa!
    Coma ti yi youpy—'

Again he stopped the chant, to stare down the slope. For the fusillade of shots sounded again—almost as if someone objected to Gavity's excellent baritone. That whimsy amused Gavity and he grinned.

'But I hardly think it's correct,' he said to

Nubbins. 'You've known me a long time, horse. You have heard me sing and you know I never have been bodaciously shot at, for bursting out in song. I suppose somebody down there is killing something—or holding target practice—or something . . .'

He was still grinning as they went down the gentle slope. But he rode alertly, a hand swinging close to the low-slung Colt in the tied-down holster on his right thigh. He leaned a little forward in the saddle and the six-three of him, added to Nubbins's bulk, gave horse and man the look of some great projectile, some huge missile that went on and could not be stopped—almost like the locomotive on that new railroad building from the east into La Fe—river and border town.

Presently, the trail climbed a tall sand dune. Gavity reined in Nubbins again, for another searching look ahead. He saw how the road dropped down a long incline on the other side. This was a country less arid, being nearer the Rio Grande. Here and there were mottes of cottonwoods and, perhaps five miles distant in a general southwesterly direction, the silvery glint of the river itself, curving like some lazy argent snake in the emerald green of the *bosque*, the tangled wilderness of cottonwood and willow and tornillo and scrubby brush on both banks.

Down the slope from Gavity some two hundred yards was a grove of cottonwoods.

Outside the trees a horseman sat negligently. He seemed to be staring at something within the cottonwoods. As Gavity regarded him narrowly, the man finished some fumbling movement at his saddle-horn. His hand jerked upward. There was the flat, metallic sound of pistol-fire.

'He's shooting at something under the trees,' Gavity told himself thoughtfully. 'A snake? Well, it could be. But he's certainly using up plenty of ammunition—and I always thought a den of snakes would be in a rocky ridge, not under a desert cottonwood motte . . . And—*Por dios*! If that's a snake he's trying to hit, it must be a tree snake! For he's aiming upward . . . Not toward the ground . . .'

He shook his head and shrugged big shoulders.

'Well! It's supposed to be a free country. If that gentleman wants to shoot off a few dollars' worth of shells, blazing away at poor, harmless cottonwood trees that never did him any harm, it's his privilege!'

While he sat watching, the pistolman seemed to finish his exercise. He returned the pistol to some place of carrying about his person and his voice carried to Gavity in a wild, somehow contemptuous, yell. He thumbed his nose at the cottonwoods and rammed his heels into his horse's sides. He jumped the animal into a gallop and surged along the trail to La Fe, going hell-for-leather.

4

'Now, now, now!' Gavity said slowly. 'I do hate puzzles and mysterious happenings—like this. Nubbins, I reckon you and your boss will just have to go see what it was that rouses up so much action down there . . .'

He tickled Nubbins with a gentle rowel and they made the cottonwoods at easy gallop. Gavity sagged in the saddle and Nubbins checked his speed. Three great cottonwoods grew close together. Apparently, they were used by the sheriff of La Fe County for a sort of highway bulletin board. Five notices gleamed upon the thick boles. Three were frayed and faded by sun and wind, but two shone bright against the rugged bark of the trees.

Gavity kneed Nubbins closer. It had come to him instantly that these notices must have been target for that vanished man. He read them carefully. One offered two hundred and fifty dollars reward for the arrest and conviction of those miscreants who had stolen from the stable of Oscar Zelman, mayor of La Fe, two fine Kentucky-bred carriage-horses. There was description of this team—details and statistics to make any horseman's eyes brighten—including the remark that each was branded upon the left cheek and on the underside of the tail with Zelman's OZ brand.

'Mexico!' Gavity told himself, out of the fullness of his knowledge as he read on. 'Yes, sir! That pair of horses is in Mexico with some rich don driving them. And there they'll stay, for all the mayor's thousand dollars gold, offered for their recovery and delivery to him. They may even have been stolen to order, because somebody saw Oscar Zelman driving 'em and decided he couldn't live without 'em.'

The other bright, new notice was signed by the Midwest Stage and Transportation Company of La Fe. In the name of the president of the company—a resident of St. Louis, Missouri, Gavity gathered from the reward dodger—the tolerable sum of twenty-five hundred dollars was offered for arrest and conviction of those men—identities unknown —who had stopped a westbound stage of the Midwest Company at Harmony Station, to kill the driver and the shotgun messenger and two passengers, wound a woman, and rob the stage itself of sixty thousand dollars in gold bullion and bank-notes, and, apparently, vanish into thin air.

Gavity whistled at this. For six months he had been secluded from the world on the Slash R cow-ranch of Bryan Ross and this robbery at Harmony Station had occurred, to judge from the notice and the date given, barely five weeks before.

Small wonder that to the Slash R, isolated as it was in the Grindstone Mountains, had come no news of even so thrilling a holdup. He stared long at the notices. That fellow with the pistol had done a good deal of shooting, first and last, at the bulletins. Now, Gavity had to thank him for the consideration shown in shooting only at the blank head and tail of each notice. He made a cigarette and lighted it. As he drew in smoke and blew it out in twin horns, something odd about the bullet pocks caught his eye. He leaned a trifle, to look at the marks more carefully.

'Well, I'll be damned!' he said softly.

Then he turned in the saddle, to glance involuntarily in the direction of La Fe, toward which the pistolman had galloped. For those round, black-edged holes in the papers spelled out very neatly what seemed mocking comment upon the offers made by sheriff and express company.

'Ha! Ha!' the pistolman had put upon each notice.

He shook his head. There was the large question, whether the man he had seen was a member of the stage-robbing or horse-stealing band, or merely a chance wayfarer who had little faith in the power of rewards, the ability and efficiency of peace officers.

He rode on toward the little border town which was his goal, and for a while he mulled the problem and considered all he had seen of this puzzling incident of the trail. But not for long . . . As Nubbins brought him nearer to La Fe, Gavity forgot the cottonwoods and the man who had shot at the notices. There was a face in his mind's eye, the same face which

7

had ridden on his saddle-horn, almost, plain in every feature, from that moment four days past when he had rolled his bed on the Slash R and turned Nubbins's head toward La Fe.

Where he rode, now, he followed in the trail of Bryan Ross the Slash R owner and the most lovely girl Gavity's thirty-odd years had ever shown him. He was following the peppery little cowman and that small, dark, lovely, and utterly desirable girl, Betty Ross, Bryan's daughter. What this following might bring, he had no slightest idea. He had only known that life on the Slash R without Betty was unendurable. So he had thrown the hull on Nubbins and come after father and daughter.

Drawing nearer to La Fe, he began to see signs of that activity which—by all the accounts he had heard—the booming border town knew these days. There were Mexican goat-herders with their flocks, carrying slings and pouches of pebbles. Farmers straightened in their little fields to watch him. And he passed occasional Anglos riding up from the river, cowboys as lean and brown and hard-bitten as himself.

When he came to a small 'dobe house set before a corn patch, he rode up to the door to get fire for a cigarette. A slender and shapely Mexican girl of sixteen or so smiled shyly up at him. She crossed the yard on bare feet, to get him a glowing stick from the beehive-shaped mud oven beyond the house. Gavity accepted it with a bow, and when he had lighted his cigarette he crooked a leg comfortably around the saddle-horn and halted awhile, to gossip with the girl in easy *pelado* Spanish.

She rolled great dark eyes admiringly up at him, seeming to study every detail of his smooth, brown face and twinkling gray eyes and wide, thin-lipped, yet good-humored mouth, his shirt of blue flannel and waist overalls and inlaid boots. The white bone handle of his silver-mounted pistol, with the ruby-eyed steer-head carved upon it, and the gold and silver plate of big-roweled, 'girl leg' spurs and bridle-bit, seemed particularly to fascinate her.

'You are not from this neighborhood,' she said after a long inspection. 'But you ride, now, for La Fe? You have come like so many others during the past months, perhaps to work with the railroad?'

'*Yo no sé*,' Gavity admitted with a shrug. 'I but know that I ride toward La Fe. What I do there will depend upon what I find to do; what pleases me. But—is there something in the town that I could send you? Even though I ride away from my work and look for more work, there is still some gold in my pocket. What shall it be for you? A *rebozo* to cover your pretty head? A *mantilla* for those also-pretty shoulders? Or would you wish a bracelet hammered from silver with turquoises fixed upon it? Tell me and—'

9

'They are very nice, those things,' she said gravely. 'And you are very kind to offer them. But the one thing I wish from La Fe, today, is none of them. It is but my brother, Manuel. If you could send him back to me—'

'A brother!' Gavity cried, then laughed. 'Now, Head of the Disciple! If that is not strange, from a niña of your prettiness. If you had said a lover— But, this brother of yours, where will I find him? Drinking, perhaps, in some *cantina*? Is he the sort to take your produce to La Fe and sell it and drink and gamble away the money?'

'Not Manuel! No, señor! Manuel is a boy of the best. Since the death of our father last year, he has been the man of our house. He is a year older than I, Lupe, who am sixteen. He is a very good boy. And he will be somewhere about the saloon of the *Americano*, Ben Miles. He went into the town afoot, early this morning. The man Miles owes him for work and—'

There was so much of trouble in dark eyes and smooth young face that Gavity bent to touch her reassuringly.

'Tell!' he said quickly. 'What is the quarrel between this brother of yours and the saloon-man?'

'Manuel worked for two weeks upon the ranch of this Miles. But when time came for paying, Miles sent him away empty of hands. Three times, since then, Manuel has asked

10

Miles for the money due him and has not had it. Miles is one of much temper, señor, a man of hard hands. Those who work for him in La Fe, in the saloon, they are of his like. Last night, Manuel said he would go for the last time to Miles. He would go this morning to the saloon. He said he would have from Miles the eight dollars for which he worked or— there would be trouble. I begged him to forget the money, but he is one of temper and stubbornness, also. He would not hear me. I am afraid, señor!'

'I'll see what I can do about it,' Gavity promised her.

Then he reached down and caught her beneath the elbows. Effortlessly, he lifted the slight weight until she swung at the level of his face. For an instant she stiffened and looked frightened. Then the small, dark head went back a trifle and she met his eyes with provocative, half-lidded stare. He drew her closer, kissed her, and set her lightly upon the ground.

'I'll have a look for Manuel, the very first thing I do, when I get to La Fe,' he told her. 'And—I think that I shall find him. Also, I think that I shall see you again, Lupe.'

'I—I would like to believe that,' she said softly.

2. 'I live here now'

Gavity pulled Nubbins in on the crest of a rise in the greasewood flat, to look forward and down upon La Fe.

From that distance the town resembled most of all a jumble of gray or brown or white blocks, strewn helter-skelter along the Texas bank of the Rio Grande, with ants moving busily from block to block.

Jogging into town he stopped again, to look about. It fairly hummed. Gangs of Mexican laborers were here and there raising the walls of new houses and stores and other buildings. For the most part, these structures were of sundried mud brick, but Gavity saw four of burned brick and as many more of lumber.

He rode on toward the center of town. The business district was composed of two streets, each a quarter-mile long. These were joined like the staff and crossbar of a capital T. The staff was Bowie Street, the crossbar was Fay Street. Both were lined with 'dobes of one story, spotted with new brick buildings of two stories. He looked and grinned.

For in the main these buildings housed saloons, dance-halls, gambling-hells, honkatonks, restaurants—and more saloons!

Cuddling in one corner of the streets' juncture was a little triangular plaza shaded by

12

cottonwoods. Upon the biggest tree—that stood beyond an *acequia*—a water-ditch that made the plaza's diagonal boundary—were placards and notices. On one bank of the *acequia* a pole held an official-seeming sign. Gavity glanced at it as he rode by:

NO
SWIMMING
ALLOWED
CITY COUNCIL

That had been the original legend. But some waggish soul had amended it, so that now as Gavity looked amusedly upon it it read:

NO
SWIMMING OR STEAMBOATS
ALLOWED
CITY COUNCIL

He looked about for a livery corral, in which he could stable Nubbins. And he found another sign, thrust out over a large, new brick saloon, just across the street from the plaza. He looked at the sign and nodded with tightening of mouth. The sign proclaimed:

PALACE SALOON
A GENTLEMAN'S RESORT
B. MILES, PROP.

'So that's the hairpin Lupe mentioned,' he said to himself. 'And he runs a gentleman's resort but won't pay a Mex' kid eight dollars for sweating on his ranch . . . I think I'm going to be interested in pow-wowing with Mr. B. Miles, Prop. . . . I do that!'

With thought of Lupe he shook his head bodingly. She was a pretty youngster. Too pretty! With the town filling, as it was, with railroad men advancing ahead of end-of-steel; with all manner of hard cases floating in, intent upon digging into the ground floor in the boom La Fe expected to continue—small chance that such a girl would long go unnoticed. She was far too attractive. Some hard-handed man would reach out and take her.

He stared thoughtfully at the saloon of Ben Miles—and suddenly observed, squatting beneath the hitch-rack and facing the Palace door, a slender Mexican youth. Gavity wondered if that would be Manuel, Lupe's brother. But while he watched the boy a face appeared over one of the swinging doors of the Palace. It showed only for a moment, a red, bloated, broken-nosed face, crowned by short reddish bristles.

Gavity could hardly see the man's eyes, they were so small and deepset. The big, coarse-lipped mouth above the heavy chin was twisted in a brutal grin as the man looked—

or seemed to look—toward the squatting Mexican youngster. Then the face disappeared.

The boy tossed away the butt of his cigarette. Then the swinging doors moved, and out upon the plank sidewalk came a man almost as tall as Gavity himself. It was the man who had looked over the door, and in the better light his prize-fighter face was even more brutal, vicious, than it had shown before.

'Looks like the Palace bouncer,' Gavity thought.

He pushed Nubbins on at slow walk in that direction, as the big man went loafing over to the hitch-rack. One of the man's hands was held behind his back. 'When Gavity pulled in no more than ten feet away, the man had halted before the boy and was speaking to him in a tone almost gentle.

'Thought I run you off awhile ago,' he drawled. 'Seems to me I told you to git and stay got . . .'

'I not go!' the boy answered defiantly. 'Ben Miles give me money—give me eight dollar—then I go. I not get eight dollar—trouble! I—'

'Well, well!' the big man cried, in the same gentle tone. 'Won't leave when you're told, huh? Well—'

His hand jerked from behind his back, bringing a heavy, braided quirt. It twitched snakily in his grip and the hiss of its lash in air could be heard across the street. The lash struck across the boy's face and fairly hurled him backward. Grunting with each terrific blow struck, the man gave him no time to rise. He seemed bent on cutting the slim figure to pieces; his arm rose and fell; rose and fell.

Black Nubbins, big as he was, had very few peers as a cutting horse. Gavity had only to lean forward and knee him and Nubbins crossed the space to the hitchrack in a rush. Then Gavity lifted slightly in one stirrup and the stampeding rush was stopped short with the black head over the crossbar.

Gavity came out of the saddle. Like his horse, he was sometimes considered by casual observers as slow, because of great bulk. Now, he laid a hand on the crossbar and vaulted it. He was swinging as his feet touched the sidewalk. He drove a terrific right-hand punch at the side face of the big man with the quirt. That worthy staggered and dropped the quirt.

The big man turned from his victim and with what seemed instinct dropped into a turtle-like shell of defense. Gavity struck furiously at him. He knew nothing whatever of boxing, but fighting—he had been fighting all his life! He pushed into the big man with both fists flashing in and out, carrying the weight of battering-rams.

As by signal, a crowd began to form and thicken about the two. Miners, townsmen, traders, freighters, cowboys, cattlemen, Mexicans—it was a picturesque, a representative, and a noisily enthusiastic gathering. Some yelled for 'Pug,' but the cattlemen and their hands were in a body Gavity's backers.

Bets began to be made. One lank cowman yelled in drink-thickened voice that he had a thousand dollars to bet on the big leather-pounder. He waved a clinking bag overhead to prove his statement. A slender and pallid man in frock coat fairly fought his way through the crowd to take that bet. Evidently 'Pug' had a reputation in La Fe.

A little of all this, Gavity heard clearly. The rest was merely noise, as he pounded away at the shell of wrists and elbows which guarded Pug. Then out of that shell came a smoking uppercut that caught Gavity under the chin, lifted him off his heels, and dropped him in a sprawl on the sidewalk. The gambler in black coat reached for the cowman's money.

Other backers of Pug yelled enthusiastically. Pug himself, thick grin contemptuous, said something drawlingly about 'cow-chambermaids.'

Then Gavity came to his feet with a wild puncher yell. He rushed the astonished Pug before the fighter could drop into his shell again. The *smack-smack*! of alternating right and left carried even above the yells of the audience.

Under that hail of pile-driving blows the flabby bouncer staggered and gave ground. He

17

wheezed, and the return punches he tried to deliver were wild and light. Gavity was hard and lean. He breathed deeply but without effort and even increased the speed of his attack.

One of Pug's cauliflowered ears was torn almost off his head by a glancing blow. His nose flattened and twisted to the side. He doubled under a right that seemed to sink in his belly almost to the leather cuff on Gavity's thick wrist. He—but nobody in that crowd could follow the blows. They only saw Gavity swinging furiously and missing hardly a blow. Then Pug dropped to the sidewalk and sprawled there like a broken toy, arms and legs limp and grotesque.

Gavity had three drinks. It would have been impossible to escape that many, among the crowd of enthusiastic admirers. The lanky cowman who had won the local gambler's thousand dollars wanted to buy champagne. When along the Palace bar something like quiet came again, Gavity asked his host if he knew Bryan Ross.

'I shore do!' the other said emphatically. 'I've bought, it's many a head of Slash R cows from Bryan Ross. Tim Free's my name, young fella; cow-trading's my business. Yeh, Bryan and me, we're old *compadres*. But I reckon he's going to be a Town Ike, now. Maybe he's smart, at that. He bought him a half-interest in Charley Jones's store—and ought to be just about a first-class gold mine! Bought him a big house out at the end of Bowie Street, too. Mighty pretty gal that is, he's got—Betty. You know her?'

'The reason I asked if you know him is, I want to ask you to do me a favor,' Gavity said slowly.

'A favor!' Tim Free grunted. 'Young fella, after that kind of fight and winning me a thousand dollars off a tinhorn, you ask anything you want to. I'd do you a dozen favors, every one of 'em seventeen hands high!'

'Thanks! Thanks a lot! Let's see, now . . .'

He grinned and considered, while he watched a reflection in the bar-mirror. At the far end of the long bar-room, staring very straight and entirely without favor at him, stood a short and round-bodied man, with fiery red face and blue eyes somewhat bulging and a bristly fringe of gingery hair around a gleaming bald head. He was swelling, precisely like a small and disturbed toad. While Gavity watched without seeming to, Bryan Ross came toward him, his mouth tightening.

Gavity whispered hurriedly to Tim Free:

'Here comes Bryan Ross, now. What I want you to do is keep him off my back. If he starts out of here for any reason, you get him by the arm and keep him in here for me. Don't let him get away from you. Give me—an hour, if you can. I'll take a half-hour, if that's all I can get. Can happen?'

'Son,' Tim Free assured him, 'it practically *has* happened! There he is!'

'What are you doing here in La Fe?' Bryan Ross demanded. 'Why ain't you out at the ranch like you're supposed to be?'

'Why, I quit the Slash R!' Gavity said in a surprised drawl. 'Yes, sir, just naturally up and rolled my bed—why, it must be four days back. And I'm here because I *live* here, now. You see, everybody's talking about the wonderful future La Fe's got ahead of it. So I decided I'd be a Town Ike, too—same as you, Mr. Ross. Thought I'd wander down this way and catch hold of some of that future. A man has got to be thinking about his future while he's young. And you know I haven't always *been* just as ambitious as I could have been. So—'

He smiled pleasantly down at Ross, who seemed on the verge of exploding. Nor did Gavity's smile calm him. When he tried to speak, he made sputtering noises and breathed noisily through his belligerent nose. When he could find words, he spoke in a voice husky and shaking like the finger he waggled:

'You— You— Now, you listen to me, Big Gavity! You stay away from me! Stay away from my house! Most of all, you stay away from my daughter! I ain't going to have any two-bit cowboy hanging around Betty. I brought her into town as much to get her away from you as anything. I— I— You mark what I'm saying: You stay away from her!'

Then he spun about, still snarling. He went fast toward the front door.

'Going straight to Betty,' Gavity told Tim Free. 'Yes, sir, just as straight as a homer pigeon. Going to give her the powders: Not to let me come inside the front gate; not to speak to me! And—worse luck!—she's a daughter that minds what she's told. Can you get him and hold him for that hour?'

Tim Free grinned and nodded. Gavity watched him hurry in the wake of Bryan Ross's fat, jiggling little legs. Then he turned and went toward the back door. He turned when he was at the end of the bar, to see Tim Free holding Ross by the arm, turning him away from the swinging doors and toward a table by the side wall.

He went on when he had seen them sitting down. He was almost at the back door, intent on finding the house of Bryan Ross as quickly as possible, to see Betty before her father found her. But at this end of the bar was a grim, black-eyed man of no particular size, but, somehow, of very obvious force of personality. As Gavity came opposite him, the man suddenly leaned with a grin, to thrust out his hand over the bar.

'I'm Ben Miles,' he said cordially. 'Didn't I hear 'em calling you Big Gavity? Well, sir! You certainly leathered that plug-ugly of mine. No hard feelings toward the house? None here. When I hire a bouncer, he better be a bouncer —the toughest man in town. He's got to take 'em the way they come and handle 'em on his own. He got just what was coming to him—just what he's handed out to plenty of others!'

Before Gavity could answer, there was a tug at his sleeve, and he looked down at the boy who had squatted beneath the hitch-rack. Across his face was a swollen weal and his thin, white cotton shirt was red-streaked. He lifted dark eyes—they were very like those of Lupe—to Gavity. He breathed gaspingly:

'I—I had to say my thanks to you, señor. But there was no chance before. You kept him from killing me, I think. And I do not forget. I am Manuel Porras, *patron.*'

Gavity nodded, then turned again to Ben Miles. He grinned, but it was not a pleasant lift of mouth corners:

'Why, I'm certainly glad you feel this way about the affair! And that reminds me: here's a young friend of mine—the one the row was about. Manuel Porras. He came into town today to talk to you about a little money due him for work he did on your ranch. He was waiting to see you when Pug sailed into him with the quirt and—I sailed into Pug. I think it may be that Pug didn't understand what Manuel wanted. It was just the money you owe him.'

There was no flicker of change in the controlled face of the saloon-keeper. But when Ben Miles stared fixedly at him, he knew very well that he had made an enemy. He could understand that Miles was a man who bore little in the way of opposition, challenge. It was plain in face and eyes.

But Miles chose not to make an issue of the matter. He asked Manuel in indifferent tone how much was due him.

'Eight dollar!' Manuel snarled. 'Like I tell you—like you know all time. Eight dollar!'

The boy's tone, also, Miles ignored. He called to a bartender and told him to bring eight dollars for Manuel. But he looked thoughtfully at Gavity while the boy pocketed the silver. Gavity grinned genially at him and looked to see what Bryan Ross and Tim Free were doing. The cowman talked earnestly, at their table, waving his hands. Ross nodded occasionally but looked often at the door.

Gavity moved quickly to the back door, Manuel trailing. He led the way up the side of the saloon and back to the street where Nubbins still stood patiently at the hitch-rack. He swung up and Manuel came to the stirrup.

'*Amo*,' the boy told him earnestly, 'you have saved my life and you have got for me this money which I could not have got. When you did those things, you made two enemies. When you think of something which I can do, tell me! And when I can think of something to do for you, I will not need to be told.'

'Why, I thank you!' Gavity answered smilingly. 'Now, take that sore back of yours home and let Lupe wash it. And—watch her, *hombre*! She is the sort at whom some man will look—then carry her home to cook his *frijoles.*'

'You—you know Lupe?' Manuel cried. 'Why—'

'I know her. I will see you both, later. Now—I have a ride to make. *Hasta la vista!*'

He spurred off along Bowie Street and Manuel yelled a good-bye to him, standing with almost dog-like posture in the sand.

3. 'We came to be civilized'

Bowie Street was the ancient trail of freighters bound from Mexico to another since earliest Spanish days, a road rutted by travelers going from Old Mexico to New, or on the return trip. Now, it was built up with the houses of early settlers and the newcomers drawn by the railroad.

Gavity hardly noticed signs of progress. He rode too fast, looking for the sort of place Bryan Ross would have bought as first move in his 'Town Ike' campaign. But he had to pull in and ask a Mexican woodcutter before he found the Ross house. It was a huge 'dobe, square, built around a central patio. It was set in a full block of ground. A high 'dobe wall, white-plastered, encircled the property.

Gavity rode up and stood in the stirrups to look over the wall. He saw clumps of shrubs and beds of flowers and toward the back of the house a kitchen garden. Great cottonwoods and Arizona ashes shaded the wide reaches of lawn. Here and there were gnarled old fruit trees dating—like the house itself—to the days of Spaniards on the Rio Grande. But it was a grape arbor that drew his eyes, arm-thick vines of the old Mission grapes covering a frame of cottonwood logs.

For beyond that arbor, asleep or very comfortable in a hammock swung under two cottonwoods, was a small figure . . .

Gavity let the split-reins fall and went like a huge cat to the top of the wall. He squatted there for a moment, waiting to see if the slight sounds of his movement had carried to the hammock. Then he dropped to the lawn and went like a shadow across to where he could look down upon the girl.

She cried out as she was lifted, hammock and all, to be held tight against Gavity's shoulder. He put his face against her slim neck and growled.

'Arthur!' she gasped, forcing back small, sleek, dark head. 'Why aren't you at the ranch? What are you doing in La Fe? You— you absolute savage! You scared me almost to

25

death—'

'But you like it,' Gavity told her placidly. 'You know you like it. How could you help it?'

'But what are you doing here? If Daddy sees you—He didn't send for you without telling me? He never did it!'

'No—that is, not exactly. He didn't send for me. But he has already seen me. And that reminds me, Miss Ross: I wanted to ask you a question . . . Are you better pleased to see me than your ancestor—our ancestor, I reckon I ought to say, since I have got to have him for a pa-in-law—was?'

'Put me down! Put me down this minute. If *he* happened to walk into the yard and see you holding me this way—'

'He won't. Besides, you haven't kissed me. And I am not going to do all the love-making in this family. Don't bother about Pa. I left him in the hands of just the noblest cow-trader you ever saw come down the pike. Old Tim Free. He's got Pa in the Palace Saloon at a table and he's talking his leg off. *I* arranged that, *querida*. You know how I think of everything. Pa can't possibly be along for a half-hour. You have got just plenty of time to do that kissing—'

'I'm not going to kiss you. I want to know all about this—your being here when you had all those horses to break. I want to know—'

Gavity separated girl from hammock without, somehow, loosening the hold he had

26

upon her, or letting her get farther from blue flannel shirt. He turned her a little in his arms so that whether she liked it or not—a question there was no way of deciding, just then—her upturned face was all but against his and she must thrust her head back to keep her mouth from his. He grinned down at her and kissed her.

'All right, then,' she yielded. 'If it's kiss you or have my neck broken, I suppose I'll kiss you.'

'Little bit glad to see a fella?' Gavity whispered, cheek against her cheek. 'Come on, now! You can say it in Spanish, even, if English embarrasses you.'

'I am glad! I—I've shown you that I'm glad. Now, put me down. I want to talk to you. If only Daddy didn't dislike you so much—more than he ever disliked anybody in his life, I do believe—there might be some hope of—He thought all this was over; thought it was just a passing fancy with us both. He believed that when we left the Slash R and moved to La Fe and you stayed there, we'd never even think of you again.'

'I could guess that much,' Gavity admitted dryly.

He let her down and straightened the hammock. She sat down, slim hands laced together, to look at him where he squatted beside her.

'He's ambitious!' she burst out. 'That's the

27

whole thing, I guess. He heard about the boom down here and the greater boom that La Fe will have when the railroads actually come in. He thought about it for months before he decided to move. He says this is like starting life all over again. Ranching is well enough, but he's never made any fortune at it. There are a hundred chances here to get rich. He bought part of a store—'

'I know. The Jones store. Doing pretty well with it?'

'They're making a great deal of money. As soon as the steel comes within sight of town, they should make ten times as much. He bought this place at a low price—and he can sell it today for three times what he paid for it. He owns some other property and has options on still more. He's been asked to run for alderman. He wants to do it. I know what he's thinking: from alderman to mayor is a natural step. He can be one of the biggest, most important men in La Fe. And so he—he wants me—'

Smooth neck, clear ivory cheeks, were suddenly flushed the color of the blossoms beyond her, on the old Spanish peach tree across the lawn. She watched Gavity.

He was making a cigarette. He looked up at her with gray eyes narrowed humorously. He nodded, as if what she told him were interesting, but not a matter of any personal or vital interest. His detachment seemed to irritate her. She leaned forward, a corner of vivid underlip between her teeth, small chin lifted angrily.

'He wants me to marry well! Some prominent business man or—or a doctor—or a lawyer—here in La Fe! A wandering cowboy, a saddle-tramp coming across a hill from nobody knows where, is *not* his idea of— of a son-in-law.'

'I reckon not,' Gavity said gravely, studying the end of his cigarette. 'I have thought more than once that his attitude is not all that a father-in-law's should be. I've even felt that he wasn't fond of me. Yeh . . . somehow I have guessed that, almost from the beginning. It wasn't so much what he said or did, but just— oh, I suppose it was just little things I noticed here and there.'

He drew smoke into his great chest and the cigarrette seemed to shorten by an inch. He blew twin horns of smoke into air above her head and when he looked at her he was grim of mouth.

'Tell me something. How do you feel about all this, *querida*? It may just be that I own peculiar notions about this loving and marrying business, but—somehow, it does seem to me that we're hearing a lot more about Bryan Ross than we're hearing about Betty Ross. I'd rather have more Betty and less Bryan. In fact—'

Now he laughed outright and flipped away

the cigarrette and covered a small hand with his big palm.

'In fact, I don't mind in the least saying that I wouldn't marry Bryan Ross, not if he was the last man in the world! Tell a fella! Do you agree with all these notions of Pa?'

'I've said it before and I say it now, again!' she told him. 'You're without doubt the most maddening person I've ever met in my life. For a saddle-tramp, you have more to say and—and—and say it! than any leather-pounder who ever came over the horizon. You—'

'Ain't you traveled much?' Gavity asked, hand closing upon her hand. 'Just plumb iggerance git you down, hon'?'

She was defeated. He always defeated her—when he was close enough to counteract Bryan Ross' snarls. She tried to keep her mouth hard and tight and disapproving, but she could not conceal the expression in her eyes. From her feet Gavity *woofed*! in the fashion of a huge and friendly Saint Bernard puppy.

'Oh! Still love me?' he demanded abruptly.

'Sometimes I wonder if I ever loved you . . .'

Her tone was indifferent, but she had to pull her hand away and stare up at the pink blossoms of the old peach tree.

'You're absolutely maddening, you know,' she went on. 'I don't wonder that Daddy dislikes you. He never decides—not in the same week—if you've said something natural and ordinary, or something he should have shot you for the minute you said it. You—that's the trouble with you: you irritate people!'

Once more Big Gavity belied that reputation which men who did not know him well were likely to give him. He twisted and came to his feet and caught her up from the hammock. He held her breathlessly close against him with one long arm and with the other jerked her hands up.

'Hold on or you'll tumble!' he whispered, and her arms came up about his neck and held him tight.

When he set her down again she was flushed and breathless and very bright of eyes. She smoothed the rumpled organdy dress and would not look at him.

'As I was saying, you're just a big savage!'

'You haven't said that for thirty-two kisses. I was keeping count by punching my toe in the ground. But go ahead! I like it. I'm a big savage and—'

'I don't know why I—I—'

'Love me,' Gavity finished for her, nodding. 'But you do, *querida*, and since you're the only girl in all this wide, wide world I ever saw that I wanted to marry—and I tell you, I've had plenty chances!—So, the question is: Would it be right for us to let a meddlesome, slanderous, bad-tempered old—you know

31

what—like Bryan Ross mix into something that, rightly, is none of his business? Now, that's what I ask you. I ask you—'

'What? What are you asking me?'

'Well, here I am in La Fe. Just like Bryan Ross! That is, in that way. Suppose I go to him and I say—in a sweet and gentle and reasonable way, understood—that I think he has got the loveliest and the most beautiful and the—the—well, anyway, the girl *I* want to marry? Suppose, then, that he listens to me patiently and—'

'What? Patiently? Daddy listen to *you* patiently? He—'

'Then, he says: "Uh-uh! Uh-uh!" Meaning "no," of course. All right, then! Suppose, just for instance, I come back to you and I say that you have got for a father one of the blindest, meanest, stubbornest, most cantankerous, old ancestors even I have ever seen. A man who hasn't got the vision to realize what it'll mean to him to have a Gavity in the family—'

He leaned to her and held her tight again.

'Darling—if I tell you what he says he won't hear about our getting married, will you marry me, anyway?'

'I can't do it! Oh, I just can't do it!' she whispered miserably. 'I—I admit that I've thought of that. I thought of it on the ranch. I've imagined you coming in as you have come, today. I've tried to see myself running away with you. But—I just can't do it, Arthur.

He's watched over me since I was a baby—after Mother died. He's been like an old hen with one chick. If I thought he'd get over it afterward, when he knew it was beyond his control, I—I might.'

'He would! Texas horses don't run against rope! Texas men don't buck something that's settled. He would get over it!'

'No, he wouldn't! I know him better than anyone in the world. He's the most stubborn human being in Texas. He never would forgive me and—and it would just ruin his life.'

'Of course,' Gavity said thoughtfully, 'it's perfectly all right to ruin *my* life and *your* life! Little things like that don't count. It's just *Daddy* who's important. Why, that old—I can't even call him what he is, because by some absolute accident, he happens to be your father! He talks a lot, but he'd get over having me in the family, even. I know his kind. Lord, Betty! I've rambled this country over, from Milk River to Cananea; from here to there! I've seen plenty, and I certainly have seen all the different breeds of Man. I know Bryan Ross's kind. He'd squawk, but he'd give in.'

She shook her dark head decidedly.

'No, he wouldn't. He really doesn't like you. He really and thoroughly and completely dislikes you! You're a stranger—nobody knows where you came from. You're an impudent young squirt (he says) without proper respect for your elders. You come out

33

of nowhere with a swagger and you want to marry a wealthy man's daughter. And on what? He says you haven't anything; you haven't even prospects of having anything— else by this time you'd be settled down. You—'

'What did *he* have when he started out to get rich?' Gavity interrupted her amusedly. 'Somebody gave him a sore-backed pony and a speckled calf—so he set up as a cowman! He nursed nickels; he did without everything. The worst of it is, he forgot how to do anything but make money. Now, I'm different. I have spent a lot of time and lots of miles, seeing the world. I've seen things he won't know about between this and his dying day. He thinks he's a money-maker! Lord, child! I know men who wouldn't bother to live the way he's lived, who'll out-make him any day of the week including Sundays.'

'Don't interrupt me!' she stopped him relentlessly. 'He has five reasons for not wanting you in his neighborhood. I've mentioned one or two of them. The chief reason is: *he doesn't like you!* When we came to La Fe, we came to be civilized—he says. We came to be somebody. And when his grandchildren look back on us, he doesn't want them to see a hugeous saddle-tramp on the family coat-of-arms. The last and most important reason is—you're an impudent puppy and he doesn't like you!'

Gavity laughed and made another cigarette.

When it was lighted and drawing, he shook his tawny head:

'*Amor de dios!*' he drawled. 'The Ross Family has come to town and it's going to be civilized . . . Already looking at one of those coat-of-arms things and a lot of pictures of funny-faced ancestors on the wall . . . My—goodness! And also goodness gracious! But, now that I look back, I suppose I ought to have foreseen something like this . . . Didn't he put on his brand-new galluses, before ever he left the Slash R and headed for La Fe? And that bulge in his left hip pocket . . . I can see, now, that it wasn't a plug of Star Navy; it was a piece of board he meant to whittle into a coat-of-arms.'

He got up and stretched long arms above his head. He looked down at the small figure in the hammock and grinned:

'Well, I reckon I'd better be heading back for town. Now that I'm a prominent citizen of La Fe, I'll have to be considering just what line of work most needs my loving attention. I reckon I could have had a job, today . . . saloon bouncer. At Ben Mile's Palace Resort. But I got to thinking about Pa-in-Law's social standing and what a disgrace it'd be for him to have a bouncer in the family tree. So, I turned it down before it was really offered to me. All because of Pa-in-Law's standing in La Fe . . .'

He bent to ruffle the blue-black hair with a thick forefinger; bent farther to kiss her on the

35

back of her neck.

'Tell you what, sweetheart-of-mine: you be looking around town and if you see a house you think we'd like—nothing big, or expensive; not over twenty—thirty rooms; something sort of homelike—you tell me. Of course, if we don't find exactly what we want, already built, we'll just have to damn expense and build us one. Come along; Nubbins is over the wall yonder.'

She walked beside him, in the curve of his arm. He looked whimsically down at her.

'Wish me luck, *querida*? Lots of luck?'

'Lots of luck! For I know you're going to need it, with those ideas of yours.'

But she kissed him again before he vaulted to the wall and leaned over to touch her head again.

'Thanks!' he said gravely. 'I will need lots of luck. Nobody knows it any better than I do. But I've noticed that often a man makes his own luck. If I came out of nowhere, bringing nothing that Bryan Ross can see, maybe that's just because he can't see certain things. I have got the notion that some of the things I'd bring with me are going to be handy here! Be seeing you!'

He dropped into his saddle and scooped up the reins.

4. 'I intended to kill him'

It was an eighth of a mile back to the Main Stem from Bryan Ross's house. Since La Fe was to be his home for the time being, Gavity looked at place and people with more than ordinary interest—and with the experienced eyes of a man who had seen many a cowtown and boom camp. He kept Nubbins at the effortless running-walk along the sandy track of Bowie Street.

'Money,' he said thoughtfully to himself. 'It is certainly here, now; and the prospect of lots more. I'm past thirty; I've seen the elephant and heard the owl. Georgetown University is a long, long way behind me. Maybe Bryan Ross is right about all this civilization business . . . Maybe it's time I gave some thought to digging a garden-patch . . .'

Then he saw a man standing before the small but ornate Gleaming Gem Saloon, and he forgot general ambitions in consideration of his particular future.

For this man was a gorilla in build. His arms swung almost to his kneecaps. His shoulder width was enormous—greater, even, than Gavity's. He had so short a neck that his shaggy head seemed to rest upon those thick shoulders. Swarthy face and tiny black eyes carried out the gorilla illusion.

Upon his buttonless vest was a large golden badge. At his sides hung matched pearl-handled Colts. His feet were squarely set—as if he balanced himself unconsciously, ready for flashing movement. He was watching Gavity's approach.

Then the swing doors of the Gem flapped out over the sidewalk. A very usual sort of townsman came out of the saloon. He staggered slightly as he came toward the officer. Gavity dismissed him from consideration after one brief and comprehensive glance. He was considering the gorilla-like man. For he was close enough, now, to see the legend on the gold badge.

'So that's the marshal . . .' he thought. 'Let's see now; I heard his name . . . Wheelen. Yeh, that was it. Winn Wheelen. His looks bear out his reputation for saltiness, too. Though I do think that a working gun-fighter oughtn't to use pearl handles on his cutters. They're too slippery . . .'

The marshal was facing, now, the somewhat unsteady citizen from the Gem. His harsh voice carried plainly to Gavity:

'If he don't want trouble, then he better not be where trouble's likely to come!'

What they were discussing, Gavity had no slightest idea. Another man had caught his eye, anyway. He had rounded the corner above the two talking before the Gem. He was tall, graceful, very nicely dressed (Gavity admitted critically) in dark, tailored citizens' clothing. As he moved toward Wheelen, he pushed back off his pale face a black slouch hat of the sort usually affected by the gambling fraternity.

Wheelen and the other man, apparently, did not notice the newcomer. The marshal was still talking energetically in his rasping voice, about that someone who had better dodge trouble. Then the tall man called clearly:

'Oh, Wheelen! I hear you're looking for me!'

The result of his hail was explosive. The marshal whirled, and the other man—without looking in the direction of the newcomer—jumped to one side, ran toward the Gem's door, and crashed into the saloon. Wheelen's hands jerked up to the pearl butts of his Colts. They moved precisely like whipping snakeheads.

Wheelen was a Gunman! 'A gunslinger from the forks of the creek!' Gavity told himself, pulling Nubbins to a halt and staring fixedly. As a traveled young man, Gavity was more or less an authority on gunplay as a fine art, on all phases of triggernometry. So he appreciated the smooth, flashing movements of the marshal's double-handed draw. But, fast as it was, it was not fast enough. The tall man had come around the corner with a hand in a coat pocket.

39

Now, he only lifted that hand, bringing up the coat. There was the roar of the gun he gripped in the pocket; another roar, and another. Wheelen had both guns out of the holsters, but they were not leveled. He began to fall forward. His thumbs twitched on the hammers of his pistols. He fired two shots into the sidewalk as he leaned.

The man who had shot him stood with head a little on one side, his arm crooked, holding up the smoking pocket of his coat. The muzzle of his gun was trained steadily on Wheelen.

But when Wheelen fell face downward, arms outstretched, pistols under his laxing fingers, the man drew a heavy gun from his coat pocket. He held it down along his leg. Men came out of the Gem, now. They did not crowd the tall man with the gun, Gavity observed. A man said:

'Well, Binnings, you killed him, all right!'

Binnings looked down at Wheelen. He nodded. His voice was even, almost drawling, when he answered:

'I *intended* to kill him. He was a dirty louse, Winn Wheelen. Somebody should have beat me to it. He needed killing a long time ago. If any of you are interested, you can pick him up and get him ready for the coroner.'

Some gaped at him. Others moved forward, to bend over the fallen, moveless figure on the sidewalk. These last made quick examination, then shook their heads. Gavity had pushed

Nubbins a little nearer the sidewalk where he could both see and hear. One of the men who had looked at Wheelen straightened and faced Binnings.

'You certainly drilled him!' he grunted.

'I told you I intended to kill him,' Binnings repeated coldly. 'Now, the coroner can find me whenever he wants me.'

Very calmly, he turned his back upon them and began to walk west—toward the Main Stem of La Fe. Nobody moved to stop him. But, on impulse that he did not trouble to explain, Gavity tickled Nubbins with a gentle rowel and trailed the tall killer. He did not ride in close to the sidewalk. He was never foolhardy. Too, he had seen more than one killing in his days of wandering between Texas and the northern ranges. So he kept Nubbins in the middle of the street.

Somebody began to yell, behind Binnings and Gavity. It was a sunburned young man, a cowboy type. Gavity turned in the saddle to see. Binnings also whirled. The gun he was carrying lifted to waist-level.

That young cowboy ran down the sidewalk from the Gleaming Gem, after Binnings. He had a pistol in his hand. He was perhaps thirty yards behind the marshal's killer.

'Binnings!' he called as he ran. 'Stop where you are! I want you! Put that pistol down! I want—'

'What *you* want is—this, Tyloe!' Binnings

41

answered him in even, almost emotionless, voice.

His pistol came higher—like that of the cowboy, who (Gavity saw for the first time) wore a badge on his shirt. The two men fired almost together, so that the sound was like the roar of one prolonged shot. Gavity pulled in Nubbins. He guessed that Binnings could have only two cartridges left in his Colt. Tyloe— some sort of officer—would doubtless have a full gun. Gavity thought that retribution was coming up to Binnings quickly.

But Binnings fired the two shots from the gun which had killed Winn Wheelen. While he was firing, he was drawing from another coat pocket a second gun. Tyloe was shooting steadily—shooting fast, too! But the critical and observant Gavity saw no sign of Tyloe's bullets striking. When Binnings got his second pistol into action, dust jumped from Tyloe's shirt with every shot Binnings sent that way.

Tyloe slumped abruptly. His knees buckled. His head sagged downward and he clawed at the breast of his shirt, upon which a bloody stain began to spread. Grimly, deliberately, Binnings walked a half-dozen steps toward the staggering officer. He fired his fourth or fifth shot at Tyloe just as if shooting at an inanimate target.

Tyloe came to the sidewalk on hands and knees. His position for a split-second was one of supplication. But he held that posture only for a breath. Then he was sprawling on the planks before a store, hardly moving, with Binnings staring across and down at him with still face—and ready gun.

The opposite sidewalk was fairly jammed, now, with spectators of this duel. Binnings moved up to Tyloe and stood over him. He raked away Tyloe's pistol with a toe, in a movement that made Gavity think of a woman touching something distasteful. Then he straightened and turned. He seemed to ignore Gavity. He looked past him at the moveless, staring townsmen.

'And that is—that!' he said in the even voice he had used throughout both gunfights. 'I don't intend to be arrested. This was a personal affair—one between Winn Wheelen and me. Most of you know all about it. It was a case of shoot-on-sight. Wheelen and I understood it as that. As for this fool, here— Tyloe—he was nothing but Wheelen's trained poodle. Whenever Wheelen told him to jump and pick up sticks, he jumped and picked up sticks. But this was one stick that Tyloe should never have tried to pick out of the water. It was entirely too big a stick for a man of Tyloe's size. And that is what I have got to say. It's all I have got to say. If anybody wants what Wheelen and Tyloe got—'

He waited for a moment, but nobody moved. So he turned once more toward the intersection of the principal streets of La Fe.

43

He seemed to turn his back indifferently, arrogantly, upon both the two dead men and the whole town. He took slow step after slow step, and none there seemed impelled to stop him.

'It's really none of my business!' Gavity said aloud abruptly, as if someone had asked him a question. 'Not a damn thing to me, but—'

There had been no feature unusual enough about the gunplay between Binnings and Wheelen to rouse much feeling in him. It was The Code that, when a man buckled a belt about him and shoved a Colt in his holster, he gave a signal: He was ready to use that pistol; was ready to back up his convictions of any variety whatsoever by the smoke of powder and the slap of lead.

Wheelen had tried to kill Binnings. Binnings had killed Wheelen, instead. The legal angle had no bearing here. For Wheelen, as marshal, had not been trying to arrest Binnings. He had tried to kill him. No— Gavity admitted—this was straight gunplay, nothing else. There was no case to stand up in court against Binnings, in connection with anything he had done.

As for the kid deputy, Tyloe, he had come running up the street with a gun in his hand. He had come, so far as Gavity could see the situation, to halt Binnings purely because of the other, quite ordinary, shooting. If he were Wheelen's deputy as Gavity believed him to be, that changed nothing. If a deputy sheriff or deputy marshal chose to play the fool, the fact that he happened to be an officer had nothing to do with his being also an idiot.

Up to a certain point, then, Gavity thought, he felt about Tyloe's killing precisely as he felt about Wheelen's. But only up to that point where Binnings fired coldly and deliberately a shot into the already dying, practically dead Tyloe. That, somehow, waked a grim rage in Gavity.

There was something else about it, too . . . It was Binnings's you-be-damned manner. For no reason at all, the killer's contempt of all La Fe included Gavity. For he had ignored that large young man, who was not used to being stared through. The gesture had power to irritate Gavity exceedingly. And he had never been a man to annoy or irritate needlessly. He was far too much a creature of impulse—if not at all impulsive. He had only one creed: He did exactly what pleased him if nobody could stop him.

Now, as Binnings walked away and he felt that dislike of the man rising, swelling, he looked at the group that gathered about Tyloe. *They* had been dismissed from Binnings's consideration with contempt—so that calm turn of Binnings's back had said as plainly as words could have done. He was not in the least worried about anything they might do. Gavity studied them. Were they resenting it? Not in the least, so far as he could see. He shook his tawny head grimly.

'Binnings has killed two of them—the town crowd,' he thought. 'He's snapped his fingers at the rest of 'em and asked what they're going to do about it. And they won't even try arresting him. Not—any! And he looked through me just as if I—I—'

Suddenly he turned, on purest impulse. He rode along the edge of the sidewalk in Binnings's wake. As he rode, he unfastened the lariat that hung to his saddle-fork by a strap. Deftly, then, he shook out a small loop and hung it over Nubbins's neck. On that—the near—side, it was not apparent to Binnings, who walked on Gavity's right hand. Nubbins went closer . . .

Binnings turned when he heard the soft fall of the big horse's hoofs on the sandy street. He had his pistol in right hand and he lifted it a little when he stared at Gavity. He waited, frowning slightly.

Gavity returned the stare, but let his gray eyes drop to the Colt, then lift in widening—as of innocent surprise or respect—to the watchful dark face. He tried to appear the simple, almost stupid fellow who saw something that startled him. Then he nodded and pushed Nubbins on as if intent upon nothing more than getting past Binnings.

He saw the ghost of a mocking grin twitch at the gunman's thin mouth. Binnings was dismissing him now—as he had dismissed him farther back—as a man of no importance. If he had really seen him, back there by Tyloe's body! His pistol sagged again—and up over Nubbin's neck the loop of Gavity's lariat jerked, precisely like a snake's head coming from a coil. It flashed across some eight feet of space and dropped over Binnings . . .

Nubbins went off at an angle with the pressure of Gavity's knees. The lariat sang like a bowstring. Binnings struggled savagely to free himself with left hand of that tightening loop. He twisted his right hand and tried to turn, to get in position for a shot at Gavity. But it was hopeless, against skilled man and equally skilled horse. He was dragged into the street, jerked off his feet and dropped upon his face.

He loosed one shot, but the bullet from his double-action Colt merely churned sand between him and the horse. Then he was flat, with the loop tight about his arms just above the elbows. Gavity grinned as he looked back.

He left Nubbins to keep the slack taken— just as if Binnings had been a calf. Himself, he came like a pouncing cat out of the saddle and crossed the distance between him and the fallen man in a rush. He stamped upon Binnings's gunhand with a high heel, then stooped.

The second pistol he got out of Binnings's coat. This done, he lifted the gunman to his feet—lifted him with no more effort than he had exercised in raising Betty Ross's hundred pounds from the hammock.

Binnings stared at him. If he had been shaken by the unexpected drop of that loop and the dragging, there was nothing in large, liquidly black eyes to show it. He faced Gavity levelly and spoke almost without opening his teeth.

'I don't know who you are, my young cowboy,' he said evenly, harshly. 'But that one loop is going to cost you just a hell of a lot more than any common leather-pounder can afford. Just a lot more!'

'It might just accidentally turn out'— Gavity's tone was as drawling, as inflectionless, as Binnings's own—'that I am not a common leather-pounder. I might even be the man they used to model the statue. But don't bother about that. If you ever decided that you didn't like something I'd done—don't ever strain yourself. Just come collecting any old time. I'll probably be home.'

Something like a community gasp had come from the men watching that swift, unexpected capture of the killer. Now, they came surging toward the two—Gavity and Binnings. Both looked over shoulder at the moving crowd. Both could hear the beginning of that low, vicious, unforgettable muttering which is the first sound of a mob.

Gavity shook his head and looked at

Binnings.

'I have had some small experience with people, in my day,' he drawled. 'Jail—if it's a good, strong jail—ought to look pretty much like home to you, right now.'

'It does look a good deal like jail,' Binnings admitted, staring. 'That is, unless you feel like giving me back a gun. With a Colt in my hand I'll face ten thousand like that riff-raff—for as long as they can stand the music. How about it? Can I have a gun again?'

'No-o, I don't think so,' Gavity decided frowningly. 'I'd just have to take it away from you again when the noise was gone. I think I'll take you to jail. Come on!'

He twitched the loop easily from his prisoner and said that calves were harder to handle. Then he swung into the saddle and put down a hand to haul Binnings up. With the lariat still trailing in the street, he sent Nubbins at the trot, west on Bowie, to whirl about the intersection of Fay and go north. He sent Nubbins west again on Austin Street and came to a stop finally before a square, unplastered adobe building.

'Somebody told me it was here,' he informed his prisoner. 'And that sign seems to show I wasn't lied to . . . *City Hall* . . . *Jail* . . . *Marshal's Office* . . . Slide down. Here's where you get off, fella!'

'And what do we do now?' Binnings inquired. 'I take it you're a stranger in La Fe.

You wouldn't know that I might accidentally have some friends in this very place.'

'It wouldn't make a bit of difference to me,' Gavity assured him cheerfully, 'if every yellow dog in the joint wagged his tail at you. I brought you along because there's something about your particular style of face that I don't like. I am a stranger in La Fe. I don't know what the rule is. I just do as I please, more or less. So—here you are. March in!'

He followed Binnings to the ground and trailed him into the official headquarters of the City of La Fe.

5. 'La Fe needs der new marshal'

There were men sitting about a long table in the room on the left of the barred door of La Fe jail. Binnings went briskly into this room and Gavity, at his heels, noted that the half-dozen of them were quite cordial to the tall man.

A chubby and red-faced little man, round of body, nearly bald, held the presiding officer's chair at the head of the table. On this one's left was a big, imposing man in black frock coat, with wide, white Stetson pushed back upon his Henry Clay pompadour.

'Zelman,' Binnings said slowly, facing the chubby man, 'you sent to Fort Worth for Winn

Wheelen. I suppose you had your reasons?'

'I think we have der reason,' the little man nodded. His greenish eyes were steady on Binnings after a flashing glance at Gavity, silent and moveless in the door. 'And—'

'He's dead!' Binnings interrupted. 'So is Tyloe. I killed them both awhile ago.'

'Dead?' a little white rabbit of a man cried shrilly. 'Why, Wheelen—You mean—you mean you killed Wheelen and Tyloe both?'

'Keep out of this, Root,' Binnings told the little man. 'Zelman, I'm not particularly hard to get along with—if I'm properly treated. But Wheelen has bothered me a good deal and I have said up and down the streets that I don't like to be annoyed. It came to the point— don't try to seem surprised; you all knew it!— that Wheelen and I were going to shoot it out. Today, we did shoot it out. And Wheelen died. Then Tyloe decided he had to make some sort of play at arresting me. So—Tyloe is dead, too. Oh! Here is my witness. I don't know his name—'

'Gavity is the name,' Gavity said slowly, moving into the council room. 'I did happen to see Binnings do the two killings. In fact'— he looked at Binnings and, facing that mocking smile, grinned in his turn—'I decided to bring him in to jail, or to whatever you gentlemen think he ought to be. So—I brought him.'

Zelman frowned at him. The little Root—

51

from his sheaf of papers and ready pencil, Gavity thought Root must be the clerk of the council—rolled whitish eyes at him. The big man in Stetson and frock coat bit the end from a cheroot and lighted it, a shrewd eye squinted at the huge figure. But before any could speak, Binnings had the floor again.

'I knew that Wheelen intended to kill me on sight. I knew it this morning. He did nothing, today, but walk around looking for me. I happened to be out of town, else I would have got the word sooner. When I did get it, naturally I put my pistols in my pockets and came to settle the affair. I asked him if he happened to be looking for me. He drew his guns and—'

He turned then to Gavity. His smile was mocking.

'Right, so far, Gavity?' he asked. 'Tell the council! Oh! This is Mayor Zelman—"Zuzu" Zelman, he's usually called. Root, there, is city clerk. Never mind the other gentlemen for the moment. Just tell them what you saw. As a stranger—and one certainly not friendly to me, since you caught me unaware and insisted on my coming here—your word should carry weight.'

'It looked to me like a very fair fight,' Gavity admitted. 'Then, Tyloe—deputy marshal, I understand—ran up and called on Binnings to stop and be arrested. Instead, Binnings opened fire and killed Tyloe, who had a gun out.'

'And you?' Zelman grunted. 'You are der stranger, but you take der place of Tyloe, and you bring in Binnings—who has der name of der fast man . . . Why is that?'

'I don't like Binnings,' Gavity said calmly. '*I* don't think he's fast with a gun. I didn't like the way he stepped up and shot the kid deputy after Tyloe was as good as dead. And when I don't like somebody, I usually do something about it. This was one of those times. I just decided to bring him in. And—there he is!'

Binnings's face flushed. The chubby Zelman made a clucking sound that somehow carried more of amusement than a full laugh could have done. He looked from Gavity to Binnings and shrugged thick shoulders.

'Well,' he said deliberately, 'and if one that thinks of der Binnings like you—and maybe like some of der others in La Fe—he says der fight is der fair fight, I joost don't know . . . In La Fe, we have got der law; we have got der order. But, too, we have got der self-defense. And *I* don't see where you, Binnings, you break der law and der order. No?'

He looked at the others there. The little white rabbit—that was Gavity's term then and thereafter for Root, the city clerk—nodded as soon as he found the mayor's eyes on him. The big man in Stetson and frock coat nodded, also.

'Mere exercise of a gentleman's

53

prerogative,' he declared in a booming voice. 'And *that* is the way I'll write the topic in our palladium of the public liberty, gentlemen; in the *Weekly Bugle* of La Fe. A gentleman disagrees with another. He naturally arms himself—nothing else could be expected! He meets his enemy, who is also armed. So—'

Gavity looked from face to face of this section of La Fe's city council. His lips curled and he shrugged.

'There's nothing in the world like knowing where you are,' he told Zelman and the others generally. 'Self-defense is a phrase Texas well knows. Being a Texas man, I can't quarrel with it. But—I've been glancing at this book here, while you gentlemen have been talking . . .'

It was a thin pamphlet on the table under his hand. The legend on it read *Ordinances of the City of La Fe.* He pushed it with a heavy thumb and regarded Binnings with head on one side and face blank—and kept his thumbs hooked in the waistband of his overalls.

'I'm just a new citizen,' he said drawlingly. 'I don't know a lot about the town. But—here it says, under the heading of *Ordinance 64-B*, that carrying deadly weapons is a violation of the statutes and punishable by fine of fifty dollars. I am just wondering if Mr. Binnings has not come under the ordinance by packing the two guns that he killed Wheelen and Tyloe with . . . It's a fine point, of course. As the distinguished gentleman'—he bowed formally to the editor of that palladium of liberties, La Fe's *Weekly Bugle*—'has remarked, a gentleman has certain rights and privileges. But—is this ordinance ever enforced?'

Binnings stiffened and there was the flush of quick anger on his face again.

'Look here, Zuzu!' he snapped familiarly at the mayor. 'I don't know how far *you* intend to let this foolishness go, but I warn you that I'm getting tired of it! I—'

'But, Mis-ter Binnings!' Zelman checked him, in tone of gravity, even sadness, belied by the shine of the eyes turned ceilingward. 'Der ordinance is der ordinance and der law. We must joost not play favorytes, no? Der point of Mister Gavity is most well made. Please to give der clerk fifty dollars. Der council will not make of each gun what Mister Gavity has took from you der separate offense. Fifty dollars, now, please.'

Binnings looked around, but seemed to find no support anywhere. He snarled, but drew from an inner pocket of his coat a long leather wallet. From it he shook gold and dropped the fine on the table before Root.

'I said,' he told Gavity softly, 'that one loop was probably more than a common cowboy could afford. Possibly afford!'

'And I said—as I recall—that maybe I am not a common leather-pounder,' Gavity reminded him. 'Too, I said something about trying to be around, just any time you feel like trying to collect. You'll remember that? All I ask is that you come at me from the front . . .'

'I'll remember!' Binnings promised. Now his tone had thickened. 'I'll damn well remember. So will you!'

He whirled and went out of the council room. Gavity watched him disappear, then looked without pleasure at the members present of La Fe's city council.

'And that's that!' he drawled. 'If it means anything. And if you figure it suits you-all, Lord knows it ought to practically please me to death. Gentlemen! *Hasta la vista!* Until I see you again. Of course, I can hope that won't be too soon!'

'One minute, my friend!' Zelman checked him. 'For der council of der city of La Fe, I thank you. You do not know La Fe. But you do know what is fair and you know what is right, by der light you have. Now, today, you have done joost fine. And so, I have der wonder. I—'

'Don't strain yourself!' Gavity said grimly. 'I think what I want is a drink. Lord knows I need something to get a taste out of my mouth, after this exhibition!'

He went out even more stiffly than Binnings had done. Zelman called to him again. The big man in the white Stetson added his voice. As he made the street, little Root the clerk came running after him.

'The mayor says—' he began, then gave ground before the sweep of Gavity's long arm.

'Tell the mayor—and the council—to go take a running jump for themselves,' Gavity snarled.

He went across to Nubbins and swung up. Then he rode down to the corner and up an alley, to the city corral. A loafing hostler showed him a stall and locked saddle and bridle in a harness room. Then Gavity crossed vacant lots to the back door of the Criterion Saloon, which was also a dance-hall. He stood looking about the huge room—in which bar and dance-floor were separated only by a row of iron columns. Nobody danced at this hour of late afternoon. But the bar was well patronized.

He drew no particular stares when he stood drinking. But he felt better for the punch of his white-handled six-shooter, carried now against his side in the waistband of his overalls, covered by flannel shirt. La Fe, he thought, was a 'sudden' community; and he had made a deadly enemy that day, in Binnings.

He drank moodily. The lift which had come, with holding Betty Ross in his arms, had somehow died. Very well, indeed, he knew Bryan Ross—and knew Betty. How long she would stand out against her father was problematical. It seemed to Gavity that Betty had been right in her farewell: he needed plenty of luck to establish himself here in La Fe, in such position that Bryan Ross must admit him as good a prospect for son-in-law as some doctor or lawyer or banker or merchant. Betty would find it hard to argue with her father.

'And what can I do here?' he asked himself. 'I know the cow-business. It would be odd if a Gavity didn't, after these generations in Texas . . . I wonder if old Tim Free could use a roan about my size, in his cow-buying . . . I think I'll wander down and hunt him up and put the question to him. He ought to have beef contracts enough, with the railroad construction camps loaded with men, to do a lot. Yes, sir! Tim Free is my first prospect. If I can dig in with him—'

A hand touched his arm and automatically he hooked a thumb in his waistband before he turned. Then, with sight of 'Zuzu' Zelman the mayor smiling up at him, he relaxed.

'My friend,' the mayor said softly, '*I* think you are der hard man to talk with. But all der same I will talk with you. Back yonder, at der table by der wall.'

'Talk with me about—what?' Gavity demanded unpleasantly. 'If I'm supposed to testify in the case of La Fe *versus* Binnings, I'll testify in court. But I don't want to talk about it here and now. So, as I told your clerk, the bunch of you can jump off something high, for all me. I don't like La Fe. I don't care a lot for the way it's run, somehow. I—'

'And, maybe, it was der same notion that brought me to look for you,' Zelman checked him, even more quietly. 'I think you will listen to der talk I have got . . .'

There was more to the chubby little man than appeared in his round, red face, Gavity admitted. He nodded grudgingly and went to the back of the big room, slowing his long steps to accommodate the mayor's short-legged stride. They sat down and a waiter brought whisky and glasses.

They raised full glasses formally and drank. Zelman got out stogies from a coat pocket and offered one to Gavity, who shook his head and made a cigarette.

'Der town is *not* run so well,' Zelman said slowly. 'When der railroads start here, der bums start here. Der good people, too! But der bums is most. We try der man, Huckafee, for marshal. For der old La Fe, Huckafee will do. For der new La Fe and der tough times with der bad mans, Huckafee will *not* do! So we make him der deputy marshal. And we send to Fort Worth for Winn Wheelen with der two fast guns . . .'

He shrugged and shook his baldish head frowningly.

'And even now, I do not see how it is, that Binnings or somebody should kill our so-fast gunfighter! From Fort Worth we get der word about Wheelen; how nobody almost is so fast!'

'He had that name across a wide scope of country,' Gavity agreed. 'Anywhere in Texas— or on north, for that matter—you could hear tales of Wheelen's notches. He was a gunslinger from who-laid-the-chunk. But—he *is* dead . . .'

'Dead he is!' Zelman echoed him. 'And so, Mis-ter Gavity—La Fe needs der new marshal . . . Will you take der job? You do not know der town, but you will not be afraid for that. You know der kind of mans we got. You know der kind of town we want. You have do today joost fine. Der pay is four hundred dollars a month. Will you take der job?'

He fumbled in a pocket and held out his hand. On the wide palm was that gold badge which Gavity had seen on Wheelen's vest. *City Marshall*, it had been lettered. Someone had scratched off the final l.

Gavity stared at the shield, then began to shake his head. But two faces somehow came to mind—and a third. He visualized Binnings and his you-be-damned manner that irritated him. He saw Betty. Last, he pictured Bryan Ross. He hesitated. The thought of meeting Binnings with both official badge and six-shooter was very pleasant. As for Bryan Ross and his daughter—

'I'll take it!' he said suddenly to Zelman. 'I'll enforce your ordinances as long as I can keep a gun smoking. I'll enforce 'em against Tom and Dick and Harry. No favorites; no politics. The mayor and the council have got to back me or I'll quit as soon as I start. As for deputies, I'll pick 'em myself. Pick 'em with a fine-toothed comb! If that layout suits you, I'm your marshal. I came here to start in. So—'

'You are der marshal! Please to raise your right hand *oop* and I swear you—'

Gavity lowered his hand and took the badge. He turned it over mechanically and scowled. The underside was red-smeared . . . Winn Wheelen's blood . . . Binnings . . .

'What?' he said vacantly, looking at Zelman.

'I say—now we talk! About La Fe; about der troubles . . .'

They poured second drinks and Zelman, drawing slowly on his stogie, shrewd eyes narrowed, began to tell of conditions in and about La Fe. They were grave enough, as he described them in his accented English!

Murders, store-robberies, holdups, assassinations of various sorts, were everyday affairs. There were so many of them that men talked of an organized gang under intelligent and ruthless leadership. Stage-robberies like that at Harmony Station sixty miles away were common.

'And nobody has made a guess at the criminals' names?' Gavity asked incredulously. 'You can't get a line on men in town without ways of making money but who spend a good deal of money? You see, I was a deputy sheriff once; I happen to know a little about catching this kind of bird. It does seem to me that some of your people ought to be under suspicion.'

'We have got nobody under der suspicion,' Zelman said helplessly. 'You could believe der fellas rode der horse joost without der foot.'

Gavity thought of that rider who had bulleted his mocking notice on the handbills outside of town. He told Zelman of it and the mayor leaned eagerly across the table.

'You could know der man again? Der horse?'

'Too far away for me to identify him. And nothing but a big bay horse. There are too many bay horses in any neighborhood to go by that.'

He finished his drink and pinned the badge to his shirt.

'All right, Your Honor! I'll see what I can do about everything, as soon as I look La Fe over and get acquainted. I came to La Fe to be one of your leading citizens. I'll try to make a good town of it. That's the only promise I make.'

6. *'A full day'*

Gavity stood beside Zelman on the sidewalk outside the Criterion. Gavity looked down at the badge; polished it gently with a shirt-sleeve. Zelman grinned.

'I feel betters!' the little mayor said suddenly. 'About de town, I mean. You are not der bragger—like Huckafee. You are not der cold killer—like Wheelen. But I think you are der good marshal for La Fe. You—Gott! Look at der Mexican ride!'

It was a bareheaded Mexican on a barebacked horse. He came up the middle of Fay Street, having turned across vacant lots from somewhere in the direction of the Stage Company corrals. He was kicking his mount frantically. At sight of Zelman he sent the chestnut over toward the Criterion's hitch-rack.

'*Su Excelencia!*' he panted. Then, in staccato Spanish, he went on to gasp out his story. 'My *amo*, Don Timoteo Free, he has killed two men, thieves of horses both, at the corral of the Company on Midwest Street. He asks that you send someone to see the dead.'

Gavity shook his head and regarded the mayor sadly.

'It does seem,' he said slowly, 'that La Fe has just bodaciously wandered up and sat down in my lap! I'll go take a look at Tim Free's work. If he's really downed him two horse-thieves, fine! They might even be two of the bunch we were talking about.'

He made a small gesture to the Mexican and the man dropped to the ground with flash of dark eyes toward Gavity's badge. The big chestnut grunted with the impact of Gavity's weight upon his back, then lunged across the street and galloped with flash of sand back toward the Midwest Stage Company's 'dobe headquarters.

Tim Free and a critical—but altogether commendatory—audience stood outside the long building of the Midwest Company. The two dead men were sprawled just inside the corral gate. They lay some ten feet apart. Each had a pistol under his limp fingers. Tim Free nursed a burned forearm without much thought of the wound. The hat rammed back on his head had a bullet-hole in the high crown. He nodded at Gavity, then the badge caught his eye and he gaped:

'You—you—they give you the marshaling job?' he cried.

'I promised to give it a whirl,' Gavity said. 'Now, about this business. What happened?'

'I walked into the corral, here, today,' the lank buyer said reflectively. 'See these two gunies coming toward me and I recollected 'em. Reckon they done the same. You see, son, the two of 'em was hanging around a camp of mine three months back. They went out like smoke—and so did nine head of good horses, all mine! So, when they seen me today, I reckon they figured the jig was up. They jumped apart and started to slap leather. So did I! And—they are lying there waiting for the inquest . . .'

'It was exactly like that,' a dark little man agreed. 'I'm the manager of the Stage Company in La Fe, Marshal. I was with Tim Free when he sighted 'em. I dropped down behind that feed-trough, yonder. I seen it all. It was just like Tim says—to a frawg's hair. They knowed the jig was up when they seen Tim.'

'It certainly sounds like a fair shootin,' Gavity announced, looking around him. 'If we can get a hack of some kind, I'll send 'em down to the City Hall for an inquest.'

'Oh, I can give you a hack,' the manager offered. 'José! Tomás! A carriage for these men. *Andarle!*'

The crowd thickened as the dead men were loaded into a light wagon and Gavity stood superintending the job. He watched it go creaking off with a Mexican driver on the seat, then turned back to Tim Free. And Bryan Ross met his eyes. Tim Free was talking:

'One thing I can't stand or endure and that's a damn' thief! I would walk and sleep on a thief's trail till I got him, if it took me the rest of my life!'

65

He moved off and Gavity found himself beside Ross. He shook his head, staring after the tall cow-buyer.

'He's a lot like an Indian,' Gavity said, as if thinking aloud. 'If he's for you, he's for you the whole chunk. If he hates you, he'll kill you—unless you kill him first. And if that was any sample, you'd better get your killing-clothes on, before you start to wipe out his mark . . .'

'Like a damn' Apache!' Ross agreed. 'Never forgets; never forgives. I wouldn't want him on *my* trail!'

'Zelman told me he had appointed you to fill out the stub of that dead alderman's term,' Gavity remarked, looking down at the pompous little man. 'I suppose you'll stand for election for the full term, next month?'

'My friends are insisting on me standing for the full term,' Ross said, nodding. Then he seemed to recall that he talked to Gavity. 'If that's any of your business! What did Zelman make you marshal for?'

'That's really a joke on him,' Gavity drawled. 'You see, he thinks I'm as brave as I am big. So he offered me the star and—being the kind of particular idot I always have been—I took it. Maybe I'll make as good a marshal as you'll make an alderman. Won't *that* be a funny thing for La Fe! Both of us working for the good of our fair city . . .'

His one-time employer snorted:

'Well, I'll tell you one thing, right here and right now: marshal's star or no star, I don't want you around my house or around my daughter! I warn you—you stay away from Betty! I've told her before and I certainly will tell her again: no saddle-tramp is going to marry her. And she minds what I tell her!'

'You're a funny kind of hairpin,' Gavity said thoughtfully. 'The funniest cowman I ever saw. But, then, I reckon you never did care a lot about the cow-business. This city life is just about what suits you. Maybe it suits Betty, too—I wouldn't know. But I do know this: I love Betty and Betty loves me. Maybe you can mess that around, so I'll never get her. I wouldn't say as to that. I've even heard that the course of true love is not likely to run smooth—and that makes mine pretty much to order. But you can't get around the fact that we're both crazy about each other and, if I can manage it, I'll have her!'

'She's not crazy about you!' Bryan Ross cried. 'And even if she was she wouldn't marry you. Because I wouldn't let her, and she knows it! Betty is a good girl, and she'll marry the man I tell her to marry!'

Gavity watched him strut off. A queer stick! He remembered how Bryan Ross had sweated and worried about the mortgage on the Slash R; how relieved he had been when somewhere he had raked together enough to pay the notes; how enthusiastic he had been about

67

coming to La Fe.

Suddenly Ross turned:

'I'll be one of the aldermen!' he yelled. 'A fine marshal you'll make! And I'll have something to say about you keeping the job. Don't you forget that!'

'Want me to go to supper with you?' Gavity yelled, in his turn. 'It'll put me out, but you have got to suffer from relatives and I'd do a lot for mine—even the to-be kind.'

He found a Chinese restaurant on Fay Street and ate his supper. He finished the meal and went back to the City Hall. The jailer told him that the dead Mexicans were in a cell, ready for the justice of the peace to officiate, next morning, at the inquest. He added that the justice was too drunk tonight to be troubled. He was a 'stove-up' cowboy, by his own admission, this jailer.

'Reckon this ain't going to help Huckafee's feelings a li'l' bit,' he said, grinning. 'I mean, the council making you marshal. Huckafee could maybe stand 'em bringing in Winn Wheelen. Wheelen had a rep' for gunplay. But taking on a stranger is something else. You want to watch out for Huckafee. He ain't what you'd call a slouch with the hoglegs hisself. But, then, I reckon he'll have his hands full tonight . . .'

'I don't think I've seen Huckafee yet,' Gavity grunted, without interest. 'And I don't see that it's any of his business if the council appoints a marshal. What's he going to be doing tonight, to be so busy?'

'You're a stranger in town,' the jailer told him tolerantly. 'You don't know Huckafee. He's plumb poison when he gets started drinking and hating somebody. Right now, it's a tinhorn out of the Tepee gambling-hall. You see, Huckafee's stuck on a floozy at the Criterion. Sal Como Se Llama—What-Do-You-Call-Her. Never did hear her name. But Huckafee's stuck on her and she's stuck on this tinhorn, Whitey. I seen Huckafee here a half-hour back. He was looking at his pistol and talking to hisself. Putting in new loads. Somebody'd told him that Sal and Whitey was dancing down at the Criterion. Huckafee says *he'd* see about how they danced; he'd make 'em dance!'

'Goodness, me!' Gavity drawled. ' A deputy marshal, talking that way. At the Criterion, you say. We mustn't have doings like that. Might give the police force a bad name . . .'

'Hell'll pop if Huckafee catches Sal and Whitey together,' the jailer said ominously. 'He'll kill Whitey!'

Gavity went—as he had gone once before—across the vacant lots to the Criterion's rear door. He moved into much more of activity this time. The dance-floor was crowded. Girls in brief skirts and low-cut waists were whirled about by men who seemed more or less drunken. As Gavity stood near the end of the bar and looked through the iron columns from the bar-room, he observed cynically that the dances were very short and the intervals for drinks correspondingly extended.

While he stood there, watching, he saw a man in citizen's clothing and battered black Stetson hat push out on the dance-floor. The man staggered a little and he cannoned into dancers and went on as if deaf to their angry remarks. Suddenly he made a little run forward and Gavity saw his hand go under his coat and reappear holding a pistol. He snatched with his left hand at someone. A girl screamed shrilly, a high, frightened sound.

Gavity charged through the milling figures on the floor, pushing them aside even more carelessly than the other had done. He reached the knot of struggling, panting, cursing figures. The man with the gun had a pallid little man by the throat, fingers closed upon the man's flowing Windsor tie. This one gripped the other's gunwrist with both hands. Desperately, he was trying to keep the man's gun trained muzzle down. A girl also was hanging to that wrist. The pistol roared before Gavity had time to interfere. The bullet splintered the floor.

Gavity caught the armed man's hand. He squeezed gently and the pistol dropped. Easily, Gavity tore the two apart. He sent the gunman reeling backward with a slight shove and let the gasping little man go into the girl's

70

arms.

The gunman staggered, but his hand went under his coat again. Gavity crossed the three yards that separated them in a flashing jump. He slapped downward with palm-edge, to drive the gunhand from under the coat. Then he set himself coldly and drove his fist into the man's face. When he had crashed to the floor, Gavity stooped over him and jerked from a belt-holster the man's second gun, a heavy .45. He rammed it into his waistband and bent again. This time he took from Huckafee's vest a deputy marshal's badge. He straightened.

Whatever else any face in that silent, staring crowd mirrored, there was no lack of interest in him showing anywhere! He looked sardonically about, meeting eyes that were only speculative, eyes that were openly hostile.

'I take it this is Huckafee,' he said slowly. 'One-time marshal, now ex-deputy marshal. Most of you have got some idea about me—about who I am. I'll tell you what I'm thinking now: too many guns are being carried. I don't like it. There's an ordinance against it. I intend to see that ordinance enforced. As for Huckafee—when he wakes, some of you tell him that he's off the force. I don't want him. I won't have him as deputy. If he makes a move antigodlin, I'll slam him where the li'l' dogs won't possibly be able to bite him—if he's alive . . .'

Again he looked from face to face. Nobody

moved or spoke. He went without haste toward the street, and silence held until he pushed through the swinging doors. Then came a quick gabbling of excited voices. He grinned at the sound.

'A full day!' he said. 'And—I wonder what Betty will say . . .'

7. 'My name's Finch'

Gavity ate at the Chinese restaurant for the second time, in the bright light of early morning. The night had been peaceful enough—surprisingly quiet—after the small disturbance in the Criterion. He looked back upon it almost amusedly. But he knew very well that La Fe would not accept a new marshal without some display of belligerence. It was not that sort of town.

He was amused, also, by evidence of the interest the townsfolk showed in him. Here at the narrow restaurant where he sat close to other breakfasters, men looked at him with sliding eyes to his face and away again. As in the Criterion and other saloons during his patrol of the night before, there were men who regarded him smilingly, others who seemed to study him with narrow intentness, and still more whose eyes held open hostility. So, he ate placidly . . .

He had finished his meal and loafed over a third cup of coffee when a stocky, grinning Mexican came into the restaurant. He looked up and down and, when he had found Gavity, came down the room and thrust out a big hand.

'I am Pancho Ramos,' he said, grin widening. 'You have the Spanish, I hear.'

'Enough,' Gavity told him. 'And I know of you. It is told me that you are the constable. What is said of you? Oh, yes! A wise head but not one of much bravery. Is that Pancho Ramos?'

Ramos's grin seemed to split dark face from ear to ear. He pulled out a chair and sat down.

'By God!' he cried. 'It *sounds* like me. There are no fools in the family of the Ramoses. As for being brave—what would you? Will a statue feed my twelve children? If I am killed playing the brave idiot, will a resolution of the council read in the plaza do my widow any service? I am brave enough, I think. But no fool. I do my work as constable and let the marshal do what killing—or being killed!—is needed.'

There was something infectious about his grin and his cheerful self-analysis. Gavity laughed.

'*Muy bien*, then! I am glad to know you. There is, of course, some good reason—some Ramos-reason—for looking for Marshal Gavity this morning. Tell!'

'Body of God!' Ramos said, still grinning. 'You are not the *tonto* of hard fist and quick gun and no brain that some in La Fe are calling you. *I* think that you and I may understand each other well enough. But there is no reason of specialness for my talk this morning. I but wished to see what that old fox, the mayor had given us for marshal. *Amor de Dios!* With a sheriff who comes never to La Fe, but stays in Palmas safely twenty miles away, a constable needs to know who is the Law in his precinct.'

He picked up Gavity's tobacco sack and papers and made a cigarette with a *'favor, señor!'*

'I think that I may be of help to you. There are things here in La Fe which of course, you do not know. If you like, we will go about the town together and I will tell you everything. *Cuerpo de Cristo!* There is little about the place that I, Pancho Ramos, do not know! I was born here.

They went out on the street together, and before they had walked a block Gavity admitted that the constable had not exaggerated his knowledge of the town. He spoke to half the men they met; he gave quick sketches of the other half—how long they had been in La Fe, what they claimed to do for a livelihood and what he believed they did do.

Every door they passed brought equally brief and vivid descriptions. This saloon-keeper stood in with the sporting crowd; that one was a good citizen. The Gleaming Gem was owned by no less a personage than Mayor Zelman. Gavity shook his head at last. He was still puzzling over the constable's interest in him.

'You do know the town, now, don't you?' he said slowly. 'I am a straightforward man, Pancho. I say what I mean. So—why are you so interested in me? Do not trouble to lie. I am the seventh son of many seventh sons. I will know if you lie.'

'It is very simple,' Ramos confessed, grin much in evidence. 'I am a constable and I like the work and the pay. You and I must see much of each other, for my precinct is your beat. I do not wish to be killed. So, if I can be a friend of the marshal, I wish to be a friend of the marshal. Huckafee did not like me. I would have you like me. Anything I can do—'

'Except fight?' Gavity grunted.

'I might fight, also—if I were sure that need was for fighting,' Ramos disagreed. 'It would depend. And since you speak of fighting— listen! There is the blacksmith shop of Patrick O'Rourke. He is a grand Irishman, that Patrick. The best smith and shoer of horses for a hundred miles north or south or east or west. Once each month he buys a gallon of whisky—'

'You mean that shot?' Gavity interrupted him. 'That was in the blacksmith shop, wasn't it?'

'Of a certainty! As I said, once a month, no more, no less, O'Rourke must have his celebration, his *fiesta*. He buys his gallon of whisky and he drinks it. And while he is *borracho*—most drunk—he will tell those who come past that he is the most savage of men. While drunk, he is very noisy, and if one does not know he seems the most deadly of killers. For twenty-and-seven days of each month, he walks like a baby in the shadow of the sunbonnet of his wife—who is certain that the sun rises and sets in him. But for three days he is—very drunk! I think he has his pistol loaded, now. It is that time in the month.'

'Well, then,' Gavity said resignedly, 'let us look in at him. If he has a pistol he will certainly make holes in the roof of his shop. He might even shoot someone passing.'

They crossed the street to the blacksmith shop and moved through a litter of broken wagons and leaning wheels to look into the gloomy place.

Gavity stared at the gigantic, pink-faced blacksmith and grinned. Not even the long-barreled Colt that O'Rourke was waving, not even the ferocious language addressed to a smallish cowboy in a corner, could make O'Rourke anything but a play-actor at deadliness.

'I warn you!' O'Rourke bellowed, gesturing violently with the pistol. 'Do you understand me? I am telling you that I am not a man to be crossed. Me, Patrick O'Rourke! They fold up the sidewalks and nail up the windies when Paddy O'Rourke chooses to be coming down the street in La Fe. It was the same in Fort Worth and San Antonio. Do not be arguing with me, little man. Something about the face of you tells me you would argue. Do *not* argue with me!'

'I want my hawse shod,' the cowboy said snarlingly. 'I never come in for no armload of gab—'

He was nothing much to look at, with the faded coat, the worn flannel shirt, the batwing leggings and dusty hat of a working hand. But there was something about his thin face and yellowish eyes and loose, sullen mouth that made Gavity distrust him instinctively.

'Do not be talking back, little man!' O'Rourke yelled. He waved the Colt violently. 'What you might be coming in for and what you will be taking home with you might be two different things! Very well they might. A harse, you say. And what would you be knowing of harses?'

'It will be better if we go in and take his pistol?' Pancho Ramos whispered to Gavity. 'I do not know that little man, but he seems to me one of bad temper. He will not know O'Rourke—'

Gavity moved in a rush that carried him halfway across the dusky shop. But he was too late. The cowboy had moved a hand from behind him. A short Colt roared and flamed in that hand. O'Rourke's great body jerked with the impact of slug after slug, fired at that almost point-blank range.

The long-barreled pistol dropped from the blacksmith's huge hand. He turned slowly and faced Gavity. His eyes were narrowed and his mouth sagged. He put up a hand to his hairy breast and took it away dribbled with red. He opened his eyes and stared, then looked at Gavity with pink moon face a mask of bewilderment almost childish.

'I'm bad hurt!' he said slowly. 'Very bad hurt. Don't be letting the wife know of it. It would kill her—'

He came crashing forward, and Gavity barely caught him and eased him to the cindery floor of the shop. Gavity felt for a heartbeat and found it, but very faint. He looked up grimly at the little man of the yellow eyes. The cowboy met his stare calmly. He was still holding the 'stingy' gun and thin wisps of gray smoke drifted from the muzzle.

'He thought he was Something!' the cowboy said scornfully. 'Hell! He was Nothing! Ain't Nothing. My name's Finch. I'm from Tombstone where there's gunslingers that's really gunslingers. I stopped in here to get my hawse shod. He was painted up for war, he was. Full of gab. All right! Me, I take 'em like they come. Tough—or else!'

'Pancho!' Gavity called over his shoulder. 'Take this imitation hard case's horse. To ride! Get a doctor here as fast as you can travel. But—he's gone . . .'

He stood, then. O'Rourke's breathing was hardly to be seen or heard. And a stooped little woman ran through the back door of the shop. She blinked around for an instant, then looked toward O'Rourke on the floor. She screamed shrilly and ran to the big, moveless figure on the cinders. She dropped beside O'Rourke and flung her arms about him.

Gavity turned away and faced Finch. He walked over to the killer and Finch made a slight movement of the pistol.

'Don't you!' Gavity advised him coldly. 'Hand over that cutter—butt front. And don't get notions about the old Road-Agent Spin, either! I cut my teeth on that stunt. Hand it over!'

'What kind of dog-town is this, anyhow?' Finch snarled. 'I stand up before a gun that a drunk's holding and I pull a cutter and save my life—'

'Shut up! You're in the clear, of course. But just because that poor wind-raiser had a Colt in his hand, don't get the notion that you're going to be a hero around La Fe, or get a rep' as a gunfighter, because you killed him when there was no reason for shooting. Hand it over—right now!'

There were five notches, filed big, on the

barrel of Finch's Colt. Gavity looked at them with curl of mouth. Finch snarled at him.

'Shut up!' Gavity commanded, again. 'Stay right here until we've had the doctor in. Then we'll have the inquest.'

He looked uncomfortably at the little woman who still clung to O'Rourke. At the shop door he waited until a gray man came galloping up on Finch's horse. He watched the doctor's examination and kept back the growing crowd. Mrs. O'Rourke waited dumbly until the doctor straightened and shook his head. Then she dropped to her knees again, and only when a Mexican woman came in and put arms around her did she lift her face from O'Rourke's.

'Where's the body?' someone called from the door. 'Good Gemini! Man can't git a minute's rest! Inquesting all the time. Two Mexicans at the City Hall—now, this. Good Gemini! Don't know who'd want to be a justice of the peace—'

He was a bareheaded, watery-eyed little man in dirty green shirt and ancient black pants, with sockless feet flapping in Mexican sandals of cowhide. He came snarling through the crowd and looked at O'Rourke. Then he stared at Gavity and Finch.

'Well, who killed him? Who killed him? Somebody killed him! Talk up! I ain't got all day to hang around.'

'I killed him,' Finch said defiantly. 'He was

80

waving a gun at me and threatening around. So I pulled and dropped him.'

'Who seen it? Come on, talk up!' the justice snapped.

'He killed him, all right,' Gavity drawled. 'And in a way it was as he says. The only thing is, O'Rourke was drunk and playing with that pistol. He never actually pointed it at Finch. But I don't suppose it would be a bit of use to charge Finch with anything. O'Rourke did have his gun out.'

'You're the marshal, huh? Well, time we got acquainted. I'm Judge Sayre, justice of the peace. Sheriff's my brother. Nothing to do, here. If you seen it and O'Rourke was waving a gun, it's plain self-defense. That's what I call it.'

He whirled away and, with sandals flapping on the cinders, plunged into the crowd and disappeared. Finch's yellow eyes rolled maliciously to Gavity. He grinned.

'And that, like you might say, is that!' he drawled. 'I suppose I can have that gun back now?'

'You can have it back,' Gavity told him slowly. 'But you will be wise if you hang it up at the first saloon you make. You'll be even wiser if you remember one thing around here: don't give anybody in La Fe any trouble, Finch. Most of all, don't give *me* any trouble! And find something to do around La Fe . . . Don't put in your time hanging around saloons and dives, spending money when you're not making money. In fact—'

He turned to look from face to face in that watching crowd; caught eye after eye and held them coldly.

'In fact, that's going to be damn' good advice for the town in general. There's been a lot of murder and robbery going on; maybe I have got some ideas about the subject. I'll be checking up on a lot of people. So will some others here in La Fe—men nobody will know except myself. One of the things that will make me suspicious of a man is his ability to live without working. Better think about that. All right, Finch! Here's the gun. You're clear—for the time being. And the next time you have any connection with an inquest, it's my pious hope that we'll be acquitting the man who drops you!'

Finch looked as if about to make answer. But, instead, he laughed and turned to swagger out to his horse. Gavity looked dourly after him. Then Tim Free and Pancho Ramos shouldered up to him. He shook his head and faced the constable.

'I suppose we'll have to do something about O'Rourke,' he said. 'Carry him into his house and send for the undertaker. Let's get it done . . .'

When that last grim move of the tragedy was done, he walked toward Bowie Street between Ramos and Free.

'I keep seeing that poor, windy Irishman and that little woman,' he said slowly.

'You'd a damn' sight better be thinking about the live ones, not the dead ones!' Tim Free grunted. He held up a hand, fingers extended, touched the thumb with his opposite forefinger. 'Binnings! Ben Miles! Pug! Huckafee! Now, Finch!'

He ticked off the names on his fingers and nodded ominously.

'Yes, sir! For a man that hit town just yesterday, you have done right good! Five men in this town that's looking for a chance to kill you. And nothing about you to show you ain't going to make a hell-slew more of enemies, today—tomorrow! You better start swinging wide around corners and looking hawk-eyed at every swing door. Come on! What you need is a drink—about three fingers in a washtub!'

8. 'I haven't got a gun'

There were alligators in the pool of the plaza. Gavity, having had his drink with Tim Free and Pancho Ramos, shook them off and loafed under the cottonwoods by the *acequia*. Very much, he wanted to see Betty Ross. He leaned on the flimsy wooden railing that guarded the pool and looked at the moveless reptiles on the grass.

He wondered whether he had been foolish to accept Zuzu Zelman's offer of the marshal's star. All his life he had been outdoors, a saddle-tramp, a drifting cowboy going wherever impulse led him. He had made money enough, at working or at gambling, to pay his expenses.

'And then,' he told the right-hand alligator grimly, 'I hit the Slash R over in the Grindstones . . . And when I saw her, something told me that there was the woman I wanted . . .'

He had known it almost from the moment of seeing her, on Bryan Ross's lonely ranch. And she had seemed to feel much the same emotion. But—did she really love him? He tried to decide the question, but shrugged it off, at last. There had been an experienced, a worldly-wise, woman once. In the inspired glow of her liquor she had looked at the young Gavity and told him that his very bigness and ruggedness and *lack* of what the world called 'good looks' would be drawing attraction for many women.

But, she had warned him, it would exist only in his presence. He wondered if that would be—could be—true in Betty's case . . . He scowled at the alligator and shook his head.

'She acted, yesterday, like a girl glad to see a man,' he thought. 'But it does seem a good

84

deal like change, somehow . . . Bryan Ross is certainly not fond of me in any way. He has been talking to her—not altogether against me, but telling her how this man and that man will come after her. And that is certainly true; it would be a strange man who didn't want her! She could hardly help thinking about her prospects; thinking that I'm not among the best of those . . .'

'And so you're the marshal!' Betty said from behind him. 'My, my! A big, gold badge—and a good chance of getting killed before you get it shined . . .'

He turned jerkily and straightened.

'Betty,' he said, almost without thinking of what he said, 'are we engaged? Do you think we're going to get married?'

'Of course we're not engaged,' she assured him. 'You know that as well as I do. We—well, we—we like each other a lot. But—'

He thought that she was more than usually lovely, this summer nooning, in flowered chintz frock, with the delicate oval of her face framed in a new bonnet that—like her sunshade—must have come from St. Louis or New York.

'Why did you take the marshal's badge?' she demanded. Her eyes were grave. 'Don't you know that it's dangerous? Very dangerous! Don't you—'

'It was a mixture of reasons,' he told her slowly. 'Maybe the very thing you mention—

85

the chance of getting wiped out—has an interest. It would settle things and I could feel, going out under some hard case's lead, that I'd done better than if I'd snapped my neck trying to tie an outlaw steer. And that was the way I headed when I hit the Grindstones and the Slash R. Just a tramp-cowboy without much interest in being anything but a leather-pounder riding the chuckline.'

He shrugged and smiled at her. But, somehow, she seemed very far away; almost like a person met for the first time and not a girl whom he had held close against him no longer ago than yesterday. He shook his head.

'I think I'm sort of down on the world today,' he said slowly. 'I saw a poor, fumbling Irish blacksmith murdered—'

'But Paddy O'Rourke had his pistol out!' she protested. 'Even if he wasn't much of a shot, he could have killed Finch, couldn't he? It seems that Finch had a right to protect his life. I knew O'Rourke, Arthur. He was the finest old fellow in the world, sober. But, suppose in one of his drunken moments he *had* killed somebody? He—'

'I don't know! I just know that the sight of him lying on the cinders in the shop, with that poor little old woman crying over him, made me want to kill Finch right then and there! I'm just down, as I said. Besides, I've talked to your father a time or two and I suppose you're right: he dislikes me and there's no chance he'll ever change his opinion.'

He stared moodily at the alligators. She came closer; put her hand impulsively, gently, on his arm.

He turned quickly and covered that hand with his own.

'The trouble is, I'm absolutely crazy about you. I'm nothing but a big roughneck cowpuncher. But I do love you, Betty. Don't let anything, or anybody, make you doubt that. I don't know where I'm going, today. This marshal job—I don't know where it will lead. I feel like a fish out of water. Before this, I've been out on the range where I could see a cow or a man coming at me. This is different . . .'

'Then why did you take it? "Why do you keep it?'

He shrugged big shoulders and scowled past her at the alligators.

'It's hard to say . . . Partly, I reckon, because it seemed that somebody had to take it and I'm man enough to handle it. Partly because— Well, never mind that! It was for a reason you wouldn't understand. Forget it! I took the job and I'll hang and rattle until something pops. The point is—I do love you and I wonder if you love me?'

'Wait awhile before you ask me that,' she said almost nervously. 'I do believe that you mean what you say. Now, tell me about O'Rourke and Finch.'

She listened with strained attention to the

brief story. At the end, she shook her dark head frowningly.

'Poor old Paddy O'Rourke! Poor Mrs. O'Rourke! But, Arthur, you couldn't do any more than you did do. You couldn't just kill Finch because he had a pistol drawn—not when Paddy was waving his pistol and making threats. You can't really blame Finch. *He* didn't know that Paddy O'Rourke was harmless. He just took him as he looked.

'I don't know what it is,' Gavity said grimly. 'All I know is that I don't like Finch and certain others around La Fe. And I know that one day of the job has changed me. I don't feel very happy about anything. You have changed. Don't deny it, Betty. You have. Maybe it's being in town. Maybe it's what your father has said. But you have changed.'

'I have not changed!' she denied—almost too quickly, Gavity thought. 'But—things may have changed. You have to admit that. Yesterday morning you were just a cowboy looking around La Fe. This morning you're the city marshal. Everybody in town knows you. Isn't that a change? You said *you* felt different!'

'You're right,' he admitted moodily. 'I am changed. Just as you're changed. And I could almost wish I never had seen La Fe—and that you never had seen the place, either. I'd like to be back in the Grindstones, taking you for rides . . .'

'I have to go,' she said abruptly. 'Don't take too many chances, Arthur. I—I hear some perfectly awful things about La Fe. Be careful and—'

'And come to see you?' he stopped her, then laughed. 'No, I know better than that. I can't come to see you. I'll have to take my chances of meeting you on the street. Good-bye, my dear. I have got to go, too. There's going to be another inquest this afternoon. And there seems to be a lot of hard feeling about it.'

'You mean Strater's case? I heard that it would be finished this morning.'

'No,' Gavity said without much interest. 'It was supposed to be finished, but the justice was so busy that he postponed the hearing until this afternoon. What makes you call it the Strater case, anyway? Strater hasn't been accused of anything, so far. He was the foreman on Fay Brothers' ranch at Cinecue. Two Mexican cowboys worked on the place. They were found murdered in the tornillo brakes and, as I get it, Strater is just a witness.'

'I don't know why, but everybody here seems to call it the Strater case. He had quarreled with the Mexicans and—'

'I didn't know that,' Gavity grunted, frowning. 'Of course, it's nothing to do with the marshal, anyway. The murders were committed in the county so it's up to the sheriff. And from what I hear, Sheriff Sayre is not likely to look into anything if it's the least trouble. Well, I have got to sort of ride herd on the inquest. That much is my job.'

He caught her hand again and held it, looking down at her steadily, thoughtfully.

'Betty,' he said slowly, 'I want more than I ever wanted anything to stay here in La Fe. For long enough, anyway, to make some money and show Bryan Ross that he's not the only one who can take advantage of a boom. That's just a side-issue, of course. I really want to make sure of you. Don't let all this town business turn you away from me! Promise?'

'I—I think a great deal of you,' she told him hesitantly. 'I don't think you're fair to try to pin me down to something. That's being like Daddy. Yesterday, he was trying to make me promise I wouldn't even speak to you on the street! I didn't promise him that. But—'

'All right. Never mind the promises. I'll see you here and there. I suppose I'll just take my chances on anything more.'

He let her pull away, and when she had gone quickly across the plaza he turned grimly, to walk down Fay Street to the vacant store adjoining Zelman's new brick building. Here the inquest would be held, on the bodies of two Mexican *vaqueros*.

Idlers, witnesses, were gathered before the open store when Gavity came past the Teepee gambling-room and Buchanan's hardware store. They looked curiously at the new marshal's huge figure, and out of the crowd a Mexican with a badge came grinning. He introduced himself in broken English as a deputy of Sheriff Sayre, and slipped into Spanish when Gavity answered in that tongue. He was the man who had discovered the bodies of the cowboys.

'They quarreled with this Sam Strater, who is a man feared by our people,' the deputy, Chavez, explained. 'Then for three days none of their friends or their families saw them. So I rode the tornillo brakes and came upon their bodies. They had been shot. This was two days ago, before you came to La Fe. We brought the bodies to the town, here. Now, the sheriff's brother holds his inquiry. I think he will be done with it by evening.'

'There are many witnesses,' Gavity said, looking at the Mexicans who stood together, a little apart from the Anglos. 'I think you will hardly hear them all before dark.'

'Oh, many of them will not testify,' Chavez prophesied, shrugging. 'Their stories will be the same. They heard the boys quarrel with Sam Strater about wages and with the brothers, the Fays, about their pay. Our sheriff's brother, the justice, will listen to one of a half-dozen. That German yonder, Schultz, will interpret. He is very good at Spanish and English. He was once a Ranger and knows our people. He has a Mexican wife.'

'And there's the judge, now,' Gavity said, with jerk of the head toward the little man. 'I will watch for a time and see that all is quiet. Ramos, the constable, should also be here.'

'I think he will be here,' Chavez grunted. 'He has been at the other session always. He knows this Sam Strater—and knows the Fays, also. They are hard men, and their concert hall and saloon draw the hardest of La Fe's people. They do not wish to have these murders put upon their foreman, Strater. I think they have made some of our witnesses understand that . . .'

He moved toward the little justice, who came through the crowd with sandals flopping. Gavity stood outside until the proceedings began in the long, empty store. There was nothing of particular interest in the testimony as given by Mexican and Anglo witnesses. Nothing, that is, except the atmosphere of growing tension . . . Everyone seemed to know the Fay brothers, owners of the largest variety theater and saloon in La Fe, and to know Sam Strater, a huge, red-faced, and belligerent sort of man. The German interpreter, Schultz, seemed to Gavity a conscientious man. His own Spanish let him follow the Mexicans' testimony about quarrels between the dead *vaqueros* and the Fays and their man Strater as if they spoke English. Schultz, listening intently, translated exactly what the witnesses said. And those witnesses, placing the dead cowboys on the Fay ranch at Cinecue, placing Strater on a horse following them as they rode away, began to build a deadly weight of evidence against the scowling Strater, without once accusing him directly of murder.

But Gavity reminded himself that this was no business of the marshal of La Fe. The sheriff and the county attorney were concerned, if anyone were to prefer charges. He found his mind wandering to Bryan Ross—just now a spectator in the room; and to Betty . . . He recalled himself to the inquest with a jerk, in mid-afternoon, when Justice Sayre suddenly pounded with dirty fist upon his table and announced the inquest finished.

'I'll say what my verdict is, tomorrow or next day,' he told the staring audience. 'Got to think things over.'

Slowly, the crowd flowed to the street. Gavity stood in the doorway of the store. Mechanically, he watched the stocky Schultz go with Chavez the Mexican deputy sheriff toward 'Little Mexico,' the quarter in South La Fe. He saw Sam Strater beside one of the Fay brothers—a dapper little man with pale face and waxed mustache. Then Strater and Fay walked faster. They overtook Chavez and Schultz. Gavity stared, then began to move that way. Something about the bearing of Strater pushed him toward the four men. But he had still twenty feet to go when Strater and

Fay drew pistols. He heard Strater's snarl:

'You lying Dutch son of a dog! You doctored up them stories to suit you!'

Schultz began to step backward. Strater shoved his Colt into the interpreter's face, and with the roar of it Schultz dropped as if his feet had been kicked from under him. Chavez began to draw his belted pistol. Strater spun on a heel and rammed the muzzle of his pistol into the deputy's belly. It roared and roared again. Chavez whirled, hand dropping from his Colt. He staggered across the sidewalk and the men between him and Gavity ran right and left, dodging into doorways, sprinting across the street.

'Drop that gun!' Gavity yelled at Strater. 'Drop it!'

He had his own pistol in his hand. Then Strater and Fay both turned upon him. Strater fired and Fay was standing with feet a trifle apart, taking deliberate aim, when Gavity let the hammer of his .45 drop. He struck Strater with his first slug; missed his second shot; saw Fay stagger with his third. Then he was walking up, shooting with grim intent to kill.

Strater fell across Chavez. Fay dropped his pistol and with left hand held right arm, pallid face convulsed, a little lifted. Gavity came alertly up to them. Fay's gunarm was broken; he saw the telltale limpness of it. Strater was apparently dead. Gavity lifted his gun a trifle and Fay shrank back.

'Don't! Don't kill me!' he screamed. 'I haven't got a gun!'

Gavity rapped him across the side-face with Colt barrel and watched him drop, then turned about looking for other friends of Strater or Fay.

He saw none; saw nobody with pistol out. But there was a third sprawling figure across the plank sidewalk, a Mexican who lay with a small bag under his outstretched hand, a bag that let bright bits of candy strew the planks about him. Obviously, he had been struck by that slug Strater loosed at Gavity. Tim Free materialized at Gavity's elbow, so silently and so quickly that Gavity jerked his Colt up before recognizing him. Then he looked grimly at the cow-buyer.

'I sort of believed Sayre would hold Strater responsible for those cowboys' murder,' he said. 'And, maybe, the Fays. But now it won't make a lot of difference. Strater's dead—and he certainly murdered Schultz. Fay has got nothing but a broken arm. And there's the well-known innocent bystander, the one who always gets hurt.'

'All over an inquest that ought to have been through and settled yesterday,' Free drawled, nodding. 'Well, you certainly do have a way of picking out the toughest people to smack. The Fays are nobody's soft spot. But I'm glad you downed Sam Strater; he was a killer that had needed it for a long time. No doubt in *my* mind he was mixed in a lot more of our killings and thievings than most folks suspicioned.'

'Hell with the Fays!' Gavity told him indifferently. 'They hired a killer, and this one here, if no more, has found out he can't do murder and laugh about it. Not around me!'

9. 'I like shotguns'

By the time Gavity had finished his supper, Fay and Bowie Streets were a midway, T-shaped, flaming with the lights of saloon and gambling-den and those stores which catered to an all-night crowd.

There were so many people moving in La Fe that the sidewalks would not hold them all; they flowed over into the sand of the streets and walked there or stood there.

Gavity leaned against the wall of the Chinese restaurant and considered the crowds. He had seen more than one such town, but never one of so much activity. There was something about the nervous atmosphere of La Fe that impressed him. His despondency of the forenoon—caused as much by pity for little Mrs. O'Rourke as by any thought of himself—was wearing off. He looked at these people and breathed slowly.

Here were men and women from all parts

of the United States. La Fe, tonight, was doubtless the most non-Texan town in all Texas. In other ways, too, the town was of mixed population. There were gamblers by the baker's dozen; cowmen and their hands stumping along on high heels; roughly dressed miners and freighters and traders; business men of La Fe, their sober citizen's clothing topped usually by wide-rimmed Stetsons. Women were in the throng, shrill of voice and rouged heavily, for the most part in silks of brilliant colors cut very low of throat. These were always well-squired, for not yet had La Fe drawn more than a woman for every score of men, and so these forerunners had their pick of the escorts.

'All looking for fortunes,' he thought. 'It's that way in every camp. Some wouldn't know Lady Luck if they happened onto her. They'll go out of here to the next boom, and when they get old and gray they'll be like that old desert rat I met beyond Tombstone—still hunting for the Mother Lode and sure they'll fall over it on the next ledge . . . And leaving their bones out in the greasewood. And I'm not much different, except *I* know that I'll recognize Opportunity when he knocks at the door . . .'

Binnings passed him, walking with a handsome, flamboyantly dressed Mexican in *charro* garb. Neither man saw the big figure of Gavity, moveless by the wall. They went on, talking earnestly. Zelman went by. Gavity shook his head. All of them were alike in that one respect: all were trying to make a fortune. Binnings and Zelman and Tim Free and Bryan Ross. But Zelman and Free were the sort to put value on more than money; they were the sort to build towns because they looked past the chance of adding another dollar to their wealth. He grinned; considered himself.

'And what am I? A Tarrant County Gavity who knows a lot about cows—and maybe a little about men . . . A Gavity who never did the thing the old, wise heads told him was right . . . One who couldn't get along with his own people, because of pure bullhead stubbornness . . . Am I, maybe, a Town-Maker, too? Can I play a part here on the Rio Grande; turn into a respectable pillar of society and all that; help build La Fe into a Place?'

Others passed him—slinking, furtive figures that reminded him of the coyotes who trail the wolf pack and yap and cringe and pounce upon scraps; cowardly souls, but dangerous to the weak. These looked to right and left with shifty eyes. Some of them saw him and looked with instinctive hatred and defiance at the gleaming badge upon his shirt, then slunk away when he stared at them.

'My town!' he said suddenly, with a long breath. He stretched great arms above his head, and there was something like a thrill to the thought. 'I'm marshal, chief of police!'

He thought little about Sam Strater, or Binnie Fay. Little Sayre had quickly disposed of both Strater and the Mexican killed by Strater's wild bullet. Gavity had been exonerated. Binnie Fay was free on bond to nurse his broken arm, charged with the murder of Schultz. He would never come to trial, Gavity knew. Guilty as he was of complicity in that wanton killing, it would not be the spirit of La Fe to split hairs. Strater had shot at Schultz, and Strater, alone, would be called responsible. But it had been a good move to drag the wounded saloon-keeper into justice court and force his brothers to post bond for him.

It was not Gavity's first killing. Twice, in a full life, he had killed men who needed killing. He had no pangs at all about the matter. Killing Strater had been precisely like killing a rattlesnake. Men were like that. Some were innately good, others were as innately bad. Reform was a hard matter. A bullet settled the question quickly and neatly.

The only thing that concerned him was the practical side of the situation. Would the Fays now join Ben Miles and Binnings and his other enemies in La Fe, in an effort to wipe him out and, perhaps, put Huckafee in as marshal once more? He shifted his pistol a trifle in the waistband of his overalls. Then he moved out from the dusky shadow of the wall and drifted toward Fay Street. The exhilaration was still with him—like that of the first drink of an evening. He was smiling, if without much of mirth, as he met the stares of the men he met.

For his huge figure did not escape attention. Some of the glances turned on him were only curious; but as he passed into sections lighted by the windows of saloon or gambling-den and the gold badge shone, there were those who lifted guarded, speculative eyes from the shield to his face and seemed to analyze him. The eyes of some women held very open admiration . . .

He went up Fay Street to the plaza. There he turned on Bowie and crossed the wooden bridge that spanned La Fe's *acequia* at Mason. He was moving along Bowie past a little jeweler's shop and nearing the Gem Saloon when a queer procession checked him, then set him laughing.

Grunting and panting, three alligators came down the plank sidewalk with claws scratching. Behind them was Pancho Ramos, a placid herdsman, speaking admonishing Spanish.

'Devils that you are! *Lagartos diablos!* Breaking the fence of the plaza pool! Straying into the houses of decent folk! I should shoot you! How many times a month must I drive you from the veranda of the mayor himself?

100

Ah, diablos! And why will you not stay in the pool? You—'

The little column came abreast of the Gleaming Gem's door. A cowboy staggered out, looked at the alligator that all but nuzzled his boot, then yelled.

'*Godamighty!*' he said. 'Alligators!'

'Alligators?' Pancho Ramos repeated. 'What you mean, alligators? What alligators?'

'Three of 'em! Right there!' the cowboy told him gaspingly. 'Mean to tell me *you* can't see 'em?'

Gavity moved closer. Ramos was shaking his head, looking at the alligators, then at the cowboy.

'Alligators? Where you see 'em alligators?'

The cowboy moved backward, toward the doors of the Gem.

'Listen,' he said slowly, distinctly. 'I see three alligators. If you don't see 'em, something's wrong. Damn' wrong! I either had too much to drink or I never had enough.'

'Don't see no alligators,' Ramos persisted gravely.

'I think I ain't had enough to drink,' the cowboy decided—and shoved backward into the swing doors.

Ramos laughed as Gavity came up to him.

'She's funny,' he said. 'Two-three time, every week, hell! These damn' alligators bust the fence; I got to herd 'em back. Cowboys come out drunk; see 'em; think they got

101

snakes.'

The alligators went scuffing on. Ramos stared shrewdly at Gavity, in the light from the Gem. Then he shrugged.

'More than alligators are walking the streets tonight. Worse than alligators, *amigo mio* . . . Body of God! You have a way of making enemies. If you do not make friends, also, in the same way—Well! As Tim Free said, you have now to face Ben Miles and Binnings and that ugly rascal Pug, and Huckafee and Finch . . . Will you have a word of advice from a careful man?'

'I am sure,' Gavity told him gravely, 'that any word of Pancho Ramos will be worth listening to by me. For the constable who has not yet been killed—even by alligators—is a man of much good sense. What is the word?'

'Huckafee is very friend with both Winst, who owns the Criterion, and Ben Miles. The Fays, too, would like to see him marshal again. Winn Wheelen was marked for death before Binnings's bullets struck him. Then, Huckafee was to be made the marshal once more. The sporting crowd would shoot up the town, and the city council would be forced to make Huckafee marshal.'

'You mean that Binnings stands in with that crowd?' Gavity grunted. 'That the death of Wheelen was arranged and Binnings served Miles and Winst and the Fays?'

'No, I do not mean that, Binnings does as

he chooses. He is a friend of all those you speak of, but they do not give him orders. He and Wheelen were enemies and he killed Wheelen for his own reasons, I think. But if he had not killed Wheelen, someone else would have killed him. Now—you carry a pistol. But if trouble came with many men, a pistol would not be the best weapon. In the marshal's office at the City Hall are shotguns. Ten-gauge shotguns! *Amigo*, I like shotguns! It is not only that they kill for ten feet to right and left of the man at whom you shoot; it is that men who will stand before a pistol or rifle will not face a ten-gauge Greener . . . I would say, the marshal of La Fe, tonight, should think of those shotguns and carry one, rather than his Colt . . .'

'An idea! A good word!' Gavity agreed. 'I go now to the City Hall and look at those Greeners.'

'And I take my pets back to the pool and hammer up again the fence,' Ramos sighed. *'Hasta la vista, amigo!'*

He hurried off in the wake of his alligators. Gavity made the City Hall through the thickening crowds. There was a wall-rack in the dingy marshal's office and from it he took two ten-gauge, sawed-off shotguns. Then he rounded the corral and entered the Legal Tender Saloon by a rear door. Matt Ryan, owner of the Legal Tender, was one recommended by Tim Free and with sight of the short, tremendously wide man, meeting his round, unwinking blue eyes, Gavity agreed with Free's recommendation of the saloon-keeper. He shoved up to the end of the bar and Ryan nodded to him.

'I suppose you know me by the badge,' he told Ryan. 'Tim Free told me to count on you and—I feel like doing that. Will you hang this to the back-bar and see that it's here if I happen to need it?'

'You'd get no bet from me if you was to say you thought you'd need it,' Ryan assured him. 'I'll be glad to keep it for you, Gavity. I hope you won't be calling for it, but—like I said—I wouldn't be giving anybody a bet on that.'

Gavity nodded with thin smile. He left the Legal Tender by the back door and moved along the rear of saloons and honkatonks that lined this west side of Fay Street. By alleys and cross-streets he made the Gleaming Gem Saloon of Mayor Zelman. The Gem was by no means the largest 'gentleman's resort' of La Fe. But it was agleam with electric lights generated by Zelman's own tiny steam plant. The like of its mahogany and plate-glass furnishings was nowhere else in the southwestern country. As for the mahogany panel on the end wall—with a half-size longhorn steer made of silver dollars, the eyes and nostrils, the horns and hoofs, made of gold pieces—cowboys stood by the hour gaping at the shimmering wonder of it.

Gavity passed the longhorn and the usual group of gabbling watchers and spoke to the bar-tender nearest him. This was a lanky man, with a tiny curl plastered on his forehead. He looked at the shotgun and nodded wisely.

'Is it—loaded?' he asked in low, confidential voice, accepting the Greener. 'I ain't gun-shy by no means, Gavity. But it makes a lot of difference in the way a fella handles a Greener, whether's she's loaded or not.'

'It's not loaded,' Gavity said in the same tone. 'If I need a riot gun, I'll need it sudden—and need it a lot. I can't take a chance that somebody hasn't fixed the shells in it. So it's empty. You just push it under the stuff on your back-bar, and if I gallop in here and lift my hand, just fill it—with that sweetheart! I'll have the shells in my pocket. I have got a scatter gun, now, on each side of wherever trouble might start. I can catch up the closest one and load it and—I *know* the gun will shoot!'

He went back through the mixed crowd, across the bridge on Bowie Street, and around the corner of the Teepee Gaming-Rooms. Between the Teepee and the long store of Mayor Zelman was a narrow building of 'dobe with brick front. This was the Buchanan Hardware Store, and Gavity wanted ten-gauge shells—new and deadly—for his riot guns. He passed the big gambling-house and in

Buchanan's doorway was halted by a lounging, bareheaded man who hummed 'Buffalo Gals' without much of tune or feeling.

Gavity had never seen Buchanan. He did not know whether this lounging one was the hardware-man or no more than a loafer. He stopped and said he wanted shells.

'Shells? Shells?' the bareheaded man repeated, as if he had never heard the word before. 'Oh—shells. Why—uh—why, we ain't got a one in the place tonight. But when the freight comes in next week we ought to have a bunch of 'em. Sorry!'

'That sounds like a sad lack, in a town like La Fe,' Gavity told him. 'Well—'

He was about to turn away when, chancing to glance over this man's head, he saw a white-haired man sitting in a chair, far down the store, plain in the light of a wall lamp. He happened to recall what Zelman—or perhaps it had been Tim Free—had said about 'old' Buchanan. Then this bareheaded man must be a clerk. For Buchanan was an Original Settler in La Fe; a member of the city council; all in all a tall man of the town.

He thought that it would be no more than right to introduce himself to one of La Fe's honest citizens. It seemed a good thing to know this minority.

'Think I'll talk to Buchanan,' he said to the man beside him. 'He—'

But as he moved to go past, the bareheaded

man threw off all pretense. His hand came up—and behind him it had been holding a pistol. He snarled and rammed the muzzle of it into Gavity's breast.

Gavity reacted instinctively—and flashingly. He whirled to the side and slapped with his left hand at the pistol barrel. There was the bellow of the shot and a bullet rapped a plank at his foot, stinging the sole through his boot. Then Gavity whipped out his own Colt from the waistband of his overalls. He let the hammer drop as he leveled it and thumbed it back again. The bareheaded man dropped, his hand jerking as he tried to lift his pistol again.

As he shoved past the falling figure a man came into his range of vision—a man with a pistol, standing behind the long counter on his left. Still another man—Buchanan had never moved, in the chair—bobbed up, farther along this counter. He, too, had a Colt in his hand.

There was no hesitation on the part of these two. They began to fire at Gavity as fast as they could lift hammers and drop them. Tinware hanging above and behind him jangled and rang with the impact of their lead.

Gavity had never been given to nerves. So he set himself mechanically, there in the cluttered aisle of the store. He drove his bullets with grim accuracy at those two. The man closest to him fell forward across the counter, slid down from it. The other ducked below the counter and Gavity guessed that he would scramble toward the back of the store. So he ran forward and fired the last shot as the man came to his feet and dived toward the back door.

He yelled and caught his ear with right hand, but continued to run. Gavity followed, fast, snatching his second Colt from the shoulder holster that carried it. But when he got into the darkness of the alley there was only the pound of running feet to show where the man had gone. So he stopped. There was no point to trying pursuit, in the crowds and the darkness of La Fe. He went back into the store, and old Buchanan regarded him with something like sardonic amusement.

'Been expecting to meet you,' he said. 'But maybe not exactly like this. Don't know as I could be gladder, though, at that. Them scoun'els had my safe open. They come in and they rammed a gun into my belly and I figured all the things I still had to do. So I opened up for 'em, and, if you hadn't wandered along looking for ten-gauge shells, they'd have been gone with everything in it.'

10. 'One-half of nothing'

The store began to fill with men, staring at the dead robber across the sill and at the pall of smoke which canopied the ceiling. Buchanan ignored these gaping ones and talked briskly to Gavity—just as if robbery were a matter of course to him. He was weathered and craggy of features; Gavity thought that dead men were no novelty to him.

'You know these men?' Gavity asked of Buchanan.

'Not a one of 'em. I looked at 'em good when they first come in—and better'n that when they stuck me up. No . . . What with the riffraff coming in all time, to La Fe, man's hard put to recall all the scoun'elly faces he sees.'

Gavity put the same question to the curious men crowding in. But except that one or two recalled seeing them loafing about saloons, neither of the dead men could be identified.

'Then we might as well get 'em up to the City Hall,' Gavity said at last. 'If we can find somebody with a hack—'

An officious spectator caught a Mexican passing, driving a cartload of mesquite roots for sale. The wood-cutter was persuaded to dump his load of roots and take the bodies to the marshal's office. Then Gavity thought of his original errand.

'How about ten-gauge shells?' he asked Buchanan. 'It was really a pure accident that I came in here, at all. I wanted a little buckshot for some of the would-be hard cases. So—'

'Got plenty of 'em!' Buchanan assured him. 'Just got a new shipment in. Haven't even unpacked 'em yet. They're out in the storeroom. Wait a minute and I'll fix you up.'

Part of Gavity's talk had been directed to the pair standing in the forefront of the thinning crowd—to the dark and handsome Binnings and a slender, well-dressed young man whose most conspicuous features were his light eyes, close-set against a great, hooked nose, and whose mouth curled in what seemed an habitual sneer. But the remark about buckshot for hard cases drew no retort from Binnings. His manner was courtly, as he came forward to lead the hook-nosed man up to Gavity.

'Prather,' he said, with jerk of dark head toward Gavity, 'it certainly is time you met our new watch-dog. Since you had nothing to do with his appointment, it should be the more interesting. Mr. Gavity, this is Mr. Prather, prominent member of La Fe's bar and—more important!—an alderman. Gavity is a very serious sort of fellow, Prather. I'm not precisely sure just where Zelman found him and rescued him from, but—'

'Zelman!' Prather snarled, looking Gavity angrily up and down. 'Zelman, this! Zelman, that! An immigrant German saloon-keeper and store-keeper! He is going to find himself in hot water very quickly. He thinks he's the two-for-a-nickel autocrat of La Fe. He thinks he can run the town just as he pleases, without troubling to consult the rest of us—who happen to be members of the city council. He's due to have his tumble. As for his appointees, they will go as quickly as they come; or—'

Gavity laughed abruptly.

'You said: Those of you who *happen* to be members of the city council . . . I like that word. Sometimes it explains things that just can't be explained by anything else . . . Go ahead, Mr. Prather. Don't let me stop you. For this is one case where the job certainly came hunting the man, not otherwise.'

'I—imagine!' Prather snarled. 'You didn't ask for the marshal's star, of course! You didn't come here to get it. You—'

'My—goodness,' Gavity drawled smilingly. 'It certainly has got windy in here. To be so quiet, outside. You're probably very good at imagining, Mr. Prather. A certain type of— lawyer often is. But, and yet, it's as I said: Mayor Zelman thought La Fe needed a marshal and he came to me.'

From the back of the store, where Buchanan had gone into darkness, there came the sudden and furious sound of swearing. Gavity decided that Buchanan must have served his apprenticeship among muleskinners.

Then the store-keeper came stumping up the long aisle. He had a box of shotgun shells in his hand, but seemed not to think of them. His narrow blue eyes were bright and angry.

'Somebody busted into the storeroom!' he cried. 'I don't know, yet, what all they took. But two kaigs of blasting powder's gone. I swear, I don't know what La Fe's coming to nowadays. Ever since the railroads started building our way, we've had the damnedest flood of riffraff pouring in! Gutter-women prancing half-naked down the streets, going arm-in-arm with elegant, drunken *gentlemen* that never have any means of support the town can see, but always got their pockets crammed with money!'—he looked squarely at Binnings—'and cheap little shyster-politicians that'd kiss a *pelado* Mexican's— *foot*, to get him to vote a couple times extra, and that run with every scoun'el tinhorn and saloon-keeper—'

This, it seemed, was addressed to Prather. He glared at Buchanan, who matched the glare.

'If you're talking about me,' Prather cried, 'I'll tell you—'

Then he seemed to realize that he had given himself away and his face turned furiously red. He rushed at Buchanan and struck the old man in the face.

Buchanan laughed, jerking his gray head back and roaring. The remnant of the crowd laughed, too. Buchanan put out a gnarled hand and caught Prather's lapel. He shook him. The blow had been a limp gesture such as a woman might have made. But Gavity came gravely forward and loosed Buchanan's grip.

'Let me have him,' he said. 'That was an entirely unprovoked assault. You make a charge against him and I'll see that he pays his fine or works it out in the street, alderman or no alderman! This business of blustering up and down, intimidating the citizens—'

'Intimidating!' Buchanan yelled, gaping at Prather. *'That?* Intimidate *me?* The man-imitator assault a grown man? Charging that with assault'd be flattering him. It wouldn't assault a sick Chinee laundryman without written consent—and .a lot of help! Assault! Give him here to me! I'm going to show him, now, what assault really is. I—'

He caught Prather's lapel again and the lawyer pulled back and slapped again at Buchanan, who moved at him with grim smile, right hand coming up doubled into a knotty fist.

'Give him to me!' Buchanan told Gavity again. 'Let me take him in charge, Gavity. I want to show him things he never learned in no school, but that he ought to know—and will know—'

But Gavity, holding a straight face with difficulty, moved a shoulder slightly and Buchanan was pushed off. Then Gavity took Prather by the sleeve and, with a sort of remorseless ease and deliberation, turned him about. Prather snarled and his hand jerked under his coat. Gavity's hand followed whippingly and closed upon the lawyer's gunhand—that gripped a short pistol of light caliber.

'My—goodness!' Gavity said reprovingly. 'Carries a gun, too! Probably a desperate character from somewhere on Bitter Creek. Goes around bullying people—maybe shooting 'em!'

He squeezed gently and Prather, with a pained oath, let the 'lady's gun' drop. Gavity released his hand then. He took Prather by the back of his waistband and lifted him high off the floor. His expression was one of serene concentration as he waved the alderman— Prather kicked and twisted and cursed—above his head. He marched down the store to the front door.

'Give us room, friends!' he called to the passers-by on Fay Street's east sidewalk. 'This ringtailed, rip-snorting Terror of the Prairies needs miles of space for his elbows. A li'l' bitsy place like the store is crowding him. He has got to get out where his flaming breath won't set the grass afire. One side, folks, or you might lose a leg or an arm! Whoop—and he goes!'

He took two long steps across the sidewalk and threw Prather into the street. As the dazed alderman rolled over and propped himself to a sitting position with one hand, Fay Street roared enthusiastically. Through the crowd came Tim Free the cow-buyer. He was in his cups and he stood swaying before Prather and shaking his head.

'Git up from that, Prather!' he yelled. 'He can't do you that way! Git up from that and tell him so! Come on, now! Git up and tear him limb from limb! I want to bet on Prather! Two-bits he can lick Gavity with one hand. Any takers? Looky, Prather! You got him scared—he's running from you! Look at him dodging back in before you can git to him!'

Gavity turned back into the store and walked down to Binnings, who had stood with impassive face through the scuffle. But when Gavity halted before him, thumb hooked in his waistband, Binnings's dark eyes narrowed slightly; became watchful.

'That was just foolishness—as you well know,' Gavity told Binnings. 'Just cowboy monkey-business. But what I've got to say to you—'

He dropped his chin a trifle and squared great shoulders. Binnings took a half-step backward and his face was pale. Then he caught himself and stiffened.

'Don't you put a hand on me!' he said thickly. 'If you raise a finger in my direction—'

'I've been having ideas about you,' Gavity interrupted him. 'A lot of ideas—and more coming in all the time. If you insist on staying around La Fe without having any visible means of support, but having a good deal of money to spend, I will probably make up my mind about you . . . Now, you bite on this: When I feel that I have got reason to put my hand on you, your squealing "Don't touch me!" won't stop me—not enough for anybody to see.'

'You're piling up a big score, aren't you?' Binnings inquired softly. He was not afraid; Gavity knew it. He had control of himself now; he met Gavity's stare steadily. 'As I told you in the street, sometimes a loop costs a saddle-tramp more than he can afford. I can promise you that in your case that is going to be exactly true!'

'You've been strutting too long,' Gavity said contemptuously. 'You think you're a gunman. Well, back in some short-grass land you have possibly stacked high at leather-slapping. Possibly you've seemed big and bad. But to my notion you're just some good family's naughty little boy who's been kicked out of his home. Along the Rio Grande, I think you amount to about one half of nothing. If you want to disagree with me—pop your whip, fella! Pull and try.'

Binnings only stared. Then the corners of his thin mouth lifted. He turned away, hands swinging easily at his sides.

'Don't try to arrange things, Gavity,' he flung back over his shoulder. 'You're not clever enough. 'When I'm ready, I do whatever I decide to do. I shoot when I'm

116

ready—just for instance. I can't be hurried and—so far—I can't be stopped . . .'

'What you really mean is—you haven't been stopped,' Gavity said, amusedly. 'What happens from here on will be brand-new to you, Binnings.'

Tim Free came into the store and brushed Binnings in passing. Something that Gavity did not hear was said. Free stood, instantly, with both hands at his hips. He wore no visible weapon, but Binnings backed out of the door as if Free had covered him. The cowbuyer watched alertly, even after Binnings had disappeared. Then he turned with a snorting sound of contempt. He came down to stand beside Gavity and Buchanan.

'That slick scoun'el!' he said angrily. 'That's the kind I would like to see hanging to every lamp-post in La Fe! But try to make some of our leading citizens see it! Bryan Ross, just for instance! *Agghhh!*'

'He's slick, all right,' Buchanan agreed. 'And dangerous as any sidewinder coiled around the mesquite bush you pick for a shady spot. Well, Gavity, like I said awhile back, it's certainly been a pleasure to know you—the way you come in. I do like the kind of inquests you arrange—Strater; now these . . .'

11. 'I own two guns'

La Fe, it would seem, was violently supporting or opposing the new marshal. Gavity found himself interested in the way men looked at him.

'Well,' he confessed to himself, when Justice Sayre had conducted another inquest and exonerated him of all blame in the killing of the two robbers—even sourly complimented him upon his marksmanship, 'I suppose I have sort of made my mark on the town. Binnings would say so. Huckafee—and that reminds me! I haven't seen anything of our ex-marshal, ex-deputy, for some little while . . . I wonder if he's just drunk, or planning some devilry . . .'

He went wandering. Betty Ross was not in sight upon the streets. He wondered if she were at home and was much of a mind to drop over the Ross wall again. But something held him from that visit. He had lost his happy-go-lucky view of La Fe and the Gavity future, since telling her so carelessly that she was to choose her house—their house.

'I never knew there was so much to town life,' he thought. 'I've rambled and trambled a lot, as the song puts it. But I never felt so downright damn' serious in all my life. Maybe a cowboy oughtn't to come to town . . .'

Buchanan hailed him. The old store-keeper

wore a grim smile today. He beckoned and Gavity went over.

'Come on in,' Buchanan invited him. 'I got something for you. Maybe you won't want it— I don't know. But if you do I certainly want that you should have it . . .'

Gavity watched him unroll a skeleton vest of softest Russian calf, on which were sewed slantingly two pistol holsters. He began to shake his head, for he knew the price of those John Wesley Hardin holster-vests. Buchanan snarled at him sideways:

'I don't give a whoop what you say! This-here vest is the finest thing a man like you could have—if he could use it.'

'It's not that,' Gavity confessed. 'I can do the cross-arm draw. But I haven't got the money to pay for it—'

'Money? Money?' Buchanan fairly yelled at him, pounding on the counter. 'Who said anything about money? Listen! I been around this river and around Texas, for that matter, it's just a many's the year. First time I ever heard that a man can't give a friend of his something, if he wants to! And after I had that useless Talaberto, the saddler, alter this to your size, I don't want to hear a lot of yammering. Don't give me no trouble, you. Put her on! And here's the match to that Colt of yours—'

'Thanks, but I own two guns—matched and tested. I— Oh, damn it! I like the outfit,

119

but—'

'There ain't a *but* about it!' Buchanan checked him. 'I want you to have that vest. I only hope you'll have time among us to do some drawing out of it that'll make the like of Binnings and Prather good and sick!'

'If you put it that way, I'll accept it,' Gavity said gratefully. 'I'm going to get out of this rig, anyway. I'm too conspicuous in overalls and boots. And this will fit under a coat just about the way the doctor would order . . .'

He moved from Buchanan's to the clothing store of Ike Cohen, two doors along Fay Street. Cohen grinned at him and remarked that the pleasantest sight he had seen in La Fe had been the dead robbers from Buchanan's.

'We got plenty of clothes,' Cohen said doubtfully, 'but in your size—I just don't know, Mr. Gavity. But we'll see . . .'

Gavity was fitted, at last. He looked down at his gray hand-me-down and shook his head.

'Last time I wore a rig like this,' he told the little clothier, 'I was walking up Market Street in San Francisco. My job was bodyguarding a California rancher who wanted to collect an inheritance. I recall that coat was ruined on Nob Hill. There were some people who didn't want my boss to collect. They were very good shots, too. They just ruined that coat and came very near to ruining me. I hope I'll have better luck with this outfit.'

'And plenty of us, now, we hope so, too!'

Cohen assured him. 'We got it a fine town, Mr. Gavity. But if these gonuffs, they get us on the run, it won't be so good. We got to have a man like you, now. Winn Wheelen—he was too quick on .the shoot. He had, I would say it, too much reputation, now. A good officer, Mr. Gavity, he's got to know how about not shooting, just so much as how about shooting, you understand. And when everybody's coming into La Fe, just for the hope of killing our marshal and making a big rep'—that's not so good for business!'

'A gunfighter hasn't got a lot of chance for days off,' Gavity agreed. 'Sick or well, he's got to be ready to hold up his end against any comer—and there's always somebody after his scalp. He's always a target. I never wanted a name for gunplay. So—'

'And you're not getting a name for gunplay now?' Cohen cried. He laughed, with both hands over his round little belly. 'Big Gavity, now, he's just the plain cowboy . . . Don't be funning! Me, I have been plenty of time in Texas, since I come to this country, you understand. Lots of cowboys buy my clothes. Maybe I don't know cowboys . . . Maybe! But—'

A little man came into the store. He looked furtively at Cohen, then at Gavity. He held a package, and this he extended to Gavity.

'What's it?' Gavity demanded, staring at the white tissue wrapping and the great bows of black silk ribbon that decked it.

'Uh—just a li'l' something the boys wanted to give you,' the little man said hesitantly. 'They—uh—well, they wanted to give it to you, so they told me to hunt you up and say it ain't much, but it's meant sincere and—and they hope you'll use it.'

He thrust the package into Gavity's hands and fairly ran from the store. Gavity shook his head, looking after the messenger. He put the gift on Cohen's counter and began to untie the ribbons. Cohen hovered near, head on one side, shrewd eyes curious. Then he stepped backward.

'It could maybe be a bomb, now?' he grunted suddenly.

Gavity laughed and went on with his fumbling.

'I don't think so. Buchanan gave me the holster-vest and you sold me the suit and all at cost—or practically cost . . . It just seems that the town wants to fix its marshal up in fine shape, in case he has to be buried without warning—'

He lifted the lid of the cardboard box and stared at the printed sheet, adorned with gold seal and purple ribbon. Then he laughed, leaning on the counter and holding his side. For it was a deed—a formal and authentic deed to one cemetery lot in La Fe Cemetery.

Cohen made a shrugging gesture of displeasure.

'Me, now, I don't see the funning. It gives me the creeps, you understand. I tell you, Mr. Gavity, there's just plenty of men in La Fe that would help you use that lot, now. I don't see the funning.'

'I'll save it,' Gavity told him, still laughing. 'It might even be that I'll use this lot in a way they don't expect—my good friends of the sporting crowd. I may need the space for a man or two of their bunch who can't afford to buy a lot!'

He was still amused when he went out upon Fay Street. He looked for Binnings. There was small doubt in his mind that the idea had come from that black sheep of some good family—as he considered Binnings to be. But he saw nothing of the tall, graceful figure. Sight of a chintz skirt in the doorway of Jones & Ross and went that way with a pleasant lift of pulses. He hurried up to Betty, and when he called her name from behind her she whirled quickly, hand on heart.

'Why—why, I didn't expect you! You startled me!' she said huskily. 'You—'

'Well, anyway, you say that just as if you meant it,' he stopped her. 'And since you're even more beautiful than you looked yesterday, or the day before, or the day before that, I'll play that I believe you.'

He looked down at her and to himself he said that she was more lovely than he had ever seen her, with the delicate oval of her face framed in another soft bonnet, and the slender curves of her figure half-shown, half-hidden, by the new frock.

'I don't know,' he told her lightly. 'I just don't know . . . Maybe your father had to come into town and start making money, lots of money, to buy these frills for you. And I don't know if a would-be cowman like me—acting marshal for the minute, of course—can afford you. But—you're certainly lovely.'

Abruptly, she sobered and put her hand on his sleeve.

'Never mind my looks! Why *did* you do it, Arthur? Take this awful job, I mean. Already you've had to—Well, it's a kill-or-be-killed job. You told me you were going to start here and become a citizen and build—'

'You don't mean to tell me that I'm, not a prominent citizen?' Gavity protested, smiling. 'It seems to me that, for the small time I've been in La Fe's middle, I've accomplished quite a trifle, thank you! Tim Free tells me that I now own the outstandingest list of enemies any man on the Rio Grande might ask for. That's something! More, if the small schemes of some of La Fe's sporting crowd work out—the ideas of Binnings and some others—I'm due for the really big funeral of the town. They sent me the deed to a cemetery lot, just awhile back.'

He poked her arm with clumsy forefinger.

'Yes, sir! If some of those schemes don't

124

happen to run into .45 slugs and get stopped, the funeral is practically arranged. As for why I took the job, I tried to tell you that, just south of the biggest alligator in the pool. I was more or less shoved into the job. Frankly, it was Binnings as much as anything. I don't know whether or not you know him—'

'Of course I know him! And I'd like to know what you mean by classifying him as one of the sporting crowd!'

Gavity stared at her face, so abruptly hardened. It had not occurred to him that she might be acquainted with that handsome and well-dressed and suave—to his notion—good-for-nothing.

'Mr. Binnings'—she hesitated, face flushed —'is—What did you mean by saying that he had schemes for your funeral?'

'Who introduced you to Binnings?' Gavity demanded. He kept his voice even, though he was growing angry in his turn and hardly knew why. 'Your father? Does Bryan Ross know Binnings?'

'I don't think he knows him very well. They were acquainted somewhere, long before Daddy came to La Fe. But that doesn't answer my question. Mr. Binnings is a gentleman! He comes of a good family. He has education and brains and—and—and breeding. He has money to invest in La Fe and he is very likely to become one of the town's leading citizens. I want to know what you mean by bracketing a man like Binnings—a very good friend of ours—with the toughs of the sporting crowd!'

'Well,' Gavity said slowly—then stopped.

He fumbled in a coat pocket for tobacco and papers and killed time making a cigarette. Something warned him to be very careful, here. A quarrel with Betty, now, could open a breach that would be hard—if not impossible—to close again. And she seemed very ready to quarrel, he thought. She was treating him as if he were the casual acquaintance, Binnings the old friend—or more than the old friend. He asked himself how he could hope to overcome both Bryan Ross's hostility to him and her leaning toward the impressive Binnings.

'Well,' he repeated—then faced her squarely, holding his unlighted cigarette. 'Look here, Betty! Am I losing out? With you, I mean! Are you beginning to believe—have you already begun to believe—that I'm not the sort of man that Binnings is? That I'm not the sort your father wants you to marry, the sort *you* want to marry? I told you, somehow you do seem changed since you came down here. You're—Oh! You act as if you'd outgrown everything behind La Fe; everything on the Slash R. Maybe you have. I don't know. But I want to know. I have got to know!'

It seemed to him that the dark eyes softened as she looked up at him. But he had caught sight of a gorgeously dressed young

Mexican who loafed along the opposite sidewalk with a sort of negligent, jaguar-like grace. He watched the *charro* absently, even while he waited for her to answer him. And when she spoke her voice was both level and—cool:

'Of course I've outgrown certain things. Anybody does! As for outgrowing you—what I felt about you on the Slash R—that's not a fair question. You remember what we said when we were riding through the Grindstones: you were going to get Daddy's consent to marry me. Then you were going to come to me. You haven't got his consent! He dislikes you, today, more than he did on the ranch. You're farther from me than you were out there. Last night you insulted a good friend of his—Mr. Prather! Today you call a good friend of ours a tough of the sporting crowd. Daddy says you were always an—an impudent puppy. Now, he says, you're worse than ever. Because you're swelled up over that marshal's badge and you spend your time strutting. Well! Is that a change in me, or in you?'

Gavity was suddenly amused. He scratched a match and set the little flame to the end of his cigarette.

'I'll have to admit that, if I'm swelled up over this star I'm wearing and if I spend my time strutting and insulting people, that's a change in me. For it's something I never did before, in all my long and noble life. As for insulting that hooknosed little shyster—and coward!—Prather, there's a thing or two that even I can't do. And insulting him by calling him just anything is one of those impossibilities! Prather—'

12: 'Now—he 'ave die!'

That dandified Mexican had halted on the opposite sidewalk. Gavity watched him, in his jacket of shimmering scarlet velvet and his wide-bottomed *pantalones* of blue velvet with crimson seam with silken sash of blue and red. The man pushed back his gold-embroidered sombrero a trifle and turned to stare at Betty with full-lidded, insolent appraisal.

'That son of a dog!' Gavity said to himself. 'I think I will enjoy slapping him off the planks—just about a block, I want to slap him . . .'

'You—' Betty began. Then she saw the direction of his stare. 'Why, that's Don Cesar Saltillo! I didn't know he was in La Fe. He's been in Chihuahua. He—he's what they call a grandee, down there. He's a very close friend of Jack Binnings. And a very dangerous man, if he's provoked. He's killed three men here in La Fe, they say, in the past six months. A deadly pistol-shot and also a knife-fighter—'

'I still think I'll slap him into the street,'

128

Gavity said softly, almost under his breath. 'I don't like the way he looks at you—as if he *might* buy you . . . A friend of Binnings, is he? That makes it all the pleasanter . . .'

Saltillo turned away again. A man came at the run past Betty and Gavity. He was panting as he went by them and crossed the street. Gavity saw him as a stocky, chocolate-brown, and square-faced Mexican. He was within ten feet of Saltillo before that dandy turned. He lifted a hand and shook the clenched fist.

'Liar! Hypocrite! Seducer!' he screamed.

'It's his left hand he's shaking,' Gavity said absently to himself and began to run that way. 'Can't see his right hand, so—'

The hidden right hand came in sight now. It held a pistol. Gavity, fast as he was running, was only in mid-street when the pistol roared and flamed. At that point-blank range, it seemed impossible that the Mexican should miss.

But Saltillo had moved with a sinuous twist of trunk and bending of knees. He was squatting on the planks of the sidewalk before the shot waked echoes on Fay Street. Somehow, he was out in the street in a jaguar-leap, catching at the other man's pistol-hand.

A dagger had come into his own fingers. The two strained, there in the sand, while Gavity came on toward them. There was incredible strength in Saltillo's slender body. He forced the pistolman's arm up and up. His own left hand was thrusting forward. When Gavity reached the pair, he saw Saltillo's face over the man's shoulder. Saltillo was laughing while he held the man rigid and drove his slender blade time and again into the pistolman's breast. Then he stepped backward, sombrero'd head on one side. He watched the other sag.

Gavity looked at the falling man. Saltillo seemed now to see Gavity for the first time. He laughed and played with the dagger.

'He 'ave fonny idea,' he said, motioning with booted toe toward the man he had stabbed. 'He do not on'erstand that, when a Saltillo of Miraflores in Chihuahua touch his wife, it 'onor the dog like him. So—he 'ave die. He think to kill me, Cesar Saltillo, with a clumsy pistol. Now—he 'ave die!'

Calmly, he moved forward. Gavity, pistol in hand, stiffened. But Saltillo only wiped the red blade of his stiletto upon the moveless one's shirt. He straightened, grinning at Gavity. He lifted dark brows inquiringly.

'It is very good that you can claim self-defense,' Gavity said in Spanish. 'Else I should have pleasure in kicking you down the street to *el calabozo*—and begging you, all that way, to try upon me the point of that woman's weapon, the knife. As it is, I arrest you. Perhaps it would please you to say that you do not wish to be arrested?'

'You—you arrest me, for killing this cur of

the alley? You say in one breath that it is self-defense; in the next that you arrest me! And why shall I be arrested?'

'For the wearing of a weapon prohibited by the law of La Fe, the dagger. Now, if you choose to resist arrest, it will be my pleasure to first kick you for one full block down the street—while you try to turn your dagger upon me—then take from you that prohibited weapon and kick you the full distance to the *calabozo*. You will please yourself. Will you resist?'

Saltillo hesitated briefly, his full, red lips snarling. But when Gavity moved his pistol slightly he forced a smile and bowed formally. Then he extended the dagger, hilt first.

'Señor, it is for you to say and for me to do—this time. We go to the City Hall and there make my bond, or pay my fine?'

'You will go, to tell the recorder—you know him, the man Root?—what it is that I charge you with. I take only the important prisoners there, and such as this I cannot find important. If, of course, you do not report to the City Hall, it will be better that you bestride a fast horse and ride across the Rio Grande into Mexico—and do not come back . . . '

'I have no thought of riding into Mexico,' Saltillo assured him politely. 'I will go to this City Hall of yours and pay the fine for carrying my knife. Then—I will see you.'

'I will have nothing but pleasure, to see you

at any time,' Gavity said, as politely. 'No matter what you may have in your hand. I will be pleased to—see you . . .'

When Saltillo had gone at his insolent, rolling walk in the direction of the City Hall, Gavity drew a long breath and suddenly recalled Betty. If she had seen the killing, he thought that it must have shocked her. He looked at the dead man in the street and at those who had come to stare. Then he lifted his eyes to look for the girl. He stiffened and frowned.

In the doorway of the Jones & Ross store she was still standing. Too, she seemed unnerved, for she had turned her back to the street and one arm was across her eyes. But close beside her, with a hand comfortingly upon her arm, was Binnings. He faced Gavity, and as their eyes met Binnings put up a hand to pat Betty's shoulder.

Bryan Ross came out of the store and said something to Binnings. He crossed the street quickly, short, thick legs moving fast. Gavity turned away and hailed a passing hack. He was superintending the loading of the body into the carriage when Ross spoke behind him.

'Well, that's the kind of riddance we can stand,' Ross told Gavity. 'Don Cesar Saltillo is one of the finest—a Mexican gentleman of manners and money and—'

'He makes me think of one man, in

132

particular,' Gavity said, without turning. 'I think both he and Binnings are alike. Both men of—manners and money—'

'Exactly!' Bryan Ross agreed promptly. 'But I thought you didn't like Binnings—'

'Take it down to the City Hall,' Gavity directed the hack-driver. 'Then get Judge Sayre on the job for an inquest. Tell him I'll be along as soon as he's ready. But it's a case of self-defense, nothing more. Turn your bill in to Recorder Root. Tell him I said it's all right.'

He turned back to the little rancher-turned-merchant. He looked Bryan Ross thoughtfully up and down. Then he looked once more across the street.

'There are so many things that you don't know—and I don't know,' he said, as if thinking aloud. 'My advice to you would be: Don't trouble your head about 'em. I have got to find Judge Sayre, if he's on the street. That hack-driver, somehow, doesn't look too energetic to me.'

He swung off to round the corner of the Teepee and go up Bowie Street past the plaza. A group of men seeming to ring around some excitement quickened his steps. He had only to look to find the sandaled justice. Sayre was fairly hopping on the edge of this little crowd.

Gavity pushed through until, in the center of the group, he saw two men upon the sand of the street. One sat upon another and aimed furious, but wild, blows at the smaller man. Between terrific swings that missed more often than they landed he addressed the target viciously.

Justice Sayre was crying out to the man on top:

'Isbell! Isbell! Stop it, now! Don't you know who it is you're scuffling with? That's Finch, the gunman from Tombstone! Isbell! Listen to me!'

'Listen—nothing!' the portly, red-faced man on top grunted, between blows. 'I know well enough who it is: it's the man that tried to shove me off the sidewalk. And . . . he's going to get pounded if it's the last thing I ever do!'

Gavity grinned, regarding the strained face of O'Rourke's killer, as Finch dodged frantically. Then he tapped Isbell on the shoulder. He knew Isbell as a dealer in ranches and town property, some sort of Georgia aristocrat new in La Fe.

'All right, Isbell,' he drawled. 'Let him up. You've pounded him enough for a shove on the street. Besides'—he drew the bigger Isbell up with grip on his arm—'he's not much of a muchness. Only time you need to watch him is when he's behind you. Let him go, now.'

Finch staggered to his feet. He was a sorry spectacle, with his shirt out of his overalls and red marks upon his face where some of Isbell's blows had landed. He snarled with all the viciousness of a sidewinder at them both.

But when Gavity looked hard at him, he turned, picked up his dropped hat, and staggered away. Isbell stood panting. Then he laughed:

'These two-for-a-penny gunfighters!' he said. 'I never carried a pistol in my life, but I suppose I'll have to start, in La Fe. Thanks, Marshal. I see you're a man of perception and discretion. I wouldn't mind paying a fine for wiping up the earth with—what did you say his name is, Sayre? Finch . . . Well, I think I'll go on about my business, Gavity, if you don't mind.'

Gavity nodded and turned, to find the editor-publisher of La Fe's *Bugle* watching with shrewd green eyes, white Stetson shoved back on his pompadour. Adoniram Quince beamed upon Gavity and moved over to side him on Bowie as Justice Sayre flapped along in his sandals.

'A most interesting item for the *Bugle*,' Adoniram Quince told Gavity. 'Finch had no opportunity to draw a pistol. Consequently, it was a matter of man-to-man and—Isbell proved himself far the better at fisticuffs. You agree, Judge Sayre?'

'Finch'll kill him,' Sayre snarled. 'Maybe not tomorrow or the next day. But just you wait! Finch'll kill him.'

'Not while I'm able to walk, he won't!' Gavity disagreed, very grimly. 'In fact, now that we know Finch around La Fe, I don't

135

think he'll do much killing here. Oh! I suppose you haven't heard about Cesar Saltillo killing a Mexican a while ago? It was self-defense, of course. I sent the body to City Hall—and sent Saltillo there, too, to make bond or pay a fine for packing a dagger.'

'Good Gemini!' Sayre cried. 'Another one! I swear, it used to be that a man could get some sleep around La Fe. But ever since the railroads started in, I just had one inquest after another. You say it was self-defense? That-there Saltillo, he's way up in Chihuahua. Friend of Jack Binnings, too . . .'

'Another item for your palladium,' Gavity told Adoniram Quince. 'You can write that Don Cesar Saltillo, grandee of Chihuahua, killed the husband of a woman he'd trifled with. But it had to be called self-defense because the husband didn't know the first thing about killing snakes.'

'I'll be glad of the item,' Quince said solemnly. 'It happens that I know Saltillo. He's a—well, rather deadly person with either pistol or knife. Going to hold the inquest now, Judge? If you are, I'll go down with you.'

'Yeh, might's well—and have it over with,' Sayre grumbled. 'If Gavity seen the business and calls it self-defense, it ought to be simple enough.'

'If anything is simple around La Fe,' Gavity drawled.

13. 'I'll stick with you'

Gavity was amused to do 'night herd' on La Fe that night. He walked a regular beat until the faces of bartenders and gaming-house employees and dance-hall bouncers and patrons of the various establishments showed that he was expected when periodically he stepped into one place or another. Then he altered his beat; zigzagged and showed himself at other intervals. They began to look furtively, or as if startled, with his reappearances.

He stood in the shadows beyond the Fay Brothers' big variety theater on the extreme southern limit of La Fe's busy section, a little after midnight. His mind was not on the policing of La Fe just then. He had a picture—of Betty being comforted by Binnings.

'She ought to be asleep now,' he thought. 'Probably she has got over the effect of seeing Saltillo kill that Dominguez. 'What a girl . . . And how far away she begins to seem . . . I was a damn' fool, that day in San Antonio, to flip a coin over my direction. For it was that dollar coming heads that sent me to the Grindstones—to meet her. If it hadn't fallen heads, I'd have gone on back to California and never seen her. And what you never know, you never miss . . .'

137

He tried to decide whether her manner, before Saltillo's knifing of Dominguez had interrupted, had been affectionate or the reverse. But it was hard to make up his mind about her.

'She did seem loving enough when I picked her up out of the hammock,' he told himself. 'But when it came to my mentioning Binnings—well, that was not so good. I—wonder! Is Binnings making some moves in the Ross direction . . . I—'

A terrific detonation from somewhere to the northeast of him jerked his thoughts back to the present. Automatically, he jumped forward and began to run up Fay Street. There came to mind memory of that blasting powder stolen from Buchanan's store. Blasting, he told himself, argued a safe being blown somewhere. The First National Bank of La Fe was on Bowie, opposite the plaza. But when he reached the bank, having whirled around the corner rather like a charging elephant, the bank was quiet and dark. But farther up Bowie, at the corner of that street and the sandy thoroughfare named for the mayor, he saw flames shooting high in air.

He ran on the faster, with others falling in beside or behind him. So he was accompanied by twenty or thirty men when he came to that ordinary 'dobe house that burned.

He stopped on the sidewalk to stare.

What—he asked himself—would there be about that house of mud bricks to blaze so fiercely? Unless it were filled with something inflammable, there would be nothing about the place to catch fire except the *vigas*—the rafters of cottonwood log—which supported the flat mud roof. Then he smelled grease afire. He stared frowningly. A man beside him voiced his own puzzled thought:

'How-come,' this townsman asked, 'that explosion never wrecked the place? It never! You can see nothing but the fire bothered the walls . . . That is, if 'twas from here the explosion come . . .'

A man in shirt-sleeves seemed to notice the twinkle of Gavity's badge. He pushed up to say that this house was empty and the property of Mayor Zelman. He lived opposite it and the explosion had come from somewhere behind it. Or so he guessed from the sound. He had noticed the smell of burning lard oil and had been puzzled by it, because of the emptiness of the place.

'I don't know—yet,' Gavity told him absently.

He began to poke about while La Fe's volunteer hose company charged up and pumped water on the blaze. But he could find nothing around the house to explain that explosion. There grew in him a disturbing feeling that something more was afoot than this meaningless blaze. His uneasiness sent him, at last, back into the shadows. He went at the trot back toward the center of town. As he ran toward the juncture of Fay and Bowie Streets at the plaza, he told himself that more than the fire was important. He felt it in his bones!

But for minutes he could find nothing to support this feeling. He poked about alleys and cross-streets and they were quiet and almost empty, most of La Fe's floating population having gone to the fire. Then he came into the alley behind Buchanan's store. He stopped short with sight of a sudden red glow in the rear of Buchanan's. It was a dull flash, and was followed—from inside he thought—by a muffled explosion hardly louder than the report of a shotgun.

He went quickly, silently, that way. It was not Buchanan's store from which the explosion had sounded. Buchanan's store was closed. But next door was the general store of Mayor Zelman, and he could see, even in that darkness, that the door stood ajar. Then he stumbled over rubbish in the alley, and before he had straightened men jumped from that door into the alley. There were two or three of them. He could not say.

'Grab him!' a man cried snarlingly. 'Grab him—quick!'

But someone chose to shoot. Gavity had come up the alley with his pistol drawn. He twisted it now, toward the nearest dark figure.

He let the hammer drop and the alley rang to the sound of firing.

He had the advantage of darkness near the wall. These men before him were vaguely silhouetted by the shaft of light that came from the stores and saloons on Bowie Street. He could see them, if vaguely; they could hardly see him at all. There was the blaze of firing from his pistol and from their pistols. Then he was standing and there was nobody before him.

He jumped to the door of Zelman's store and collided with a close-packed group coming out. There was a savage hurly-burly; blows felt, not seen. The pistol in his hand was empty and he had not the time to jerk another from the Hardin vest. He swung viciously, clubbing blows with the empty gun. Someone shot at him, the muzzle so close to him that he was scorched by powder flame, his shirt set afire. He was knocked off balance and the men rushed past him. He straightened and got out the second Colt from his holster-vest. He whirled and began to shoot after the running ones.

Men came running into the alley—men returning from the fire and attracted by the shots. Gavity yelled at them, giving his title. They packed the alley around him and he led them into Zelman's store to make a light.

The store was wrecked! In the center of the long room between the counters a huge iron safe had been blown open. Blankets and quilts from the stock had been used—to muffle the explosion, Gavity thought. Some of these had caught fire. Gavity and his volunteer aides stamped out the blaze in the cloth.

He was looking about when Zuzu Zelman himself came pushing through the staring crowd. The mayor waved short arms excitedly and, with sight of Gavity, whooped at him.

'Der money! Der money!' he cried. 'Gone? Yes? Not?'

'I don't know,' Gavity told him. 'I haven't really looked around. There are a couple of pretty sick men—if they're not dead men—in Teepee Alley out back. But I don't know about your money. Was there much in the safe?'

Zelman squatted and began to paw frantically in the wreckage around the safe. He yelled and stood, holding up a heavy cash box. His round face was split by a smile that seemed to extend from ear to ear. He waved the box and seemed about to embrace Gavity.

'Wait a minute! Keep calm about it,' Gavity admonished him. 'I take it that your money's still there?'

'Der t'ieves—dey don't take der money!' Zelman yelled at him—and at the crowd in general.

His English was thicker than usual as he explained that more than nine thousand dollars was still in the cash box; that his safe was used for depository by merchants and traders when they needed a place for their cash after the First National's closing hours; that the day before had been unusual in the number of deposits he had accepted. He waved the box:

'I tell you, my friends, by Chiminy! La Fe has got der swell marshal! Der bad mans what come to La Fe now, and tries his devilment to keep oop, he was better in hell with his back broke and one bucket of salty water for to drink! I tell you, my friends—and you know old Zuzu Zelman, he does not give you der guff—La Fe has got one—fine—marshal. Der bad mans, he will last like der paper dog what chases der cast-iron cat by hell. By Chiminy! You stick by us and we stick by you and we got der good time in La Fe while Gavity will be der marshal!'

'Let's get those hairpins in from the alley,' Gavity suggested. 'Maybe somebody will recognize 'em. It might be a lead. Don't bother about throwing all the bouquets. The only kind of flowers La Fe's marshal is likely to appreciate will be forget-me-nots—and they'll be on his coffin!'

When the two men—both dead—were brought in and put upon a counter, he looked grimly at them, then at the faces of the men who stared fascinatedly at them.

'Anybody know these men?' he demanded.

He looked for any small sign of

nervousness, or recognition, while the dead were studied. But whatever suspicion he had, that this robbery (like that at Buchanan's) was a well-planned stroke made by a brainy, organized gang; that here in these observers were members of that gang; he had to shrug inwardly and confess defeat for the time being. Suspicion was one thing, proof entirely something else! When he found the gang and hit smashingly at it, he must have absolute proof.

One by one, the men in the store shook their heads and disclaimed anything but the vaguest knowledge of the dead. They were known—their faces and their status as saloon-loungers of the type only too common these days in La Fe. But no more was discoverable about them.

At the last, Gavity shook his big shoulders and turned to Mayor Zelman. He said that the two might well go down to City Hall and await an inquest.

'Sayre won't be pleased about it, of course,' he grunted. 'But it's you old-timers—Sayre and the rest of you—who let this riffraff get a jump on you, so you had to hire a gunman for a marshal—'

'Gunman?' Zelman cried. 'Der marshal we have got, he is not der gunman—not like Winn Wheelen. But he is der marshal of der kind La Fe needs. And Sayre, he will hold der inquest and if he will growl, we will ask him what his brother, der sheriff, *he* have done in La Fe! You stick by us, Gavity; we stick by you! And we will have der good time in La Fe!'

'All right,' Gavity said in a flat, weary voice. 'You've made a gunman out of me, whether I like it or not. I suppose it can all be chalked up to the Cause of Law and Order, or something. I never thought my pistols would earn my living. But since it's going that way, I'll stick with you. Now—I'm going to turn in. Let's get a hack and get it over with . . .'

When he had sent the bodies to City Hall, for Sayre's inquiry, he went out and walked the street for a time. He was not concerned with the mere killing of two human wolves, who had died while trying to kill him. What it was that depressed him, he could hardly say— except that he wanted to see Betty Ross; talk to her; hear her say as she had once said on the Slash R that she would wait for him to bring her father about to their way of feeling. And that, somehow, seemed very distant tonight.

'Ah, the hell!' he said at last, when block after block of tramping brought no lightening of his gloom. 'I'd better take a good, big drink and turn in—but not in the same room I used last night!'

He had his drink in the Gleaming Gem, then twisted and turned until he reached a cheap rooming-house across from the Gem.

There he put the washstand across the door and sprawled across the bed with a pistol under his hand.

14. 'Who is Mrs. M'Ree?'

While he ate his breakfast in Wo Lee's restaurant, Gavity saw that tall and portly Kentuckian, Adoniram Quince, editor of the *La Fe Bugle*, come toward where he sat at the counter. Quince beamed, this morning. His green eyes were almost childlike in their friendliness—and Gavity was not in the least deceived.

'Good morning, General!' he said blandly. 'How is that palladium of the public liberties, our *Bugle*, getting along? And is this an official visit, or—is it ham and eggs that brings you in?'

'I would like to receive at first-hand, suh,' Quince replied smilingly, 'the details of the robbery at Zelman's. I think I may record the affair under a heading of classic Latin: *Culpam poena premit comes* . . .'

'"Punishment presses a close attendant on crime," if I recall,' Gavity said, grinning.

'What? A Latinist *and* a triggernometrist!' Quince cried with what seemed honest amazement. 'The age of wonders is not over! And where did you get your Latin?'

'I read a book, once—or dreamed I did,' Gavity told him. 'Never mind that. It will be an odd day in this community of yours, General, when a spiky Greek root will take the place of a .45 slug! Don't try to hoorah me. What's on your mind? No matter what I may have tried to learn, here and there, in this school or that, I have accomplished one thing: I can read men's faces. You can open up with me—speak with what the old boys called freedom and frankness. You want something out of me or you wouldn't have come chasing me into a Chinese hashorium. Oddly, I wanted to ask you a question. Now, if we can trade . . .'

'And what is that question?' Quince countered. His florid face and twinkling eyes alike were very shrewd.

Gavity rolled the spoon about in his coffee-cup and grinned. He thought that Adoniram Quince might—doubtless did—play politics in La Fe. That would be natural to any Kentuckian. But in any matter not running counter to his own interest he might be trusted—if he liked the man he dealt with. In reason . . .

'What is the question?' Quince persisted. 'I—think I'll try to trade with you,' he added, after a slight pause.

'I'd like to know why Binnings killed Winn Wheelen,' Gavity told him, turning to stare directly into the green eyes.

'Oh, that! Yes, of course. Certainly. Why did Binnings kill Wheelen? Or—if I may be permitted—you would like to know why each was so ready to kill the other . . .'

He fished in a breast pocket of his frock coat and got out a stogie. While he bit the end from it and fumbled for a match, he looked anywhere but at Gavity.

'Odd . . . Very odd, suh . . . Odd, that you should ask that question—of me—this—very morning . . . For—Why do you ask it?'

'I'm just one of those curious—even inquisitive—folk you hear about,' Gavity said, shrugging innocently. 'Sometimes, that is. The more I think of it, it does seem a trifle strange to me that, after Binnings killed Wheelen, he told the whole town about the hard feelings they knew about—trouble between him and Wheelen . . .'

'Yes?' Quince drawled. 'He did say something like that.'

'But,' Gavity went on thoughtfully, 'I've asked a few questions, here and there, on that point. The peculiar thing is, nobody I've met thus far seems to know of any trouble between the men. Nothing, that is, beyond a natural sort of dislike; nothing that would explain a killing. Now, I'm peculiar in some ways . . . When something odd flops down in my life, I want to get it made as plain as possible. Would you happen to be a man like that, General? Would you?'

148

'Ummm . . . In moderation, perhaps . . .' Quince admitted cautiously. 'Within the bounds of discretion, I might say. Suppose we let that point go, for the time being. Mrs. M'Ree wants to see you, Gavity. That was what I intended to say to you this morning— or not say, dependent upon what I decided after talking to you. But, since you ask me the question about Binnings and Winn Wheelen, I think I had best deliver her message, suh. Mrs. M'Ree—you may have heard this—was Wheelen's very good friend.'

'And who *is* Mrs. M'Rees—besides being the ex-friend of the ex-marshal?' Gavity demanded suspiciously. 'You know, I'm still practically a stranger in town. It would be terrible if some of you established and respected citizens got me tangled in affairs that would be troubling to a poor cowboy.'

'Oh, nothing like that! There would be nothing embarrassing to you in a meeting with Blonde Rose M'Ree. She's the—ah—relict of the late "Bet-You" M'Ree, a leading gambler of La Fe and half-owner of the Teepee Gaming-Rooms.'

Then, catching Gavity's steady stare and facing the lift of Gavity's brows, he nodded.

'Oh, yes, of course. But that hardly enters, these days. Rose is a person to be relied upon. M'Ree, as I said, owned a half-interest in the Teepee. He fell out with Huckafee during the latter's incumbency as marshal. Huckafee then shot his enemy in the back of the head. It was this action—plus his too great intimacy with the Fays and other leaders of the sporting crowd—that led to his demotion and Wheelen's hiring as marshal. I counsel you, suh, to call upon Mrs. M'Ree. Any questions you have to ask, about La Fe in general, certain residents in particular, she can answer. It is even possible that she *will* answer them!'

Then he stood—rather as if afraid he would say more. Gavity looked upward at the shrewd face and nodded slowly. He let Quince go without trying further questions. When he had paid Wo Lee for his breakfast, he went out of the restaurant and wandered along Fay Street.

In the store of Jones & Ross he saw his ex-employer fussing importantly about packages that clerks were unwrapping and opening. He loafed in and leaned upon a counter. Bryan Ross looked suspiciously up at him, then his head jerked toward the rear of the store, and when he looked at Gavity again he was scowling. Gavity looked toward the rear of the store and held back a smile. Ross's manner assured him that, somewhere in the dusky background, Betty stood.

'Morning, Mr. Ross,' he said genially. 'Catching the loose trade, I see. My— goodness! A St. Louis store wouldn't have a better stock. Maybe store-keeping would be better for me than marshaling. I wonder if I couldn't start an opposition store, in the vacant building across the street . . .'

Bryan Ross snarled vaguely and corrected a clerk who was stacking shirts on the counter. Gavity began to move around, looking innocently from one thing to another, but getting closer the while to that place where Betty should be. She came from the back room, carrying lengths of bright print cloth across an arm. She smiled faintly to Gavity.

'Dodging me?' he asked her in a low voice. 'I thought you could hear me talking to your father.'

'Of course not!' she said quickly. But there was a sudden flush of color in her face that made him sure his charge had been correct. 'I—I was picking material for a dress. I don't know why I'd dodge you.'

'You—got over that—business of Saltillo? It was too bad that you had to see it.'

'I didn't see it, really, but— It was bad enough to know that it was happening.'

She shivered and shook her head. He stood close to her, now, and was putting out a hand to her arm when Bryan Ross snapped at him waspishly. Gavity let his hand sag and turned.

'I said,' Ross told him irritably, 'that it's time for the council to meet. I think it will be just as well if you attend the meeting, Gavity. There's going to be—some interesting discussion. If you're ready to go, come along.'

'It certainly sounds like Father inviting Willy into the woodshed,' Gavity said bodingly. 'Come on up to the council meeting . . . Interesting things'll happen . . . And *you* are wanted . . . Yes, sir! I wouldn't be surprised if Mr. Prather and some others intend to ask for my resignation. Well, goodbye, Betty. If the council fires me, I'll have more time to see you.'

She said nothing; only glanced uneasily at her father. Bryan Ross stood uncompromisingly watching Gavity.

'Let's go, Councilman,' Gavity said with a cavernous sigh. 'Might as well get it over with—and find out about the rent on that vacant store across the street . . .'

They walked down to Austin Street together, Bryan Ross's thick, short legs somehow conveying utter disapproval of his companion and most of the things seen on the way to City Hall. Gavity was mildly amused. He had received no warning of any particular fireworks to be exploded at this morning's council meeting. He wondered why Zelman had not warned him. But it might be that the mayor had received no intimation, either, of more than a routine assembly.

'I'll be in my office,' Gavity told Bryan Ross when they entered the 'dobe building. 'If the council wants me for anything, I'll be ready.'

But he looked in, a few minutes later, from the hallway. The council was not a full body. Zuzu Zelman sat at the head of the long table, and it seemed to Gavity that the council was marshaled rather as to factions; and that Zelman's backers were in the minority.

Prather's face was skinned, his sneering mouth less attractive than usual because of swollen lips. One of his eyes was almost hidden by a bluish discoloration; the other glared malevolently at the mayor. Gavity grinned at sight of these marks of his hand. Prather reminded him of an angered sidewinder. Zelman wore his placid smile and seemed not to note anything unusual about Prather.

Gavity knew the council by now. Behind Prather would be Hook, called a satellite of the hooknosed alderman; Luis Benedetto, a ward-heeler who was close friend of Ben Miles the Palace Saloon owner; two or three others, including Bryan Ross.

Whether Prather's plan was a complete surprise to Zelman, Gavity had no way of knowing. But almost instantly, when the meeting was in movement, Prather rose and moved that the office of marshal be declared vacant. Instantly, Hook seconded the motion. But Zelman grunted and looked around the table. Gavity saw the round face turn innocently upon Adoniram Quince, who sat beside him. Gavity could have sworn to the wink which lifted the editor from his chair.

Then Zelman began to talk in a drawling, reasonable tone. Before such an important motion was put to the vote, discussion was in order.

'Der future of La Fe, my friends,' he said slowly, 'perhaps it depends on der motion.'

'Just the point I make!' Prather interrupted.

'Just the point I make, too,' Buchanan the hardwareman grunted. 'Let's hear what the mayor's got to say. We can vote any time.'

'Der town like La Fe,' Zelman caught up his speech again, 'it is not der town like other towns. Der marshal of La Fe, he will not be der marshal like other towns can have. And so—'

He amplified; he discussed the special qualifications which must be possessed by the chief of police, in such a place as La Fe or other boom town. Prather interrupted. Zelman turned a bland face upon him.

'All this is very true!' Prather said. 'And I have a list of candidates who possess every qualification you're mentioning. Finch, a most reliable man, has just arrived in La Fe. He is willing to accept the office of marshal. Luis Benedetto, here, a man known to us all, is another candidate. Even Mr. Binnings, whose qualifications perhaps outweigh those of any other candidate in the field—'

'We'll vote on 'em,' Buchanan checked him. 'That is, after we decide whether we can use another marshal. Go on, Zuzu! I'm *awful* interested in what you was saying.'

Prather subsided, while men began to come through the door out of which Adoniram

Quince had gone so quietly after receiving the mayor's signal. Gavity saw how Prather glared at each newcomer, then at Zelman. For each of those men sat down close to the mayor . . .

Prather scowled with what seemed to Gavity perfect understanding of Zelman's maneuver, while the mayor talked on and on, for more than a half-hour, about the past and present and future of La Fe, going into the tiniest details. Then Zelman looked about the table and suddenly banged his fist down.

'As for me, my friends, der marshal we got is der marshal I think we need. But der motion and der second are right. We have der vote, now.'

Alderman by alderman voted and Zelman turned sadly to Prather, who was glaring at him.

'And so, Mr. Prather, der marshal we got is der marshal we keep, no? And I think it is better so . . .'

'I got a motion,' Buchanan put in. 'I move we ought to give Mr. A. Gavity, the marshal, a vote of thanks. He's started out his career in La Fe in the finest possible way. He's honest and he's efficient and he certainly ain't one bit afraid of the sporting crowd or any of the shysters that back 'em up! Do I hear a second?'

'Seconded—with pleasure!' Adoniram Quince boomed.

That motion carried with only Prather and

Hook and Mullins and Benedetto for *noes.* Gavity was called in to receive Zelman's congratulations and commendations. He looked around the table and, catching in turn the stares of three enemies, smiled pleasantly.

'Now, this is downright fine of you,' he said. 'It makes a man want to go out and do a lot better job than he's done—maybe a better one than he ever hoped to do. That's the way I feel about it, anyway. I will police your town for you just as well as I know how. The only way I'll be stopped is by lead. And'—he looked straight at Prather—'unless that lead is from around a corner or out of the dark from behind, it won't be one-way shooting . . .'

He found himself walking beside Adoniram Quince on Austin Street. The editor of the *Bugle* turned twinkling eyes upon the taller, bigger man.

'Gratitude, suh, is one of the chief pearls, if not the great and lustrous pendant pearl, of that opalescent necklet of all the virtues worn by humanity . . .'

'You won't get any arguments from me on that subject,' Gavity agreed. 'Zelman is the kind of man you feel like sticking to, because you well know he's sticking to you!'

'One of that breed known as Nature's Noblemen,' Quince said in best Kentucky manner. 'A diamond, suh; rough, yes! But one *needing* no superficial polish to reveal his innate worth!'

156

'I couldn't put it in just those words, but that's the way I feel about him. And how is the *Bugle* going? You ought to have enough news, these days, to make twice your size of paper.'

'A plethoral! A very plethoral! More than I have room to print. And—how is your engagement with Mrs. M'Ree?'

'I'll be seeing her,' Gavity answered, a shade evasively. 'Anything else you'd like to tell me about the lady before I make my call on her?'

'There is little to tell. She retains "Bet-You" M'Ree's half-interest in the Teepee. But she has also built that fine brick hotel, the Rose, on South Fay Street. Two stories! I had a Rose Edition of the *Bugle* when she completed it. She has housekeeping rooms on the first floor. From these, she manages her affairs.'

Gavity nodded, staring down toward the red building of which Quince had spoken so enthusiastically. He thought that a call on the 'relict' of the gambler was in order. He was doing well enough, as marshal, in a sort of blind way. But if he intended to strike at the gang behind such robberies as that of Buchanan and Zelman, he needed to know a great deal more about everyone in La Fe. And who would know more than Blonde Rose, with her lines into the night life of the town?

'Besides,' he told himself, while Quince watched narrowly, 'she has a grudge. Where it may rest is hard to say. But since M'Ree was

157

shot in the back by Huckafee and Binnings was gunning for her other friend, Winn Wheelen, there might be a chance of learning something valuable. If her grudge sets her talking!'

He nodded abruptly to Quince and swung down the plank sidewalk of Fay Street, heading for the Rose Hotel. Presently, he was knocking on a side door.

15. 'You call on Blonde Rose'

Years of night life had not robbed Mrs. M'Ree of a fine skin and firm, full-lipped, naturally red mouth. She was a tall, shapely woman in middle thirties, yellow-haired, with large blue eyes that, Gavity suspected, masked a very shrewd brain indeed. There was a shadowy wariness, hardness, about her that warned him, while he sat in her parlor looking blankly at her.

'I'm glad you came to see me, Gavity,' she said promptly. 'From what I've heard, around town, you're a man to tie to; a man I can trust. And I want to warn you right off about some of the men you might not learn about until— until it was too late for knowing 'em to do you any good.'

She moved on the tapestry-covered couch to snap the stub of her cigarette into a brass

158

jar two yards away. She began to roll another, of Duke's and brown paper.

'Jack Binnings, just for instance—and mostly! He's a plain louse! Don't let his smooth manners fool you a minute. He looks the gentleman and he acts the gentleman when that suits him. But he's bad—as bad as they come! I'm the girl that knows these remittance men. I've known the like of Binnings it's many a year, now, in one camp and another. He's bad all through!'

She looked at Gavity steadily over the cigarette, then smiled. Her face softened amazingly.

'Yeh, I like your looks! You're not my kind—so don't get worried about my being interested in you. I like your looks and I'm going to do anything I can to help you. Maybe that won't be so little, either. Cards on the table, Gavity! Have you been wondering what the trouble was, between Binnings and Wheelen—that just about nobody knew anything about?'

'I've been wondering just exactly that,' Gavity admitted, nodding. 'I feel that there's a lot of something-or-other going on, under the surface. Not just the ordinary hell-raising that an average marshal can take care of as it pops up. But these robberies and murders that can't be traced to anybody. Like the two store-robberies I stepped into.'

'You're right! There is a lot going on under

the surface. Winn Wheelen had one of those bulldog kind of minds. It took time for him to figure something out, but he generally was right after he figured it. He was slow and sure. Well . . . it was something he was getting on Binnings that kept him busy up to the minute Binnings killed him. Whatever it was—he wouldn't tell even me about it—he wanted more, or needed more. So he set Tyloe and Huckafee onto Binnings; put 'em tracking down Binnings's doings.'

Gavity stared at her frowningly. She nodded energetically.

'Tyloe was all right, but Huckafee is a dirty bushwhacker. Even if he hadn't shot Bet-You M'Ree in the back—the sneaking dry-gulcher!—I wouldn't trust Huckafee across my thumb. My idea is, Huckafee went to Binnings with word of what Winn Wheelen was doing. So Binnings stepped out and got Wheelen.'

She eyed him coldly, calculatingly. He looked up from the end of his cigarette.

'A good many men coming to this part of the country, to a boom town, have got something on the back-trail they'd rather not see uncovered,' he said slowly.

'Even you, maybe?' she suggested, then laughed. 'Gavity, I want to see you get Binnings! Get him right! I think you can—a sight easier than even Winn Wheelen could have. Maybe you're not the gunslinger Winn

160

was—I don't know. But you're fast enough! And you've got brains and—I'd bet—some education behind those brains. That's the reason I asked Ad' Quince to send you here, after we'd talked a while about you. There's the deepest head in this town—Adoniram Quince, with his mouth full of big words! I take his judgment and it's all for you!'

She hesitated, then leaned forward impressively to gesture with her cigarette.

'So far as I know, there's just two of us alive today who know that Winn Wheelen suspected Binnings of something. Me and Huckafee! And it's mightily little that Huckafee'll tell you—after you yanking the badge off him! More likely to let you have a slug out of some alley! You watch your step cat-eyed, day and night. You're bucking something big, here. I—my notion is, Winn figured Binnings for boss of your robbers and killers. That's my idea.'

'Binnings?' Gavity said quickly, for he was taken off his guard. 'Why do you think that, if Wheelen didn't talk?'

'He's a mysterious hairpin, Binnings is. He's got plenty brains and he's always flush with money. I've seen him drop a couple thousand at the Teepee without batting an eye—and be back the next night with as much more. You know well enough that's not ordinary money. Where does he get it? Who's sending it to him from the old home town?'

'That's right. But you can't convict him on that. You can just get suspicious.'

'Another thing! You know what they're betting, right now, that you won't last three days? Even money! And two to one you won't last six days! Who's back of that? I tried to find out and I couldn't—and generally I know well enough what's going on in La Fe. I did hear, though, that Ben Miles is forted for you. You watch Ben Miles, Gavity. He's a tall boy in La Fe. He never does any of his own killing, but somehow his killing gets done, just the same.'

'I've had notions about Ben Miles,' Gavity admitted dryly.

'You keep those notions polished! The first time you make a move toward the Palace—and Ben's breaking plenty ordinances, the same as most of the saloon-keepers—he's going to be waiting for you. He's keeping Huckafee drunk, since you took Huckafee's badge off him. And that mean little gunman Finch, that murdered O'Rourke, *he* is eating and drinking off Ben, too. You watch your step when you walk into the Palace. I'm with you, up to the back of my neck. For I want you to get Binnings. Winn Wheelen was worth a million Binningses. So was Bet-You M'Ree. Two finest men *I* ever knew.'

'Who are Binnings's special friends?'

'Ben Miles and Luis Benedetto—Luis, you know, is an Italian with a Mexican wife. He's a great politician in Hogtown and Little Mexico. Prather—you *met* him!—and Hook and Mullins. He seems to be pretty thick with this new city father, Ross, too. Maybe that's because Ross has got a pretty daughter. Binnings's long suit is pretty women. Then there's that Mexican killer, Saltillo, that you arrested. Saltillo's deadly as a rattler. Hook and Mullins are not cut out for real crooks. They do plenty dirt, in politics, but it's just the regulation dirt. The others—this Ross, I don't know much about, yet—are human corkscrews. Then, there's the bunch you always see, the ones that kowtow; nobodies that hang around for free drinks.'

She got up from the couch and stood before him, looking up earnestly.

'You look into Binnings's doing, honey. I think it'll pay you—and so it'll pay me. If you need anything, from money to chalk, you call on Blonde Rose. I'm the one to help you. But, most of all, you be mightily careful! The sign's up against you and I don't want to see you go the way M'Ree and Wheelen and Tyloe went. Looks to me like it was just plain providential, you drifting into town the way you did. And now, if you get yourself rubbed out, we'll have somebody like Huckafee or Benedetto for marshal. And I'll have to kill Binnings myself!'

'I'm not fond of the thought of getting rubbed out. There happen to be two or three things I want to get done before that happens.

I'll be careful. It begins to look like a good-sized order I'm handed. If the sporting crowd is "forted" for me, I'm standing just about on my own. La Fe's like every other town, I reckon: there are more honest folk than dishonest, here. But they're not organized and the sporting crowd is.'

'And the honest folks are too busy making hay to worry much about anything they don't have rammed down their necks,' Blonde Rose agreed.

He went slowly down the street. Everywhere was truth of what they had said. The stores were doing rush business; wagons of freight creaked along the sandy track of Fay and Bowie, or stood unloading at doorways. Houses and buildings were going up with bang of hammers or slap of masons' trowels.

'No, they naturally are too busy with their own affairs to worry a lot about running their town,' he thought. 'They pass a bunch of ordinances and hire a marshal to enforce 'em—unless enforcement pinches *their* particular corns. When they do that, they think their responsibility is ended . . .'

He came past the plaza and looked across at Ben Miles's Palace Saloon. It seemed to him that a great deal of noise was coming from the Palace, for this forenoon hour. He went over and stared across the swinging doors. There was a blowsy brunette of dance-hall type, banging away at a piano. Drinkers

164

encouraged her with whoops and patted their feet in time to the tune she played. Gavity grinned with mirthless lift of lip-corners. Ben Miles knew very well the ordinance forbidding a woman in a saloon.

But when he walked into the place, it was at neither the brunette nor at Ben Miles that he looked. He found the little cowboy-gunman Finch halfway down the bar. Finch saw him at the same moment and shifted his hands slightly, so that they disappeared from view of Gavity. But he made no hostile move when Gavity bore down upon him; only watched with yellowish eyes.

'You said you hail from Arizona,' Gavity said pleasantly. 'I'm beginning to hear that you're pretty fast with the hardware. That's the word going around.'

'Never met nobody faster,' Finch grunted. 'And I have met just a-plenty,' he added significantly.

'That's interesting. But in La Fe there's an ordinance against packing guns. I'm beginning to enforce that rule. As a newcomer, you're entitled to the doubt. I know you're used to just living with those hoglegs under your coat, but I'll have to ask you to hang 'em up behind the bar here.'

'And if I don't choose to go naked?' Finch demanded. His eyes seemed trained, not on Gavity's face, but on his hands.

'Oh, but you will!' Gavity assured him. He

put his right hand on the bar and grinned. Finch watched that hand. 'You will choose to take off your guns.'

Finch gaped, with sight of the Colt which had flashed into Gavity's left hand from the Hardin vest.

'Be mightily careful about taking 'em out and putting 'em on the bar,' Gavity counseled. 'This is cocked, you see.'

Without a word, Finch reached most carefully under his coat and produced two-short-barreled Colts. He handed them over to Miles and Gavity watched narrowly while Miles turned with them, to deposit them somewhere beneath the bar.

Gavity grinned as if there had been no moment of tension. Then, and then only, did he let his eyes stray back to where the girl sat at the piano, watching him. For an instant he regarded her, then turned reproachfully back to Miles.

'You know better than that,' he said. 'Violation of Ordinance 12, that forbids a saloon-keeper to let a woman come into his place unless he runs a licensed dance-hall or variety theater in connection.'

Miles kept all emotion from his expression. But there was the tiniest trembling of his hard-set jaw, to tell of the strain he was under.

'Why, now that you mention it, I do recall some kind of fool law like that,' he admitted gravely.

'You'd better send her out. Then—better hightail it down to City Hall and make bond for appearance in recorder's court tomorrow morning.'

He waited, while Miles went out from the bar to speak to the girl. She nodded and stood with malevolent glance at Gavity. Then she crossed to a side door and vanished. Miles came back with blank face and walked behind the bar. Gavity watched. Then, very softly:

'Better drift down to City Hall right now, Miles, to post that bond,' he suggested.

'They know me well down there,' Miles answered, as quietly. 'I'll see somebody about it. Maybe in a few days.'

'You're going to drag it down there—right now!'

'My young friend,' Miles said, with marked thickening of voice, 'it does look to me like you're laying up just a hell-slew of trouble for yourself, when there's not a bit of use in it. I happen to have a good deal of influence in this town. It won't get you a thing but a skinned nose—or worse—trying to buck me. That damn' foolishness about not letting a woman go into a saloon was started by our prize jackass, Zuzu Zelman. Like this about packing guns . . .'

He brought Finch's Colts from under the bar and set them on its polished top. He did not hold them; seemed hardly to know that they were there. He was looking Gavity in the

167

eyes. But as he let his hand fall away from them, they were left in easy reach of Finch's hands.

'It's a fool ordinance,' Miles went on. 'But I'm perfectly willing to go down to the Hall and make a row about it. I happen to be busy, right now. But when I have time—'

Gavity moved flashingly as Finch's fingers twitched. He stamped upon the gunman's foot with a violence that brought an agonized howl from Finch. He swept the Colts down the bar, scratching the finish sadly. He shoved the staggering Finch out with a ramming foot and leg, to crash into the piano. He reached over the bar and caught Miles's shoulder, to drag him up and over the bar and to the floor on the outside.

'Miles,' he drawled, 'I'm sorely afraid you misunderstand my taking the trouble to be polite to you. So, I'll just haul you down to the recorder myself, instead of letting you go down like a gentleman. We won't even stop for your hat and coat.'

He looked across at Finch, but the gunman seemed to have lost his thought of helping Ben Miles. Nor did anyone else in the Palace crowd move. They opened their ranks in grim silence, to let Gavity and the struggling, cursing Miles through.

Down Bowie Street, toward Fay, Gavity marched his prisoner. By his expression he was deaf to the threats of the furious saloon-man. Crossing Fay toward the mouth of Austin Street, they met Bryan Ross and Betty, with Binnings and Prather the hook-nosed alderman. Gavity would have passed them calmly, with no more than merest nod, but Miles called to Prather—and to Ross. This last surprised Gavity and he halted.

'Put this young fool in his place!' Miles snarled. 'He comes breaking into the Palace and jerking guns and hammering customers around—'

'What's it all about, Gavity?' Bryan Ross demanded angrily. 'What's the idea of jerking one of the town's leading men around like this?'

'One of the town's leading men certainly knows better than to break the law,' Gavity said easily. 'Even more, he ought to know better than to threaten the city marshal; tell him he's got so much influence with crooked aldermen that it's dangerous to arrest him. I don't like that. I didn't like it. So I'm taking him to City Hall to post bond.'

'You're certainly trying to lay up trouble for yourself,' Prather told him ominously. 'You can't do this sort of thing.'

'That's the quaintest thing I've heard today! Because—as you can see—I am doing it. You know I'm doing it.'

'Now, listen! You'd better—'

'That'll be all from you!' Gavity stopped him grimly. 'You don't tell me what I can do.

169

Your ideas don't interest me at all. This man is going to City Hall. More! He's going with my hand on the back of his neck. He lost his chance to walk down like a gentleman, when he tried to fix it with a cheap little killer— Finch—to rub me out. I reckon it was asking too much of him—to go down like a gentleman.'

He pushed Miles past them and on along Austin to City Hall. Of officials he saw only Root, the little clerk. Root gaped at the pair of them. Miles snarled at him as if Root had been one of his bar-tenders:

'Here, you! Make me out some kind of damn' bond. You—'

Gavity lifted him a foot from the floor and shook him.

'Shut up! I'll do the talking. Root, this is a violation of Ordinance 12. If we need a judge to make out his bond, I'll be happy to slam him in jail until a judge shows up.'

'I—I can fix the bond!' Root gasped. 'Just a minute!'

16. 'I'm arresting him again'

When bond had been made and Miles was gone, Root fidgeted with the pen and ink on his desk and looked furtively at Gavity, who grinned with perfect understanding.

'You know, Root,' he said, 'I entertain a notion that this is not Mile's last appearance in your office. It seems to me that, if I was city clerk of La Fe, I'd stop worrying about the way Miles feels. It might even be, you see, that he won't be pulling wires much longer. Anyhow, I'd try to remember that walking a tight-rope is really simple, compared to trying to run with the hounds and the coyote both.'

It was perhaps an hour later that Gavity, coming along Bowie toward the Palace, heard once more the tinny clamor of the piano ahead of him. When he reached the swinging doors of the Palace he saw one of Miles's bartenders standing, as if getting a breath of air. But the man's eyes shuttled sidelong to Gavity with nervousness he could not conceal.

So Gavity hummed 'The Zebra Dun' and walked on past with only that glance at the Palace. Down to the corner of Fay he went, pretty certain that he was watched, turned there and moved past the stores of Buchanan and Zelman. At Midwest he turned again, walking faster. He slipped into Teepee Alley and from that gained the narrower, and nameless, alley which ran behind the First National Bank and the Palace Saloon.

From the mouth of the alley he had seen nobody about the back of the Palace. But when he came noiselessly closer, he heard someone clearing his throat, just inside the saloon. There were whisky barrels here at the

171

door. When feet scraped inside, he dropped to a squat behind the barrels. A man came outside and, after an instant of silence, said, as if speaking to someone in the saloon:

'Well, ain't no sign of him out here!'

When he had gone, Gavity stood again. He looked cautiously around the door-jamb and found that sentry lounging within a yard of him, back to the door, hand on a six-shooter thrust into side waistband.

Gavity leaned and caught him with both hands—by the neck and by the wrist of his gunhand. He jerked him outside, lifting him clear off the floor, squeezing his throat. The man glared at him rattily.

'Tut, tut!' Gavity reproved him. 'Packing a gun. After all you heard me say to Finch.'

He twitched the Colt from his captive's waistband and rapped him scientifically across the temple with the barrel. Then he let the senseless figure sag behind a barrel, pushed the pistol into his own waistband, and slid inside to stare about.

The place was not crowded now. Ben Miles was behind the bar and Finch stood near him, on the customers' side. The piano had been moved over to a window and turned, so that the brunette girl could sit outside and, with hands only inside the saloon, play noisily. Gavity grinned. It was a very novel method of evading the ordinance against women in saloons.

172

He looked quickly around. Prather and Alderman Hook were up the bar, near the front door. In a chair across from Prather was Luis Benedetto, a big, heavy-faced, and dark man.

Gavity took five steps up the bar-room without being noticed. Then Benedetto turned and looked at him. The Italian made a gasping sound that drew other eyes that way. Gavity could fairly *feel* the stiffening in the atmosphere. Ben Miles was moveless; Finch, also. Gavity crossed to the bar, grinning.

'Ve-ry clever,' he complimented Miles. 'But—I'm almost sorry—it's still against the law for a woman to play the piano in a saloon. We'll have to stop that new notion, too.'

'My lawyer says I'm on the legal side, this time.'

But, for all the tonelessness of Miles's voice, there was no doubt in Gavity's mind about the intention behind this maneuver. He was intended to come in; to object; to run squarely into ambush. He knew it well enough. But he continued to grin.

'The woman's in the saloon—to an extent,' he said. 'For if the hands and arms aren't a part of the woman, then what *are* they part of? No-o . . . You'll have to give this up, too.'

'Better let him alone, Gavity,' Prather counseled, without coming nearer the two. 'I have told him he's all right.'

'Now, that's just too bad! And I hope he

173

didn't pay too much for the advice—since it's not worth a tinker's dam. I'm arresting him again. Same charge.'

Then he went across to the piano, stood looking at it for an instant while the girl pounded, and spoke to her.

'Away, sister! Out you go—and don't let anybody talk you into coming back or I'll have to send you down to jail!'

She jerked her hands back and moved away from the window. Gavity caught the piano with both hands and lifted it bodily from the floor. He turned it; dropped it with keyboard facing the room. He looked at Miles—and at Finch.

'Get your hat, Miles—if you want to wear a hat on the street,' he said evenly. 'It's City Hall, again! I told Root you'd be back soon. You—'

Then he dropped behind the piano, jerking both pistols as he threw himself to the floor. He had seen the shotgun coming up, where Luis Benedetto sat. As he struck the planks he heard the roar of it and the almost human moan of the shattered piano.

Gavity propped himself on left elbow and fired at Benedetto. He saw the big man let the shotgun fall and stand and take two long steps forward before he crashed down.

Finch was coming at him, a pistol in each hand. They began to flame and a slug scorched Gavity's shoulder before he let the

174

hammer drop on his fourth and fifth shots. Finch half-turned, bent almost double under the slug that struck his belly, then staggered sideways to the bar. He let his guns go and clung to the bar.

Gavity looked flashingly around, in time to see the big bouncer 'Pug' coming from behind the bar with sawed-off shotgun. He shot left-handed at Pug and under the second or third shot the big man went backward—faceless—and as he fell let both barrels crash into the Palace ceiling.

Gavity was squatting now. He shot a man with a carbine through the hand or arm and this one fled through the back door. Even in the ring of shots that lingered in his ears, Gavity could hear his shrill screaming in the alley.

He had the Colt taken from the man at the rear door. He let one of his pistols drop and drew this gun. Miles was going down behind the bar. Gavity fired, but the bullet went over the saloon-man's head and smashed a pyramid of whisky quarts and wrecked the mirror of the back bar. Miles disappeared.

Gavity stood, mouth a white line across his tanned face. He menaced Prather and Hook and the miscellaneous loungers who gaped at this aftermath of gunplay.

'Come out of that, Miles!' Gavity called. 'Come out and go to City Hall. Come on—before I shoot through that bar and kill you. I

175

ought to, anyway. But I'll give you one chance—'

Miles rose with hands held high over his head. He was palpably afraid. But the set mask of his face he could hold unchanged. He stared almost incredulously at Gavity, then walked stiffly out, hands still elevated.

Gavity found that his vest was snagged from front to side; his coat had two bullet-holes in it; his face was bleeding from the ricocheting splinter of piano leg that had struck it. His shoulder stung where Finch's bullet had scorched it. He was in killing humor and Miles seemed to guess it.

'I got my hands up!' he called quickly. 'I got no gun on. You better be careful, Gavity! You—'

'I ought to kill you right here and now,' Gavity said thickly. 'It would save me doing the job later on. This was a nice little try at bushwhacking you made. I knew it from the minute I walked into that back door. The trouble with you is, your grab is bigger than your reach. That's something better men than you ever will be have suffered from. Come on with me! We'll let Judge Sayre hold his inquest right here. But you won't go out of my sight for one minute.'

He looked bodingly at Prather and the hooknosed man paled. Alderman Hook also seemed to find no pleasure in facing Gavity. He shrank back so that Prather was shielding

176

him.

'I suppose this whole plan was yours, Prather,' Gavity drawled grimly. 'Some more of the legal advice you gave Miles. You know—I wouldn't be a bit surprised if, eventually, that law practice of yours got you killed . . . In fact, I'll be downright surprised if you live six months . . .'

Men were beginning to crowd both doors of the Palace; to stand at the window where the brunette girl had played the piano. Gavity saw Tim Free among those in front.

'If you'll get Judge Sayre, Free,' he called, 'we can settle this, right here and now. Move over against that wall, Miles. As for the rest of you, just stand right where you are. If you want to move around to ease yourselves—don't do it! I'm in a nervous condition of the trigger-finger. I wouldn't mind a little bit if I shot one of you accidentally—you lousy drygulchers!'

While he reloaded his pistols and waited for the justice, he tongue-lashed the silent—and moveless—witnesses of the shooting. He sketched Prather's history—as judged from his appearance. He told Hook of thieves and murderers hanged in one place and another, who were upright citizens by comparison with crooked politicians.

'And you, Miles,' he said, having finished with the aldermen, 'anybody would see you in a crowd and automatically put his hand on his watch. But don't bother about that! You're not going to be around the top of the earth for long enough to really contaminate anything. I'll bet there's a yard of warrants out for you—murdering sick Mexicans to rob 'em and daring crimes like that. I'll eventually write those other places and tell 'em to cancel the warrants; that you got yourself killed in La Fe!'

'It's easy to talk when you're holding a gun on a man who hasn't got one,' Miles snarled. His face was very red. 'Maybe it won't be me that kicks off, here. It might even be you! We better wait and see. Unless you'd like to make a bet!'

'No use to make a bet when you couldn't pay when you lost—and you're going to lose that one! Well, here's the judge! We can see if you're going to be held responsible for Benedetto and Pug and Finch. Whether the coroner's verdict says so, or not, you really killed the three of 'em.'

The little justice came flapping through the crowd. He looked at the bar-room floor and shook his head.

'I swear!' he complained. 'I don't know what the town's coming to. Killing and killing and killing! Nothing but inquests. What happened? Tim Free says—'

'It was like this,' Prather began, with quick glance from Miles to Gavity. 'Miles was—'

'Shut up!' Gavity silenced him. 'I'll testify

178

and you can tell your lies later—under my eye, too, Prather. I came in here because Miles had a woman in the saloon, Judge. Arrested him and booted him to jail when he thought he was a hard case—which he never could be unless he was at somebody's back. Then he decided to get me killed—'

He told his story with vicious compliments to the address of Miles, Prather, Hook, Benedetto, and the others. At the end, Sayre shook his head and snarled.

'All right! All right! It's my finding that the deceased come to their ends at the hands of the marshal, while they was trying to kill him. Lord knows, that's verdict enough in La Fe, today. No use going into a lot of work with witnesses and testimony. Man can certainly see that they was shooting at the marshal—but they couldn't shoot quite good enough.'

'But, look here!' Prather cried angrily. 'We want to—'

'Shut up!' Gavity grunted. 'The inquest's closed!'

17. 'I speak like an oracle'

Gavity read Quince's account of the killings, in the *Bugle*. He thought that Quince must have sat up half the night setting the story, to get the printing finished.

'It must have taken him quite a time,' he told himself, 'because of the way it runs . . .'

For there was nothing in the *Bugle*'s account to connect Ben Miles with the shootings. Adoniram Quince remarked only that, as the city marshal had moved to arrest the saloon-keeper for violation of a minor ordinance, the notorious Arizona gunman Finch had decided to settle a difficulty arising earlier in the day. He had opened fire on Marshal Gavity and had been killed.

Benedetto's part in the affair—so the story said—could not be satisfactorily explained by questioning of any witness. But he had fired a shotgun at someone—that much was clear even by the conflicting testimony of observers. Whether he had fired at Finch or at Gavity; whether he had been killed by Finch or by Gavity; he was dead. So the truth would hardly be known.

Ben Miles disclaimed all knowledge of details. He had been talking to Marshal Gavity when the shooting began. He had dropped behind the bar for shelter and had seen nothing. Prather had testified that he had given legal advice to his client Miles; and that he had warned Marshal Gavity that, in his opinion, the saloon-man was not violating the ordinance against permitting women in a saloon. He had then turned away and had seen none of the shooting.

'Well, well, well!' Gavity said aloud, folding

180

the *Bugle*.

He went out of Wo Lee's and down the street. Almost the first person met was Adoniram Quince, who smiled at him genially. Gavity returned the smile with perfect understanding.

'It's all right, General,' he said. 'You and I can still be the best of friends—if only you never tell me you believe one word of all this you printed. It's not hard to see why you did it—any more than it is to understand why Prather and the rest of 'em lied like hell.'

'You made no charge against Miles in connection with the shooting, nor said much of Benedetto's shooting at you,' Quince reminded him. 'I could hardly make a charge, in your stead.'

He looked down Fay Street, along the front of that fortress of the sporting crowd. His big head moved in a slow nod.

'I wonder what they are thinking, after yesterday,' he said softly. Then his sides shook in violent laughter. 'I could give them a thought: "Let no cat now boast of his nine lives."'

'Do you happen to know whether or not the city council has sent for a new marshal?' Gavity asked him abruptly.

'What? A new marshal?' Quince grunted amazedly. 'Why—why should we do that, when we've got the best man in Texas, right here and right now?'

181

'I'm about to resign, I think,' Gavity said slowly. 'I didn't come to La Fe to be a policeman. I drifted here for—Well, among other things, I thought I might put down my roots and start making a fortune. Oh, not today or tomorrow, of course, but eventually. I thought I'd sort of grow up with the town. All I've done, so far, has been to serve you people as a good, new broom, sweeping clean! I want the council to get another man.'

'You mean that—ah—the young lady in question, who is "among the other things" you came to get, isn't inclined toward gallant lictors? My young friend, let an old and wicked and sometimes kindly man counsel you: Do not take at face value any look of disdain cast toward the man behind the city marshal's badge. For, let me assure you, many a proud, disdainful face is carried above an admiring, even a loving, heart!'

He tapped Gavity's arm and nodded vigorously.

'I am old enough to be your father. Very well! If *my* son were in those boots of yours today, I should say to him: "My son, I could not recommend to you as a career the life of marshal in La Fe or any other town. But La Fe is a town in its formative state. Almost more than anything else, it needs a city marshal who can be neither bought nor bluffed!"'

Gavity shrugged and fumbled with tobacco and papers. Quince shook his big head gravely.

'Listen to me! Let me assure you that you are as surely aiding the building of this city as is any man here—Zelman or any other. For without your bravery and your guns—without your willingness to stamp on snakes—there can be no foundations dug. So, wear that shield a time longer. Tame or kill or run out the riffraff, then lay the foundation for that personal fortune you desire. If I be any prophet, coming generations will not belittle the work you are doing.'

He laughed suddenly and brought out a cheroot.

'Lo! I speak like an oracle. I do that sometimes—when not too drunk and not too sober. But remember what I said about a girl's face as contrasted to a girl's heart. Now, I will leave you to Tim Free. He is coming toward us with an expression I know too well.'

Gavity turned to watch the lanky buyer swinging their way.

'When Tim Free has swallowed five drinks,' Quince explained, 'no more, no less, he is moved always to speak upon one subject, the finest herd of mules Texas ever saw. Goodbye! I have heard the story many times, I will let you hear it, now.'

Tim Free stopped before Gavity. Exactly as if resuming a conversation unavoidably interrupted, he wagged a thick forefinger at Gavity.

'The finest mules this country ever see! And three as good Mexican boys as ever I hired, too. Then these damn' thieves come along, the gang of 'em. They killed my herders and they run off the mules. Run 'em over into Mexico, I reckon, and sold 'em for half what they cost me; a tenth of what they was worth. And I had 'em sold before ever I bought 'em, too.'

Gavity nodded grave sympathy. He saw Manuel, Lupe's brother, coming along Fay Street from the direction of that Mexican quarter known generally as 'Little Mexico.' He thought that Manuel was looking for him.

'Yes, sir! Sold before I bought 'em,' Tim Free went on angrily. 'To a grading contractor on the railroad, you see. This fella says to me he wants the finest mules he can get. So I says to him I'll gather the finest mules in the country. And I done it. Then they killed my boys and they stole my mules! A year back . . . But I'll come up with them thieves if I have to wade Jordan River in my shirt-tail to come back across and git 'em. I am lots like an Injun, Gavity. Man hits *me* in the nose, he better hit awful hard—so hard I never will wake up to hit him back. I always pay my debts.'

Gavity nodded again. There was much of truth in that. From all that he had heard around the corral of the Midwest Stage Company, from Bryan Ross and others who

184

had known the old buyer for years, Tim Free had precisely that reputation. He evened old scores.

Manuel came up and stood with blank face while Tim Free talked on. When the buyer had swung on, going toward the Mint Saloon, Manuel's expression changed abruptly.

'*Patron,*' he whispered, 'I have word of those carriage horses which were stolen from the mayor. It was a man I know, one of scarred face who works for the beautiful *señora* of the Hotel of the Rose, who told me of them. He was ordered by his *patrona* to look and listen for any word that might be of use to you. This Arturo Griego is a friend of mine and when he knew that I serve you, he said that I might help. A while ago he told me to go into a *cantina* in Little Mexico, while he went to still another. And I played that I was drunk. So I heard four men—Mexicans—talking. They *were* drunk! Their tongues were loose. *Patron!* I heard of the horses. But also I heard more.'

He looked quickly around and sidled nearer.

'They perhaps know little of more than what they have done. But from their talk it seems to me that here in La Fe are the men of that thieves-gang which has committed so many robberies of stages and banks and stores; so many murders! Each man of the gang, I think, knows a few others. But no man

185

of the ranks knows all the members of the gang.'

'That would explain many things,' Gavity said slowly, frowning. 'It would explain a great many things about which I have wondered . . . The biggest robbery of all—that of the stage at Harmony Station, for one. But the mayor's fine horses? What of them?'

'They laughed about it, these men who stole the horses. They said that the mayor spoke in council one morning, talking most bitterly against the gang of thieves. That day, for a great joke, they stole his fine team. They hold the horses in the town, now, looking for a buyer in Mexico. One is to look at the horses soon. Perhaps tomorrow. Two men of the gang guard the horses always.'

'You have not learned where, in La Fe, they are held?'

'Not yet. But I will know, soon. For these men are still in the *cantina*. They will be there for some time, drinking and talking. When they leave I will be at their heels.'

'Do you think they were of the gang which robbed the mayor's store?' Gavity grunted suddenly.

'No. I am sure that they had no hand in that. But certain ones of their gang did the robbery. They know that much, if not the names of the men who had part in the robbing.'

'*Muy bien!* Go back and follow them to

where they have the horses, if they go that way. But, Manuelito, much care is needed in these things. These are not men to face without a pistol in your hand. You have one?'

'No, *patron,*' the boy shrugged. 'I have not had money for pistols. If you will loan me one—'

Gavity drew from left holster one of his matched Colts. With almost sleight-of-hand speed he passed it to Manuel and saw it go under the youth's shirt.

'*Vaya con dios, hombre!*' he said smiling. 'Be very careful. But, if anything should happen, do not worry about Lupe. I will care for her.'

'That rich one from Chihuahua, Don Cesar Saltillo, he has seen her,' Manuel told him with quick frown. 'Don Cesar has always had from our sort what he wished. I think it has surprised him that, in our house, he has done so little. Of course, in Lupe's mind is set another picture. Else she would have been honored by his visits. Your picture, *patron!* So, she looks at Don Cesar with never more than one eye, her other being upon you . . .'

Gavity threw back his head and laughed.

'My—goodness!' he cried. 'Lucky at cards, unlucky at love, the saying is. The first thing I know, I'll begin to drop money at poker. Never mind, Manuel. You go back to this drinking-place and follow those thieves to the place where the horses are. Then come to me with the word and we shall see what we can do

187

toward setting that team back in the mayor's stable.'

He thought a good deal, that afternoon, about Adoniram Quince's description of La Fe and his part in the formation of the town. He drifted with seeming purposelessness about the streets, but actually was alert as any wolf.

'A part in the building of the town . . . Without my guns—and my willingness to use them—there wouldn't be any stores here, because the thieves would steal the people blind, intimidate them . . . I suppose he was right! But a man never wants to think that he's a killer . . . And yet—if you've killed one rattler, then step into a den of the things, you have got to kill and kill fast . . .'

Some solid, substantial citizens of the town—for the most part friends of Zelman and members of the Zelman faction in politics—stopped to shake his hand and say that they were pleased with his work; begged him to keep it up. One prophesied, even, that La Fe would one day build a monument to its present chief of police. Which brought a laugh from Gavity.

'That monument,' he said amusedly, 'is much likelier to be set over my grave. You know about my cemetery lot?'

There were other citizens, apparently just as substantial and respectable as the Zelmanites, who regarded him with a studied

188

lack of expression, even with downright, lowering malevolence.

Prather was one who lowered—but Gavity would have expected that. Hook and Mullins also were certainly anti-Zelman. But there were store-keepers and saloon-men and other miscellaneous townsmen who—he thought—should appreciate an honest administration, who were obviously his enemies.

Twice in the afternoon he saw Betty. Once she was with her father. He would not put himself in her way. But when for the second time he looked up a street and saw her standing before a little jewelry store, he moved quickly toward her. Before he could cross Bowie to where she looked into the narrow show window, Binnings came around a corner, to sweep off his wide, black hat and bow to the girl.

Gavity thought that she had not seen him, because she was facing Binnings. It hurt him, somehow, to see how she smiled up at the tall, handsome gunman, around whom hung so much of mystery. Then Bryan Ross came out of the jeweler's with a package. It seemed to Gavity, watching steadily, that the little man was not too well pleased with the sight of Binnings holding the girl's hand.

On impulse, Gavity turned and walked into the Coney Island Saloon. He went through with a nod to the bar-tender and various drinkers. By way of the alley he came back to

Bowie Street and crossed. So the party of Bryan Ross had to pass him. When the three came to him, Binnings stared straight ahead as if Gavity's big figure did not exist. Bryan Ross's red face grew redder still and he muttered something under-breath. Betty smiled slightly, nodded more slightly still, as if she had never been held close against Gavity's shoulder; as if they were no more than the most casual acquaintances.

Then they were by and Gavity, pivoting slowly, stared after them. He swore almost soundlessly and recrossed to the Gem of Mayor Zelman. Zelman was in the saloon and he greeted Gavity with wise smile. They had a drink together, then another.

'Our sporting crowd, my friend,' Zelman said in an undertone, 'they are very mad by you. Yes! You must be very careful. They are like der rat; they bite from der dark; they bite from der back. We cannot lose you, Gavity!'

Gavity nodded—as if he were listening to the earnest little man. But to himself he was saying:

'Many a proud, disdainful face is carried above an admiring heart . . . Well, Adoniram Quince, I do hope that you're right. Even if I hardly believe you can be . . .'

When he could leave, he went out to wander again. He was passing the corral of the stage company on Midwest Street when Manuel came trotting up to him. Gavity drew

190

a long, slow breath. At least, here was action. He was tired of thinking; tired of trying to persuade himself that Quince could be right.

18. 'You get der thief?'

Manuel was panting. He grinned up tensely at Gavity and slapped the bulge of the pistol under his shirt.

'Come with me, *patron!*' he whispered. 'The horses are in a shed in Hogtown. I have seen them!'

'*Muy bien!* We go to that shed now,' Gavity told him.

Manuel led the way out Midwest Street to a point almost opposite the house of Bryan Ross. At Zelman's block-square place he gestured to the south. There lay 'Hog-town,' a huddle of 'dobe houses halfway to the lazy curves of the Rio Grande.

Manuel was a hundred feet ahead as they approached this ancient settlement of the Mexicans. Presently he beckoned imperatively to Gavity. He stood flattened against a large and very dilapidated 'dobe wall, ear to a crevice between the mud bricks. Gavity went quietly and cautiously up to the boy. When he put his ear to the crack in the bricks, he could hear voices.

'We can go around the corner now,' Manuel

whispered. 'I went that way when I was here before. This stable is behind a long house.'

Gavity followed him through a shabby yard and at the corner of the stable looked across at the house to which it seemed to belong. A fat woman drowsed, sitting in a chair with rawhide bottom, at the back door of the house. An ancient man nodded beyond her. They edged around the corner and toward the stable door. Then a tall man—a hard-faced American—came out of the stable. Gavity recalled him as one seen loafing about various saloons, but particularly in the Palace and Criterion. This man stared narrowly at them.

Before Gavity could speak, he took a half-step backward and was in the stable door again. He called to someone inside. Another American—also a saloon loafer whom Gavity had seen—appeared instantly. The two stood watching.

'I'm looking for a stray horse—or maybe it's two stray horses,' Gavity told them smilingly. 'Thought they might have strayed this way and been caught.'

'No horses here,' the first man said quickly. 'But, come to think about it, we did see a couple go by. It must be half an hour ago, ain't it, Joe?'

Joe only nodded and continued to watch Gavity.

'They was kind of drifting toward town, these was,' the speaker went on. He had a broken-toothed grin, but his eyes were pale and watchful.

'Those wouldn't be the horses I want,' Gavity told him, with smile as wide. 'These I'm after—the ones I'm going to take back—have been drifting south ever since they were stolen. Drifting toward the river and a market. If I didn't happen to be seventh son of a seventh son, I might go on by. But there's an itching under my left shoulder blade that tells me our horses—Zelman's horses, that is—are right behind you in that stable. Probably they crawled in through a crack and you didn't happen to notice 'em. Those things happen—not often, but occasionally . . .'

Joe shifted position a trifle and glared at him. His hand was out of sight, now, behind him.

'He told you there ain't no horses in here!' he snarled. 'Now, you're maybe marshal, fella, but marshaling's like lots of other things: it only goes so far! You ain't coming in here and you better make up your mind about that! You—'

Mexicans were appearing as by magic, as if drawn by some magnet, around the chair of that fat woman who, now, was very much awake. Gavity whipped out his pistol. Manuel drew his. Gavity went forward in a long, lunging step. Manuel whirled at his command and covered the Mexicans who were at Gavity's back. Joe and the other man jumped backward into the stable, yelling to the Mexicans.

Gavity reached the door and dropped quickly to his knees. He expected the men inside to shoot—and shoot they did! But his crouching posture sent him below what they expected for target. The flashes of their shots gave Gavity perfect targets. He fired twice at each flash, having that split-second of advantage which in gunplay means the difference between living and dying. He scrambled inside, keeping low, calling to Manuel.

'I am here, *patron!*' the boy answered fiercely. 'These thieves will not come into the stable!'

He appeared in the door, firing at the Mexicans, who seemed to be reinforcing Joe and his companion. The two guards at whom Gavity had fired made no further sound. Gavity left Manuel to hold the door while he reloaded his pistol and hunted the horses. They were in a stall adjoining this large room that was piled with hay and sacks of grain.

He ran back to the door and helped Manuel check the Mexicans, who had taken cover in the yard and were firing wildly at the stable. Manuel called for cartridges and Gavity handed him loose shells from a coat pocket.

'Now,' he said, when the reloading was done, 'you hold them from the door for two

194

minutes. We must get the horses away, else there is little point to this fighting.'

He looked quickly around the feed-room and at the heavy roof of mud-piled saplings. There was firewood here; cottonwood poles and mesquite roots. He found a sapling thick enough for a lever, jammed the end of it into a crevice of the rear wall. He heaved away furiously, straining great shoulders, until a section of that wall gave and he could attack the edges of the hole left.

From lariats he fashioned two *jaquimillas*, turns of rope about the horses' necks and noses. He led the horses through the gaping hole he had made. Manuel was firing away through the door, husbanding his shots, cursing like a veteran when the others' bullets knocked dust into his face.

Gavity called him and the boy came at the run, grinning through blood and grime that masked all but his brilliant eyes.

'Look at those *ladrones* who fired at me,' Gavity directed him. 'If they are alive, I will take them to town. If not—so much the better!'

Manuel jumped to explore the sacks. He called that one man was dead, the other vanished.

'Then, no matter! Let us go! After all, we have the horses of the mayor and we will take them to his house.'

They swung up bareback and the big half-bloods jumped under the heels ramming their sides. Behind them as they galloped they could hear the yells and scattering shots of the Mexicans, who seemed afraid, even then, to make a direct charge on the stable. Across vacant ground the big horses ran, to bring up before Zelman's stable in the rear of his big house in a swirling cloud of dust. Zelman came running across the yard.

'Der horses!' he yelled incredulously. 'My horses! How is it you get 'em back for me? You—Der shooting by Hogtown. It was you, yes? I hear it. And I see der *stre-e-eaks* come this way and— It was you! You get der thief?'

'One of 'em. Maybe one or two more. But there's no way of telling. They were over in Hogtown. Been over there since they were stolen, probably. Now, I'd like to know who owns the house and the stable where we found 'em. Who can go with us?'

'Ricardo!' Zelman called. Then, to Gavity: 'Ricardo will know der house and der man. He has been in La Fe der sixty year.'

An ancient Mexican with a hoe hobbled across to his *patron*. He listened to description of the house and stable and nodded calmly to Zelman:

'But yes! Everyone in this part of La Fe knows that old house of the Saltillos of Chihuahua. Don Cesar has lived there sometimes. But he has other houses also. I think that a man not of his family now lives in

196

the house with cousins and others. I have not seen him there for many weeks.'

'But, just the same,' Gavity told Zelman grimly, 'I want to talk to Don César Saltillo. It might just be that he knows something of that stable holding your stolen horses. Anyway, we'll certainly see. I'm going to town, now, to look for him.'

'You go to town, yes!' Zelman said, grinning. 'But you go in my carriage! I want to show der thieves we can get back some of der things they steal.'

So it was in state that Gavity and Manuel went back into Bowie Street. For Gavity the ride was spoiled, despite Zelman's almost childish joy in recovery of his 'beau-ti-ful horses.' As the ornate carriage passed Bryan Ross's house, he happened to turn his head and see, walking up and down under the cottonwoods that bordered Ross's sidewalk, Betty Ross with Binnings. She held his arm and they were talking so earnestly that neither even heard the carriage. Or so it seemed from their manner of preoccupation . . .

'I owe you der reward and tomorrow in der council I pay it,' Zelman told him, beaming at the surprised faces of men on the sidewalks of Bowie. 'And Manuel . . . If you want der job with old Zuzu Zelman, Manuel, der job with Zelman wants you.'

Manuel thanked him. Gavity hardly listened. Partly, he was looking for Saltillo

197

among the men who gaped at the carriage. But he thought more of Betty and the proprietary way in which Binnings looked down upon her and how she held to his arm . . . At last, at Bowie and Fay Streets, he dropped from the carriage and took up the search for Saltillo.

'Saltillo?' a bar-tender at the Mint said, grinning, 'I ain't seen the man since he killed that fella and you made him go to City Hall. Hard to say just where you could find him. You'd have to know what woman he was chasing!'

It was the same elsewhere. The bar-tender's phrase recurred to Gavity—and Manuel's remark about Don Cesar going to see Lupe. He went to the city corral and saddled Nubbins.

'You old crowbait, you!' he told the horse affectionately. 'About time you got some exercise. And—it may just be, before long you'll get plenty of it. The way things look around town—the part of town I'm really interested in—I might as well straddle you and keep on riding.'

He sent the big horse at a lope out of town and along the road by which he had come— ages ago, it began to seem—to hunt for Betty Ross.

'And make my fortune!' he thought sardonically. 'Ah, well! Town life has changed many a person, so I've heard.'

Lupe came to the door of the house with the fall of Nubbins's feet on the hard dirt of the yard. She stared, then ran across to stand at the stirrup. She was smiling vividly.

'*El Grande!* The Big Gavity!' she cried. 'I am very glad, now. Manuel has told me of the things you do; of the bad men who try to kill you—but die before they can. I am very glad to see you. Will you get off the great horse and come into the house? I have not thanked you for saving Manuel—'

He swung down, but only let the reins drop and stood smiling at her. For her honest pleasure was infectious. He could not help comparing it to Betty's manner. And there were so few places where a welcome seemed real that he was touched.

'I am glad that you are glad,' he told her. 'But I am here only to look for a man. You know Don Cesar Saltillo? Manuel said that he had been here. Be careful, Lupe . . .'

'I have been very careful! But he is not here. He has not been here today. I thought that he rode back to Mexico on business. He is a *caballero*, *El Grande*, but also a man of the worst. We know much of him, Manuel and I. Why do you hunt him?'

'I think he knows a thing which I wish to know. But if he has not been here today, then I must go back to town and hunt him elsewhere. If he went across the river, there will be someone to say so. Do not trouble

199

more about Manuel, Lupe. He is now a friend, both of me and of the mayor. He will have work in the town. And you—why, you will find a good young man to take you to the priest and to his house.'

'I do not want a young man,' she said slowly, looking directly up at him. 'Since a day when—when a great man on a tall horse came riding up and took from me light for his *cigarro* and kissed me, I have known what man I wanted. . . Tell me, *El Grande*, is it true that the lovely *americana* in the town is the girl whom *you* will take to the priest? This is—certain?'

'It is not certain!' he assured her, with grim tightening of the mouth. 'I fear that the lovely *americana* does not feel for me what you say you feel.'

'Then why do you hold your hands from me?' she whispered, coming closer. 'It is not merely that you helped Manuel; from the instant that you rode into this yard, I knew what I felt.'

'You are only a child,' he said—a shade uncomfortably. 'I do not bargain with little girls.'

'A child? I am nearly seventeen! In this land—but you know that. It is the *americana* who holds you back.'

'Perhaps! But something holds me. Now, I must ride back to town, Lupe. But I will see you again, soon.'

On impulse, he bent and kissed her lightly, then turned to Nubbins. She was standing there, watching, when he looked back from fifty yards along the La Fe road. He waved and she lifted her hand in reply. He shook his head scowlingly.

'The poor kid!' he said aloud. 'She and I seem to be in the same boat—and a leaky craft it seems to be!'

Then he shrugged off thought of everything connected with love-affairs. There would be work to do tonight. He felt it in his bones. Too much had happened to the prestige of Ben Miles and the Fays and other leaders of the sporting crowd for them to let much time slip. There would be trouble soon, he knew.

19. 'Huckafee won't talk'

Blonde Rose M'Ree was in the Teepee when Gavity reached the big gaming-house on his first round after dark. She stood talking to an egg-bald little man in the rear of the room. When Gavity came back she introduced the bald man as 'Pueblo Charley' Ull, her partner in the place. Ull's inscrutable dark eyes narrowed slightly. He shook hands and told Gavity that he was glad to meet him—a statement that Gavity could not accept or reject, as to truth. Ull's tone was too inflectionless.

He went on about his supervising of games. Gavity told Blonde Rose that the place must be a gold mine; it was already fairly crowded and more men were coming in.

'Yeh, it's good enough. Ull's a wizard at running a place. About the only thing he ever has done, I reckon. But ne' mind that. What I want to tell you is, watch your step tonight! Something is hatching. I don't know what it is; couldn't find out. But there's one of those lull-things you hear about. You know—the kind that goes before a storm. Too many of the sports are packing guns. And we can't have *you* getting shot in the back.'

He nodded and asked her about Saltillo.

'Haven't seen him around. But he may come in. Sometimes he bucks the tiger here. What do you want of him?'

He told her about the horses—and thanked her for having Griego look around. She shrugged and regarded him with what seemed almost affection.

'I told you I was going to help. And I suspicioned all the time that Zuzu's team was still in La Fe. Generally, I know a little about what's going on. Want to walk with me as far as the hotel? I'm tired tonight. I think I'll turn in early with a box of candy and a novel. I got a dandy in from St. Louis, today. Think it's about a duke and a seamstress; that's what the picture on the cover looks like.'

Then she looked up at him and the red mouth twisted.

'That is, I'd appreciate you siding me if you think it'll not wreck your reputation. That Ross girl might be looking . . .'

'I'd risk it, even if you happened to be right—which you certainly are not. I count it an honor to escort Rose M'Ree on the street.'

'Thank you! A right pretty compliment. It's not that I'm worried about being bothered. I've got a cute little seven-shooter handy for that kind of thing. And I can stitch buttonholes with it. But I don't get the chance of walking with a man like you—looks and size and all—every day. Come along, then.'

They went through the Teepee and many eyes turned to them. On the street he looked automatically to right and left. Blonde Rose nodded slightly. Then they were elbowing through the crowds on their way down Fay. Gavity observed, as he had done on previous nights, how the disappearance from the streets of most of La Fe's solid citizens coincided with appearance of the sporting crowd and those of the town's residents and visitors off whom the sporting crowd lived.

'Gives me notions,' Rose said abruptly. 'A boom-camp like this reminds me, kind of, of a big snake. Lord knows I have seen plenty of 'em, honey. Rough places. But I reckon it was in me not to stay on that Connecticut farm and raise kids and put up preserves. I was off and on my own when I was sixteen—and that was nearly twenty years back. Yes, sir, I have looked at 'em high, wide, and handsome in those twenty years. From north to south and Connecticut to California, I have seen the elephant and I have heard the owl . . .'

'Too much itch in the feet?' Gavity inquired, smilingly.

'Too much Me,' she said cryptically. 'What I like about my novels is, they're so different from what I know. Sometimes I let out a big laugh over what the writers think living is. Look at it! You're tall enough to see over the crowd. Ain't it just like a big black snake with yellow splotches?'

He had to admit that Fay Street very closely fitted the description, where it lay under the lights of saloon and honkatonk and gambling-house and variety theater and other fortresses of the sporting crowd.

'It's got a voice all its own,' Rose went on.

'It has!' Gavity admitted. 'Queer! I have seen a camp or two, since I rolled my bed up in Tarrant County when I was beginning to shave. But I never thought about it in just that way. You're right!'

He listened to the tinny clamor of dance-hall and saloon piano; to the twanging of stringed instruments; to the wheezing semi-melody of an asthmatic old organ somewhere on a side street. There was the wild, high yell of some exuberant miner or cowboy or freighter; the distant cackle of some one of the rouged women, laughing; the strident, angry muttering of men who quarreled within half-open doors. Too, for undertone, there was the smaller sound of rattling chips and the singsong call of dealers. All blended to make—as Blonde Rose had said—the Voice of La Fe.

Then he forgot her fancies. For they were going slowly past the store of Jones and Bryan Ross. A buggy turned in the street and he saw Ross and Betty in the seat. They saw him at the same moment—and saw Blonde Rose. For the two were outlined by light from the Stag Saloon behind them.

He could not see Betty's face. But she was staring at him. So he lifted his hat very gravely and the buggy went past. He said nothing as he walked on with Rose. But the tall woman made a clucking sound.

'That's too bad!' she said quickly. 'I oughtn't to have done it, Gavity. Made you walk with me. I'm sorry!'

'What about?' he snapped. 'I have a right to walk with anyone I want to walk with. Do you think for a minute that you'd have talked me into walking with you, if I hadn't wanted to? Don't talk like a nitwit!'

'Yeh, but what she thinks is, I've caught me another marshal. Girls are like that—her kind of girl, anyway. She'll be combing you for this, don't you think she won't! And—you're crazy

205

about her. You know you are!'

'Right! I am. But what difference does that make? Bryan Ross never did like me. The fact that a tramp-cowboy has got to be marshal of La Fe makes not one little bit of difference to him. He won't let me come inside his gate. And she—sometimes I think that she feels the same way about it.'

'All the same, I'm sorry! For Jack Binnings is going to bump into what it takes to stop him cold. After that, it'd be you. And Bryan Ross is just the kind of hairpin to ride with the crowd. You're making friends around here; old Zuzu Zelman and the ones that are going to count in La Fe. You're on the way to being a big man in La Fe. I know it! So—I'm sorry!'

'You're just like a hen, clucking over one egg!' Gavity told her—and laughed. 'Don't bother about it. I'll walk anywhere, any time, with somebody I like. If the Rosses don't like that, they know what they can do.'

At the door of her rooms in the Rose he touched his hat-rim and smiled down at her.

'I think you're a good friend of mine, Rose M'Ree,' he said. 'Now, you trot in and get your candy and your novel and stop bothering about me. If I'm not big enough and ugly enough to shoulder my own affairs, you never will see anybody who can. I'm going back to ride herd on the town and earn my pay.'

'You be careful, though! Remember what I said, about something hatching. Walk like a cat, honey!'

'Don't worry! They'll have to come at me from the back.'

'That's just what I expect 'em to try! You be careful!'

But as he made five rounds of the town there was no sign of any hostile movement against him. Apparently, little attention was paid him, as he looked into or walked through the saloons and dance-halls and gambling-houses and such merchandise stores as were still open.

Then, near eleven o'clock, on his sixth trip around the 'beat,' he came down Bowie Street toward Fay. As he reached the corner opposite the plaza, he stopped for an instant. On the corner of the plaza was a pile of 'dobe brick and other rubbish of a building torn down.

The street was getting quieter. Most of the people were indoors now, at the games or elsewhere. He could hear the clatter of chips inside the Teepee, against which he stood.

Then a blur of movement behind the rubbish on the plaza caught his eye. He could not make out the shape of it, but automatically his hands went under his coat to grip the butts of his Colts in the Hardin holsters. But before he could draw, there was an orange flash from that pile of brick on the plaza, then a great roar.

He identified the sound instantly and

mechanically as that of a shotgun, both barrels fired together. He had no doubt at all that he was the target and as the gun was fired, he was going down to a squat, pulling his pistols. Like echo to the bellow of the shotgun he heard a guttural sound overhead, from a window of the squalid rooming-house above the Teepee, half-cry, half-groan.

Something thudded heavily on the sidewalk beyond him. He felt a spattering of wet drops, like a shower of rain, upon face and hands. He looked flashingly sideways and saw a dark mass on the sidewalk.

But he gave that sprawling figure only the one glance. He began to shoot at the rubbish pile on the plaza. There was no reply. But from the mouth of that alley on his right came a blast of shots, stabbing flames and the heavy roar of many pistols or rifles. Bullets churned the sandy street in front of him, or smashed into the planks of the sidewalk beyond him.

He twisted on his heels and began to fire his left-hand Colt. Furiously, as once he had held a cow-camp single-handed against a rush of settlers, he emptied his pistol. Then he came to his feet, hard-faced, teeth shining in a snarl. With a wordless roar he charged the alley-mouth, swinging his Colts like clubs. Lead buzzed waspishly past him, but he ran on at the bush-whackers in Teepee Alley.

There was a sudden halt of the firing. He heard the patter of running feet in the quick silence that followed; harsh cries that carried the note of alarm.

'Stand still! Stand still till I can get you!' he yelled at the runners. 'You sons of dogs! Stand still!'

But there was only one of the ambushers in the alley. He was dead, sprawling across a Winchester.

Gavity bent over him and, sure that he was dead, snatched the Winchester from the ground and threw the lever. It was still loaded. He reholstered his pistols and with the carbine across his arm he crossed the street to the plaza. Here, too, a man sprawled, lying across the 'dobe bricks. Gavity glared around. Men were beginning to come around the corner of Fay Street; to crowd the doors and windows of the Teepee.

He scratched a match and looked at the sprawling one, turning him roughly to see the face. Then he laughed, recalling what Blonde Rose had said about Wheelen, Tyloe, and Huckafee, and what they might know of Wheelen's suspicions of Binnings. He straightened.

'She was right. Wheelen and Tyloe were dead when she said it. And—Huckafee won't talk . . . Not now!'

He went back to the Teepee sidewalk, where men stooped over that huddle from the rooming-house window.

'What happened?' Tim Free demanded,

209

pushing through to Gavity. 'That-there dead one is a Chinese boy that works upstairs in the lodging-house. How-come he got killed?'

'Poor devil was looking out of the window at the wrong time,' Gavity said curtly. 'As for the rest of it, Huckafee's over on that pile of brick in the plaza. You can smell the liquor on him, even if he is dead. Some of the rats around La Fe primed him to bushwhack me. But they made the mistake of getting him too drunk to hit me, even with a double-barreled shotgun. And some of them waited in the alley, yonder, to give him a hand, if he needed help. They couldn't stand facing a man, though. So, when I charged 'em, they ran like the sons of dogs they are. I killed one. He's in the alley. This is his gun.'

'But—but who killed the Chinaman?'

'Huckafee must have. Let go both barrels in the air and tore the window out of the rooming-house.'

He drew a long breath and let the carbine down. From his holsters he got the Colts and ejected the empty shells. He only grunted impatiently, in answer to questions. With loose cartridges from his pockets he reloaded the Colts. This time, he did not replace them in the Hardin vest, but let them sag in his coat pockets. Tim Free called after him as Gavity moved away from the crowd; asked where he was going.

'To make a little visit—and an

announcement. Maybe to kill one of the crowd that primed Huckafee so carefully!' Gavity snarled.

He was followed at a respectful distance by some of the men from the Teepee. He came to the Palace and smashed through the doors. Ben Miles was behind the bar. He faced Gavity steadily, but the pulse in his throat hammered. He was very pale. Gavity went straight back to him, after a quick glance around at the nervous drinkers and loungers.

'You couldn't get there, could you?' he snarled at Miles. 'I told you about reaching and grabbing. You tried to hire Finch to rub me out. That didn't work. So you poured Palace whisky into Huckafee and told him he ought to kill me, so he could be marshal again. And that didn't work!'

Miles said nothing. His hands were out of sight, under the bar. He stared almost glassily at Gavity.

'Why don't you try doing some of your own killing, for a change? You've got your hands on a gun, right now. Pull it! Take a chance, for once! Get it out and try killing me yourself! Here—what more do you want?'

He slapped both big hands on the top of the bar and leaned toward the saloon-keeper. But Miles was moveless. On his pale forehead was a sudden twinkle of perspiration.

'You won't? Won't even take that much of a chance? Then, come out of that! Come over here!'

He caught Miles as he had done that other time; by his neck and his arm. He stood on the brass rail for a better lift and jerked him out. Then Miles tried to bring a pistol with him. He cried out gaspingly to the others to help him, but none seemed inclined to move against Gavity.

Over on the floor he sprawled and Gavity kicked the pistol from his hand. Then he jerked Miles to his feet and carefully held him with left hand. His right flicked over, not smashingly, but only hard enough to rock Miles's head. Again and again he struck him, then let him go and hammered him back up the room, to send him crashing out through the swing doors, a bloody, senseless wreck, into the men crowding there to watch.

'And that goes for the bunch of you!' Gavity snarled at the Palace crowd. 'I can straddle the lot of you, one-handed!'

20. 'Just plain suicide'

He brushed past the men on the sidewalk. Tim Free yelled at him and he snarled his answer without turning. He crossed the street to the Gem and men gaped at him. At the bar, he beckoned one of Zelman's bar-tenders. The man whitened, then came at the trot, to stare fascinatedly at Gavity's face.

'Give me a quart of whisky!' Gavity commanded. 'No! Two quarts! There might be somebody else around who can handle one.'

He took the liquor when he had replaced in their holsters his two Colts. He rammed a bottle into each coat pocket and told the bartender to charge them. Then he walked down the room and went through the back door.

By back streets he made the city corral and there saddled Nubbins. He swung up—the hostler gaping as all of La Fe seemed to be tonight—and rode out. Down the sandy road toward the house of Manuel and Lupe he went, first at the trot, then at the tearing gallop. He pulled in before the door and yelled for Manuel, giving his name.

They both ran out and stood peering up through the darkness. He swung down and put the reins in Manuel's hands.

'What is it, *patron*?' Manuel whispered anxiously. 'They do not come after you, from the town? If they do—'

'No, nothing like that. But I am sick of that town for the time. I have killed Huckafee and one other tonight. I have thrown the saloon-keeper Miles into the street. I have come here because I feel safe here. I have brought whisky. I will drink it and forget La Fe.'

It was Lupe who pushed close to him and told Manuel to hide the horse in the mesquite behind the house, Lupe who caught Gavity's arm and drew him toward the 'dobe as if she, not he, were the elder.

'But of course,' she said almost crooningly. 'You come to us because you know that our house is your house. There is in it nothing that is not yours—altogether yours. Come in, *El Grande*. Manuel will put the great horse where he cannot be found, but where he will be at your hand if you need him. Bring the whisky and drink it; forget the dead men in La Fe. Not that they matter. For if they had not tried to kill you, they would be alive at this moment . . .'

In a cool, dark room Gavity sat upon a rawhide-laced cot and uncorked his whisky. Manuel slid in presently, to say that Nubbins was in the mesquite 'islands' behind the house. He would not be found in a month of search, except by himself.

He brought earthen cups and drank with Gavity, who told of the affair with Huckafee. He whistled and swore softly under-breath when Gavity described the fight. Lupe, curled at Gavity's feet on a bright *zarape*, said nothing. She only watched and, when he looked down at her, smiled at him.

They drank the first quart. Manuel got up unsteadily and said thickly that his head was going around. Lupe rolled cigarettes for Gavity and herself and lighted them with matches from Gavity's hat-band, on the floor beside her.

'And now, what will you do, Great One?' she asked him. 'Go back to that place, to kill for those who fear to kill for themselves, and in the end to be killed yourself? Or—'

'Now, I will drink the rest of the whisky,' he said. 'And thank you for your hospitality.'

She only watched, in the dim light of the kerosene lamp. He sat with the bottle in his hand, the second quart.

'I have been in many places,' he told her. 'Before this, I have killed men. Not because I wanted to kill them, but because they were the kind of men who understood nothing but killing; men who would kill until they were killed. But I begin to be afraid of this La Fe. There is so much of killing!'

'It is a town of the worst,' she agreed. 'Why do you stay there, the watchdog of those fat storekeepers? Out in the open is the place for a man such as you. Why do you not go back to the ranches, to ride and work?'

'I cannot tell you,' he confessed. 'I—It is something within me that holds me when I am about to ride the horse to the ranges again. I—'

'It is that *americana!*' she said between her teeth. 'It is because you love her, and hope that she will love you, that you stay! You said to me that I am only a child. *Muy bien!* It may be that I am no more than that. But I am old enough to see that you love this one. You—

215

Drink the whisky! There is nothing that anyone might say, nothing that I might offer, that would keep you from La Fe—and from her. I—'

She got up, with lithe, graceful movement. She was gone from the room before he could put out a hand to stop her—even if he had wanted to put out a hand. He sat and drank. Darkness deepened. She did not come back. He finished the quart and stood a little unsteadily. He called her and she answered from the yard. He went out and found her sitting beside the house. He dropped to the hard ground beside her.

'I am sorry,' he said thickly. 'Life is the thing that is given us and which, in some way, we shape. But we cannot make of it what is in neither material nor thought. I—I— My dear, I am very drunk. I do not like to kill men. I—'

He fell to the side, and when next he moved, there was light in his eyes—the sun. Manuel, swollen of eyes, but grinning, stood over him. Gavity found himself under a blanket. He sat up and looked around.

'Manuel,' he said huskily, 'I have been drunk. Something tells me that I have been very drunk. Let—me—see . . . There were two quarts of whisky . . . I had them of the mayor's bar-tender. You and I drank one, together. Then you were drunk and you went to sleep. I drank the other quart, alone. Lupe was here. She must have covered me when I fell in the

216

yard.'

'It was like that,' Manuel agreed. 'Except that I do not know of your falling in the yard, because I had fallen before. I am not used to whisky. But Lupe says that you dropped here. And now what, *amo*? Lupe sent me to ask if you would eat with us? There is not so much, but—'

'I would eat the side of a cow; both sides of a pig,' Gavity told him. 'I feel very well, Manuelito; very well, indeed! For quickly ridding oneself of foolish notions, I know of nothing like whisky. But, I warn you, never try it too often! The good effects wear off; only the bad remain. A man—'

He got up and stretched; yawned.

'Where is the water—for washing, not for drinking?'

Manuel showed the way to a horse-trough in the rear of the house. Gavity splashed and wiped himself dry with a piece of sugar sacking that Manuel held. He reached for his shirt and Manuel clucked admiringly as he stared at Gavity's thick chest and heavy shoulders.

'*Amor de dios!*' the boy said woefully. 'It is only the wonder that you did not kill that Pug, when you hit him with those arms. And those scars!'

'Never mind!' Gavity grunted. 'I am hungry—and at peace with all the world, now. I will eat and go back to La Fe. The little

217

justice will hold an inquest and I will be worried not at all. So much for the drinking, my son. But, as I was saying, a man should drink a little every day—not too much! Four, or it may be five, drinks. Else he should not drink at all except for medicine, then get very drunk, indeed. What is for breakfast?'

'Eggs and steak from a goat that Manuel found straying in the mesquite,' Lupe answered from the kitchen. 'Coffee, of a certainty. Does it please the Great One?'

He stopped inside the kitchen and put an arm about her waist. She smiled up at him and he shook his head.

'You were a very lovely one, last night! I will not forget it, ever. But—one makes of his life what one can . . .'

'I—I think I understand,' she told him softly. 'And if—if ever there should be reason to feel otherwise, I—'

'I will not forget! Now, I will ride back to the town. I am free of those things which sent me out here.'

They ate breakfast, Gavity and Lupe laughing at Manuel, who could only drink coffee. Then the boy went for Nubbins and brought him back saddled. In the yard, Gavity put silver into Manuel's hand and waved aside his protests.

'You will soon work for the mayor. But, until that time, money is a good thing. If something should happen, if I should die

218

under their bullets, this would be no more than something found and stolen by the first to reach me. Now, I know that it is in your hands. *Hasta la vista!*'

He rode back to town—having waved at Lupe—very much at ease. Huckafee and the other bushwhackers were of no importance. He held no particular dislike for the sporting crowd, even. When they showed their heads he would strike at them. Until they did he could forget them.

In the corral the hostler who had brought Nubbins out was still on duty. He blinked at Gavity and shook his head.

'I almost thought you'd rode off for good,' he said. 'In fact, when the mayor and old Tim Free come hunting you, I as much as told 'em that. But Zelman knowed about you packing two quarts and he says you went off som'r's to get drunk.'

He looked curiously at Gavity's beard-stubbled but otherwise unmarred face. He shook his head again.

'But I reckon he was wrong. *You* ain't been ory-eyed.'

Gavity saw Nubbins in a stall, then walked across a vacant lot to the little barber-shop next the Criterion on Fay. He sprawled in the chair and the barber forbore to question him, or to comment on the night before. Not that he did not want to. From beneath the towels Gavity could see the fat little man directing attention to him with gestures and contortions of face.

He got up at last, smooth-chinned and combed, to face Zelman and old Buchanan in the doorway of the shop. He went to meet them, and Zelman beamed upon him.

'Now, this is joost fine, Gavity,' he said, putting out his hand. 'When that nitwit in der corral, he say that you have rode away and look like you will not come back, I tell him he is der damn' fool. But—'

'But you worried, same as the rest of us,' Buchanan told him dryly. 'We got the best marshal in Texas—and some of us know that—and you was scared stiff he'd got disgusted and gone off. Glad to see you, Gavity. Gladder, still, the way you handled them dirty dry-gulchers last night. How you feel?'

'Good enough,' Gavity grunted. 'I suppose there'll be another inquest today . . .'

'Oh, sure,' Buchanan agreed. 'And if Sayre's got a lick of sense—which sometimes I do doubt—he'll bring in the only verdict he could bring in. He'll say: Just plain suicide!'

He had more to say, as the three of them went toward City Hall. Zelman nodded and grinned.

'They're staring at you like you was some special kind of side-show freak,' Buchanan told Gavity. 'You see, even Winn Wheelen, that was supposed to be extry-special with the

220

cutters, he only bumped into one gunplay in La Fe. That wasn't a lot, either; just a would-be hard case in the Fay place. But you have had more slugs chunked at you, in your days of marshaling, than most men have shot at 'em in a long life. But nobody has more'n burned you, yet. They don't know what to make of you.'

'Der charmed life!' Zelman cried. 'They think you have der charmed life and it is no *use* that they shoot at you! Yes. And you take Ben Miles and you *vli-ip* him out on der sidewalk because he have got Huckafee drunk, but you do not kill him as you could have killed him. I tell you, Gavity, der sporting crowd know now what I said in der council: Der bad mans what come to La Fe and try his devilments to keep oop, better he was in hell with der back broke. Yes!'

In the door of City Hall was the little justice. He looked at Gavity with something like the fascination that others showed. Mechanically, he jerked a thumb toward the room inside.

21. 'Big Pedro is chief'

Gavity stood at the long bar of the Criterion with Buchanan and other leading men of La Fe. He moved his whisky aimlessly before him and answered briefly when a question was put to him directly. He was conscious of the stares turned on him by friend and enemy alike.

That curiosity did not surprise him. He had been in too many towns like La Fe, where a gunslinger unusually efficient wore the official badge of the police. Always, these were stared at.

'It's the same sort of curiosity that's roused by a man who's going to be hanged,' he thought now, as the mumble of talk went on to right and left of him. 'A man who's killed a man—and particularly a man like that who's probably going to be killed—is always the object of stares. I'm a freak, just as Buchanan said this morning. I've killed several in the shortest possible time—even for La Fe. The chances are, I'll be killed. Yes, to these people I'm simply a freak.'

Then he felt someone staring at him—and that was odd, because of the other stares, of wandering citizens and of satellites of Miles and the Fays. There was something about this which turned him slowly. It was Binnings, coming up the bar-room. The tall figure reeled just a little. His eyes were glassy, his face more than usually flushed. In the lapel of his coat was a rosebud—a vivid, scarlet bud. He looked blankly at Gavity. Then a man at the bar spoke to him:

'Well, Jack!' this one cried. 'Roses, huh? Been robbing somebody's garden, I'll bet you. Unless—a woman gave it to you . . . Of course, you wouldn't admit that!'

'Why wouldn't I admit it?' Binnings said, with the merest shade of thickness in his voice. 'It was given me by a woman—a girl, rather . . . A very lovely girl! She gave it to me as a token. It's a—a sort of shadow of—of something—much lovelier that she's promised me. But we won't even hint at names.'

Gavity met the smile and sardonic shine of Binnings's eyes. Then he turned back to his drink. He held the bar with one big hand and the knuckles shone white. He was shaken by a sick rage and he drew a long breath, to keep himself from stepping out and catching Binnings by the neck and handling him as he had handled Ben Miles. He felt that he could break Binnings's neck with one easy squeeze, this evening. But he had to control himself here. After all, he was only guessing that the rose had come from Betty; that Binnings intended him to believe that.

'I'm going to walk!' he said abruptly to Buchanan.

He left his whisky untouched, and as

Binnings went on to stand farther down the bar he went quickly out to the street. He crossed Fay, walking fast. He went up Bowie and looked over the swinging doors of the Palace. There was some small satisfaction in missing Ben Miles from the bar; in looking at the wreck he had made of the back mirror. Then he went on. He had thought himself free of the despondency of last night. But now he found nothing pleasant about life. Betty had put a rose in Binnings's lapel—a token of more to come from her . . .

At Mason Street he turned south toward the corrals of the stage company. When running feet struck the plank sidewalk behind him, he pivoted mechanically and drew a pistol. Then he saw that it was a woman—a Mexican, by the *rebozo* that hooded her. He waited, expecting her to pass him. She had come either from Bowie Street or from some doorway on Mason.

But she did not go by. Instead, she stopped, panting, a hand upon her breast, within two yards of him. He could make of her only a slender shape, but there was something about her that made him think her young.

'What is it?' he asked her at last. 'What do you desire?'

'You are the marshal,' she said gaspingly. 'I have seen you upon the street. I—I have something to tell you. But I cannot make up my mind to tell . . . I—All day, I have thought of it: Shall I tell? Must I tell? Can I tell? Then, no more than minutes ago, he struck me! Look! Do you see the print of his flat hand upon my cheek?'

She came closer and flung back the square of dark cloth that had hooded her. Gavity drew in a breath. This was no woman of the peon class. The faint light from Bowie Street showed a thin, ivory-hued, aristocratic, and beautiful face. Her great, dark eyes were blazing furiously. Her full-lipped red mouth worked convulsively.

'I cannot see the print of a hand, no!' he answered quietly. 'It is not easy for me to believe that any man would put upon a face so lovely the print of his hand. What is it you have to tell me? If I can help you, I will be glad to help.'

'I have much to tell! I will prove to him that he cannot toss *me* aside like—like the stub of a cigarette which he has smoked! Señor, I know—more than any honest woman could know! Because I hate Pedro Grande as once I loved him, I will tell you a great deal. Not all! For there are some to whom I cannot and will not be traitor, even to show this robber and murderer, this Pedro Grande, that Carlotta has claws as well as rounded arms . . .'

'Pedro Grande?' Gavity repeated. 'Robber and murderer . . . What is this talk? What do you mean?'

'I will tell you enough to let you do the

thing you desire to do—let you take the man who is chief of all the robbers and killers about La Fe, who sit here in La Fe and make their plans and strike their blows about the town and the country around it—as at Harmony Station!'

Gavity stiffened, looking down into the lovely, furious face. Harmony Station! Chief of the robbers! He knew enough of women of this race and kind to understand that, when they believed themselves wronged, they moved quickly and savagely to take revenge; moved without thought of consequences.

If this were the woman of the gang's leader—and somehow he had no doubt of that—and she had quarreled with her lover, then she was a sharp tool for *his* hand, a perfect tool. There flashed into mind a picture—memory of that notice on the bole of the cottonwood outside La Fe on the road, the notice into which a tall graceful rider had fired, biting with bullets into the paper his mocking comment.

Twenty-five hundred dollars reward for those robbers and murderers from Harmony Station, the notice had offered. And the vanishing rider had added 'Ha, ha!'

'This Pedro Grande,' he said slowly, trying to decide how best and soonest to draw her out without alarming her or causing a change of mind. 'He is the chief of the gang? The men who stopped the stage and robbed it and did the murders at Harmony Station, they are here in La Fe—tonight? Then, what of—Binnings? What of Saltillo?'

'I do not know them. But in the band are both Americans and Mexicans. Some are known here in La Fe as notables, even! Señor, you know that you have gone up and down the town, asking—oh, so carefully!—concerning these robbers. And the men of whom you have asked have shaken their heads; they have shrugged most gravely; they have told you that they know nothing. *Bueno!* But within minutes of the time you asked them, every word of your talk and your questions has been told to Pedro Grande! He has known everything that you suspected, everything that you did! His spies are everywhere in La Fe.'

'I can believe that,' Gavity admitted. 'But there was no help for it. I had to ask the questions and, if he learned of my suspicions, there was nothing to do!'

'He knew! This attack upon you, made last night . . . Who, think you, planned that, ordered that? Why, Pedro Grande! He is like the great cat. You are the mouse between his paws! He has not yet really tried to put down his paw hard and smash you. Not yet! But at this moment the paw is lifted and is ready to pin you, dead, to earth. Señor, you walk this night in the very shadow of death! You think that certain ones here, whom you know, may be trusted. I assure you—I, the cast-off one of

227

Pedro Grande—that you can trust nobody in La Fe! One is a tool of Pedro Grande; another is afraid because his interests will suffer. You can trust nobody! Had Pedro Grande not struck me and thrown me aside, today, your life would be a matter of minutes, not hours. The sun might strike your face, tomorrow, but the light would not disturb your open eyes.'

'But you are willing to save my life?' Gavity asked her, grinning slightly. 'You are willing to help me?'

'Because I hate him! Yes, I will save your life; I will help you; I will show you how to destroy him and I will laugh above his dead face! Tonight, he sits with two Americans in his house. They are tall ones in the band. The house is in what La Fe calls Little Mexico. You can take him there, because he has with him only these two. It will be better to have with you more than one man; better, because safer. But you must be as quiet as cats. For at the first sound he and they will vanish. He has ways of disappearing.'

Gavity considered. It seemed the part of wisdom to take someone with him. But he could not decide upon those men. Besides, he would lose time, perhaps attract attention. He shrugged at last. After all, he had always lone-wolfed it . . .

'I will go with you,' he told Carlotta. 'I will not take anyone with me. I will go with you now, if you will show me the house.'

'That will make less noise. But there are three of them,' she answered doubtfully. 'Still—you are the very devil with guns, so Pedro Grande said this morning. It may be that you can take or kill the three of them single-handed.'

They continued south on Mason Street until it became a winding, sandy track with the lights of Little Mexico—not many showing at this hour—ahead of them.

At last, Gavity asked her how much farther, but she only hissed at him for silence and hurried forward. In and out, around the corners of 'dobe houses in the tiny settlement, he followed her without much thought of direction. After all, it made little difference. He had his guns and this might be the chance he had hunted, to wipe out the robbers who had troubled La Fe. That was all he cared about now. Then she stopped and leaned close to a wall. She seemed to listen.

Gavity could hear nothing but pigs or dogs that passed, snuffling. From faraway sounded the howling of a cur. Once or twice a dark figure padded softly by. He wondered what she expected to hear. Then she came closer to him. He caught the faint, disturbing perfume of skin and hair as she tiptoed to whisper softly:

'Wait here a small minute, until I can see if he is still with those *americanos*—as he should be.'

229

She was gone before he could object. Gavity waited grimly, hands under his coat on the butts of his pistols. A minute passed draggingly, then suddenly there was a strangling cry from around the corner:

'Help me! Help me! I—I die!'

He had been thinking that such a man as this chief of the gang whom she had described would hardly be one to show mercy toward even a woman—particularly if he had reason to suspect her of treachery. So he jumped forward now, both of the Colts whipped from his holsters.

Within a yard and before he had seen anything, he tripped over a rope stretched knee-high. He went sprawling upon his face and dropped his left-hand pistol. He had the sickening feeling that he had been trapped— and easily, by a clever woman, working for her lover.

The darkness seemed to erupt rushing figures, heard rather than seen. Desperately he scrambled to his knees and, while he leveled his remaining Colt he groped for the other. He found it, within a yard of the spot where he had fallen. He drew back the hammer with practiced thumb. The men seemed to be charging him from all sides. He began to fire and, at that range, there was small chance of missing! For the circle closed about him. They were ahead and behind and on both sides.

He felt the retreat before his rain of bullets. Then he came to his feet and charged those behind him—between him and town—with a roar, just as he had charged the killers in Teepee Alley the night before. His last two shells exploded, sending slug into the vague mass before him.

Then he swung the pistols like clubs. His hands rose, fell, the barrels smashing down upon skulls and bodies. It seemed an endless battle. There were always men before him and men coming up behind him. He panted as he flailed down with the Colts. Bodies brushed his, but he flung them off and his great height and the tremendous blows of those long barrels kept him from being swamped by others' numbers. He even beat them off and beat them back.

But as he hurled them off, a woman's voice rose furiously from somewhere in the darkness.

'Dogs! Fools! Let him escape and the Chief will flay the hides from you! There are enough to swallow him! Kill! Kill!'

So it was the trap he had suspected! He hurled himself at the remnant of attackers between him and the corner around which he had run. They stood stubbornly, but he clubbed them down and back. Behind him the woman's voice was lifted in shrill threats. But this pack, it seemed, feared Gavity's lashing blows more than it feared any prospect of future punishment. They would not close in.

Gavity found the way suddenly clear before him. He ran on, gasping painfully, going in what he thought was the general direction of town. As he staggered along the sandy track, he began to hear a faraway shouting, what seemed the distant rattle of shots.

He halted briefly to listen. The sounds came from the east somewhere, not from within the town. He shook his head and trotted steadily toward La Fe.

When he reached Midwest Street the corrals of the stage company were on his left. There was much noise from the corrals and he went automatically that way, but stopped forethoughtedly at the corner to reload his pistols. Then he went forward at a walk.

There was a crowd in the gateway of the corrals, plain in the light of the office windows. The men babbled excitedly, and before he reached them he caught snatches of talk about raiding Mexicans.

'What's the trouble?' he demanded of the nearest man. 'What do you mean, Mexicans raiding?'

'A whole gang of 'em! Word just come to town. They're going to hit us a' lick like they done at Rosalia in the Salt War. Going to wipe out La Fe and rob the stores and the bank and kill off the Anglos—'

'My—goodness!' Gavity drawled. 'They must have sent you a letter, to tell all that.'

He saw Zelman coming through the crowd and worked toward him. Zelman was sputtering furiously:

'Where der devil you have been?' he demanded.

'Little Mexico,' Gavity said absently, looking around. 'Woman. Went down there with her. Now, what's the trouble?'

'Oh! Der woman! S-so!' Zelman grunted, staring. 'Well—it is der rumor, Gavity. Der Mexicans will raid La Fe. Now, we have got der men of town ready. We will go hunt for der Mexicans, no?'

'We certainly will,' Gavity assured him. 'Where's Tim Free? Buchanan? We can make up about three parties. I'll take one, they can take the others. We'll comb the river and see if this is just a rumor or the real quill.'

'Here,' Buchanan answered. And Tim Free also shouldered through to him and answered.

'All right, then!' Gavity called to the waiting, watching crowd. 'Let's divide up! Some with Buchanan, some with Free, some with me! File off your front sights and throw your spurs away. We'll have a look at these Mexicans. Of course, if we run onto 'em, some of you brave gladiators will probably be cold in death tomorrow. But you don't care about that! It's all for the glory of La Fe.'

The three parties formed and moved away. Gavity led his group in a primitive skirmish-line toward the Rio Grande. They shuffled through ankle-deep sand, through greasewood and mesquite and cactus. They disturbed grazing stock and waked sleeping Mexicans in outlying houses, but found no trace of the Mexicans until a shot was fired at them from the river itself. And that was hardly a skirmish. Whoever fired, ran quickly.

22. *'I'm going to spin a loop'*

Gavity sat up in bed when someone came pounding frantically at his door. He was still sleepy, for after the firing had stopped on the river, he and his men had hunted back and forth for hours, hunting the ambushed man or men.

'What's it?' he inquired drowsily. 'What's the trouble?'

'Mayor wants you at City Hall right off,' a voice replied imperatively. 'First National Bank was robbed last night and Louie Hook— Alderman Hook's brother—was murdered. They're having a hot session of the council and they're trying to vote— Well, the mayor says hustle on down!'

Gavity scowled, then rolled from the bed. He splashed hands and face with tepid water in the tin washbasin on a rickety stand, then got into his clothes.

As he went down the stairs of his lodging-house and turned toward the Hall, he told himself that, at least, he had been no bigger idiot than the rest of La Fe. He had only been fooled, as the rest of the town had been fooled, by that shooting on the river. For he thought nothing, just now, of any connection between 'Carlotta' and the robbery of the bank.

He went into the council room to stand grimly at Zelman's elbow. The little mayor looked up uncomfortably at him.

'Gavity,' he said slowly, 'you tell me last night that you are by Little Mexico with der woman. Today, Prather and Hook they tell me der same thing. It is so, yes?'

'A Mexican woman!' Prather snarled. 'He told you the truth—even if I don't see how he happened to admit it.'

Alderman Hook and Mullins nodded agreement.

'And while he was helling around Little Mexico with some slut, my brother Louie was being murdered at the bank!' Hook cried, banging the table with his fist and glaring at Gavity.

'Wait a minute,' Gavity grunted. 'Who was your brother? I mean, how did it happen that he was in the bank?'

'He was the watchman! And while you was—'

'Watchman! You mean, he had a pistol on him? Well, well! And for what did he wear it?

235

Why didn't he pull that big, trusty six-shooter of his and kill him a few of these robbers?'

'A good idee!' Zelman cried in his turn—and banged the table. 'For der watchman, your brother was not the so-much! For why does he carry der pistol, if not to shoot der thief? Why *don't* he kill some thief with his pistol?'

Gavity ignored the mayor's outburst.

'Yes, I was down in Little Mexico for a while, last night. I went down there with a woman, too, just as I said. It was this way—'

Briefly, almost tonelessly, he told the story of Carlotta and her promise to deliver to him the chief of La Fe's robbers. At the end of his account Prather and Hook and Mullins sneered openly.

'An odd tale; almost, one might say, a weird tale,' Prather remarked in faraway tone. 'But not too hard to check . . . Or it shouldn't be . . . Let's see! José Franco, the jailer, lives in Little Mexico. He's here in the Hall. I saw him as I came in. Let's have José in, your Honor. All this savage battling should have disturbed him. He must know all about the terrible battle between our marshal and the assassins. Why, even if the fight didn't wake him, he must have had to step over the bodies, as he came to town this morning!'

Without waiting for Zelman's approval, he lifted his voice, bellowed for José Franco. But when the jailer appeared, a squat, fattish man, with tiny, shrewd dark eyes in broad chocolate-hued face, Zelman took the procedure from Prather's hands. In Spanish as good, almost as Gavity's, he asked Franco if he had heard the sounds of a battle in Little Mexico the night before.

Franco shrugged and shook his head. He had not. He had slept peacefully the night through. Then, to Gavity's thought, he rather gave himself away. Without being asked, he said that any noise must have waked him, for he was a light sleeper.

'I can tell that,' Gavity assured him. 'It is written upon your very face. A light sleeper. But, even so, you could not have heard the shooting on the river when half the town searched for a band of Mexican robbers. For—'

'Oh, but I did hear that!' Franco answered quickly. 'I only thought it a band of cowboys shooting off their pistols.'

'You heard it, even though it was ten times as far away and, by your own word, you slept the night through,' Gavity drawled, with lift of sandy brows. 'Franco! Franco! In but a small moment I will begin to have thoughts about you . . . I—'

'Mr. Zelman!' Prather interrupted quickly. 'I object to the marshal's tone. It's plain to everyone, I think, that he was down in Little Mexico, carousing with some woman. He was neglecting his duties. He—'

Gavity put a hand on the table and leaned. He thrust a long arm across and caught Prather by the chin. He dragged him across and dropped him on the floor on his own side.

'*Just* to keep unbroken my record of never hitting a man while he was sitting down,' he said gently.

Then he slapped Prather's face, twice.

Hook and Mullins jumped up, swearing. Others of the council came to their feet almost as quickly. Some protested Gavity's action, others objected to Prather's words.

'Gen-tle-men! Gen-tle-men!' Zelman boomed.

'What would you? Even der alderman, he have not der right to call a man der liar unless—he have der willingness to back what he will say! I tell *you*, gentlemen all, if anybody here will wish to call old Zuzu Zelman der liar, he will *also* get der fi-ine smack by der face! Such goings-on by der council room, they are very sad. But I cannot blame Mr. Gavity for doing that which any man having not der spine of one alley cur will do. Mr. Prather! You will please to siddowun!'

'I think I have the floor,' Prather snapped. 'I intend—'

'*Siddowun!*' Zelman roared, standing himself, with fist lifted. 'Else Mr. Gavity will not be der only man to poke you!'

Prather dropped into the nearest chair. But he looked at Hook and nodded. Hook rose instantly and moved that the office of marshal be declared vacant and a successor to Gavity be appointed—from that list of names submitted at the earlier meeting by Alderman Prather.

'No. No. I am not for der motion,' Zelman commented slowly. 'It is true that last night der safe in der bank, it was blown; that der watchman, Hook, was murdered. It is true that if der marshal, he had been by der bank, he might see der robbers. If he saw der robbers, *I* know—and you know, my friends!—it would be very bad for der robbers.'

He looked around the table and those of his faction nodded.

'But I say, gentlemen, Mr. Gavity have not had time to make der Sunday School yet of La Fe. I will bet by any gentleman here five hundred dollars that, before he have finished, Mr. Gavity will have, not *joost* der robbers of der bank, but der gang of thieves which will come like der dirty dog and steal my Kentucky horses and rob der stage by Harmony Station and use La Fe for their headquarters in der dirty work!'

'I'll take that bet—and put up the money right now!' Prather snarled at him. 'You, Hook? You, Mullins?'

'We'll take him, too!' the ones addressed cried. They began to get out money and Zelman grinned. 'We'll take it, now!'

'I want five hundred, too!' Bryan Ross said suddenly, from where he had been sitting, nodding approval of Prather's words.

'Franco,' Zelman told the jailer, 'you take this, my order, to der store. You get from der bookkeeper two thousand dollar and you bring der money back. Mr. Ross, you will hold der stake in der safe at your store?'

'You put me in a sort of tough place,' Gavity told them all, generally. He looked around, facing Hook and Prather and Mullins—and Bryan Ross. 'I was about to tell you that you could take your marshal's badge and go jump into the Rio Grande. But since the mayor has expressed so much confidence in me—two thousand dollars' worth of confidence—I'll change my mind and keep the job awhile. Maybe there's a little more to it than that: I hate to be licked—and give the like of some of you the chance to laugh at me.'

He stared longest at Bryan Ross and met malicious triumph in the little man's bulbous eyes.

'So, I'm going to do my damnedest to help the mayor win his bet,' Gavity went on. 'I'm going to spin a loop and drop it over the whole gang of scoundrels Mr. Zelman speaks of—or bust a hamstring. And I don't care how many they are, or who they are, or how many crooked politicians are backing 'em'!

'Crooked politicians?' Prather snarled. 'What do you mean by that term—here in council?'

'That term always seems to worry you, Prather,' Gavity said gently. 'It couldn't be a guilty conscience, now, could it? But you'll learn, soon enough, exactly what I mean by it. I'm adding not one word to what I said. Not now!'

It came to him suddenly that there *was* more to his sudden decision than the desire to vindicate old Zelman's belief in him. If he had quit now, with La Fe laughing at the simple way in which he had followed that Mexican woman into an ambush, that would irritate him for the rest of his life. But—the rosebud in Binnings's lapel was somehow tangled in his decision also. He hardly knew how Betty and her likes and dislikes were involved in this matter of being marshal. But she was. So he looked grimly around the council, then went out to the dingy little office that was the marshal's.

Zelman came in, alone, after a while. Franco had brought back the money. Bryan Ross had taken it to the store of Jones & Ross for deposit in the safe. Zelman sputtered angrily.

Prather and Hook and Mullins were getting too 'uppity.' This new man, Ross—a mayor's appointee, at that!—was lining up with Prather's faction in the council. Gavity nodded without much interest. He got up from the pine table that was his desk and stretched long arms above his head.

'I'm going to get breakfast,' he said.

Zelman went up Austin Street with him, still fuming. At the corner of Fay he continued up Bowie toward the Gleaming Gem. Gavity was about to cross to Wo Lee's restaurant when he saw a buggy standing before the Jones & Ross store. A Mexican boy sat in it, holding the reins of Bryan Ross's team. On impulse, Gavity went that way.

Betty Ross came out of the store and crossed to the buggy. When she saw him, she hesitated, moved on toward the buggy, then stopped. Her face—he could see it across thirty feet—was furiously red. Then she faced him and regarded him from under lazy lids.

'Hello!' he greeted her. 'Early for you, it would seem.'

'Your—love affairs don't seem to be prospering,' she answered. 'That is, if I can believe what I hear. They seem to be urgent, rather than lucky. Or—was it worth being kept in Little Mexico last night, even though the bank was robbed because of that?'

He looked blankly at her and she went on in the same malicious drawl.

'But I didn't think it was Little Mexico that held the attraction. I—rather thought you were living at the Hotel Rose. The—marshals seem to favor the Rose, somehow . . .'

'I've heard the tales,' he said carefully. 'Prather told that one about Little Mexico in the council room—and got his face thoroughly slapped for it. Of course, I couldn't really hit *him*. But there are some others in La Fe who won't be slapped. They'll be punched—or killed.'

He moved his big shoulders resignedly, in a gesture more emphatic than an outburst could have been.

'I really don't know whether you believe those stories—about my carousing in Little Mexico with a Mexican woman, and about Rose M'Ree, or not. So far as I can see, I'm just the same big saddle-tramp from back over somewhere—nobody has ever bothered to ask me where I'm from or why I drifted here—that I was when I hit the Slash R and you—liked me. I have slung lead at some men, before this session; been an officer. It didn't bother me much, any more than cleaning out this rattler den is bothering me because of the cleaning.'

He shook his head and watched her broodingly.

'No-o, I'm not changed—much. You're the one who's changed. I've tried not to believe that; tried to feel that it was just your father talking and the difference in the way you're living and the people you're meeting. I've tried to believe that you still care about me, even when it was plain that you don't; that you're siding with those who don't like me. But I'm afraid I see it, now, too plainly to be misunderstood.'

She looked at the toe of her small shoe and was silent.

'So, as soon as this cleaning here is finished, I'm leaving. I don't own a lot except horse and saddle and guns. But pride is one thing I happen to have a lot of. The sort of pride a man has when he's always stood with his back pretty straight and his chin stuck out, refusing to do cheap things and cowardly things. The kind of pride that won't let me—for instance—push in where I'm not wanted; or marry into a family that thinks I'm not good enough to associate with them—and thinks that without bothering to inquire about me; marry a girl who listens to everyone but the man she's supposed to love, No! I am not that kind—no matter how much I may love the girl!'

For an instant, he thought, her face softened and she looked at him uncertainly. Then a slender Mexican girl, vivid, graceful, passed them. Betty's eyes went mechanically to the girl and, with sight of the admiring side-glance bestowed upon Gavity, her mouth tightened viciously.

Before either could speak, there was the dull report of a pistol-shot, the jangle of broken glass, in the Teepee opposite them. A furious bull-roar came from the saloon and the gabble of excited voices. Men ran out of the Teepee.

Gavity whirled and ran into the street. He pushed men aside and crashed through the swing doors. Two big men were wrestling desperately against the bar. Each had a pistol drawn. Each gripped with left hand the right wrist of his opponent. On the floor—a shivered ruin—was one of the dozen chandeliers which had cost Bet-You M'Ree five hundred each and which were the Teepee's pride.

Gavity knew both men by sight. He had seen them several times walking with Binnings and Prather. They were snarling at each other—fragmentary sentences, phrases. One seemed reeling drunk, the other sober.

'Cut it out!' Gavity commanded them. 'Break away and drop those hoglegs. Break! or I'll cut the both of you in two!'

They twisted and stared at him, then relaxed. Gavity went closer, pistol in left hand. He jerked the Colts from them, ramming each into his waistband, without for an instant losing the drop. The sober man looked sideways at his companion, then at Gavity. He forced a grin:

'Just trying to—git this feller—to go sleep off his jag!' he panted. 'He pulled a gun on me—'

'You're a liar! You're a damn' liar!' the drunken one cried thickly. 'And that ain't all you are, neither! You're a damn' thief! Thought you could rob me, huh? I'll show

245

you! Ordinary, I ain't got a bit of use for no kind of tin badge. But I got less use for a dirty thief like you. I—'

A quart bottle flashed in the other's hand. He had twisted and snatched it from the bar. It swung sideways and crashed into the drunken man's temple. He collapsed under the terrific blow and began to fall, with blood oozing from his head. Then Gavity slapped the other man over the head with his pistol. He looked down grimly at them both. As he stared there came the beginning of hazy idea. It came from nowhere—except that he had seen both of these men with Binnings . . .

'Give me a hand with these would-be hard cases,' he grunted to the staring men behind him. 'Let's take 'em outside and send 'em down to the Hall.'

He had one glimpse of Betty, still standing beside the buggy, as he and others carried the two senseless figures out to the sidewalk. Then she turned quickly from the buggy and re-entered the store. He shrugged and looked up and down the street. A Mexican was driving toward the Teepee in a rickety wagon. Gavity waved him up and the unconscious men were loaded into the bed. Gavity sat beside them. A little man from the crowd jumped nimbly up to the seat.

When the wagon had creaked into Austin Street on the way to City Hall, the little man twisted to look curiously down at Gavity's prisoners.

'I—wonder!' he said softly. 'Wonder what Hurgan was about to spew when Lippy cut him short with that bottle.'

'So do I,' Gavity told him. 'What's your guess?'

'Don't drag me into this, but—you might ask Hurgan or Lippy about Harmony Station . . . Idell, that was agent at Harmony, was mighty thick with both of these hairpins, when I relieved him up there after the robbery. Idell's here, now . . .'

Then he jumped out of the wagon and ran back toward the corner, ignoring Gavity's call to him.

'Well!' Gavity said slowly, aloud, staring down at Hurgan and Lippy. 'They were thick with Idell. Idell was agent during the robbery. Idell is thick with Binnings here . . . I do think I may have something!'

At the jail, Hurgan could not be roused from his stupor. Lippy sputtered under the buckets of water thrown over him by José Franco the jailer. But he faced Gavity brazenly.

'Ain't got a notion what Hurgan was sore about,' he claimed. 'I hit him because he called me a thief. But he's always ugly when he's drinking.'

Gavity stared at him, then turned to Franco, ordering both men to be held in dark cells in the jail rear.

'They see nobody. They get no bond,' he warned the jailer. 'Else you will be very sorry. I will tell Root the same.'

23. 'Do not move, gringo'

While Gavity ate his belated breakfast at Wo Lee's he considered Idell. The one-time agent at Harmony Station was still in the employ of the Midwest Stage Company and Gavity had seen him around La Fe several times. He tried to picture Idell in his mind; decide what approach would be most likely to set the man talking loosely.

But he had no plan when he came out of the restaurant and walked up Bowie Street. He rounded the Palace and was going toward the stage company corral and office when sight of the Stockmen's Hotel, across Mason from the Palace, brought another thought. He crossed the street and went quickly into the Stockmen's narrow stairway.

There was a Mexican chambermaid cleaning the hall upstairs. She proved susceptible to a silver dollar. She looked furtively up and down, then unlocked the door of Binnings's room for Gavity. She promised to stand guard at the stairhead for him.

Very thoroughly, if quickly, Gavity searched the room. He went over the floor for sign of a

248

loose plank; hunted the washstand and the tall wardrobe through; searched Binnings's clothing and a big leather valise; tore the bed apart to examine the stitching of the mattress seams. At last he gave it up and went irritably into the hall again. There was not so much as a scrap of paper in that room to give a hint of Binnings's past or present. He questioned the chambermaid.

'*Yo no sé!*' she told him, shrugging. 'He is never in the room except at night, to sleep. Even then, not more than one night or two in the week. Sometimes we do not see him for half a month.'

'You have no knowledge of where he may be, when not here?'

She shrugged again; grinned wisely.

'He would not be the only gentleman in La Fe to have more than one *domicilio!* Men will be men and women will always be women, señor! What would you? I have worked in many houses of the town. There are things I could tell . . .'

Gavity considered that idea frowningly. Another lodging . . . He thanked the maid and went downstairs. He thought of the places Binnings might use, while he walked slowly toward the stage company office. He considered it even more when he was told that Idell was not in La Fe, but out in the country buying mules. Presently, he drifted into the Palace.

Ben Miles was not in the place. The bartender who served Gavity kept his red face blank, his manner entirely courteous. But his eyes were alert, as if he feared another such explosive time as that when Benedetto and Finch had died here.

None of the other drinkers spoke to Gavity. He moved his glass aimlessly about the bar and looked restlessly about him. So he chanced to be staring at the back door when a slender figure passed in the alley.

The Palace stood on the corner of Bowie and Mason Streets. Directly across the alley was a big, square building of 'dobe that faced on Midwest Street—faced the office and corral of the Midwest Stage Company. This building, so Gavity had been told, was occupied by someone in the town as a warehouse.

When he drifted to the back door of the Palace, the alley was empty. That slim, hurrying figure, hooded by black *rebozo* as on that other occasion when he had seen her, had vanished. Gavity considered that. The warehouse presented a blank rear wall a quarter-block long—blank except for one smooth, heavy wooden door.

'Unless she ran—my Carlotta of the pitiful tale—she had to go into that door,' Gavity thought. 'And why would she be going into a warehouse?'

He stepped into the alley, then waited a

long minute to see if anyone in the Palace were interested in his movements. Then he crossed to that door, looking right and left and behind him. He looked at the heavy pine planks. If it were barred inside, nothing short of a battering-ram could open the door. He wondered how Carlotta had opened it. He pushed experimentally, but it was solid in the frame. No sign of a latch. Then closer study found a knot of rawhide that projected from the frame five feet above ground.

Again he looked all around and found nobody in the alley, nobody passing the mouth of the alley on Mason Street. He drew a pistol and reached for the rawhide. As he pulled, a string came through a hole in the frame. With ear against the door he could hear the tiny rasping sound made by a bar lifting inside the warehouse. When he pushed, now, the door swung slowly, noiselessly, open. Inside was pitchy darkness, the smell of cloth and food. He went in, crouching, gun out. He closed the door behind him.

There was neither light nor sound in the place. He wondered if he could have been mistaken; if Carlotta had got through the alley to some other door. There seemed nothing in here to bring her hurrying. He began to inch forward toward the front wall, that on Midwest Street. His left hand was out. It touched boxes and bales and he went noiselessly around them.

Then he heard voices and moved on toward the sound. Presently, he found a thin bar of yellow light along the floor—the light from a closed room, lying upon a threshold. He reached that room and put an ear to the door. But only a mumbling, with occasional word, carried to him. He eased himself to the floor and with ear to the threshold made more of the talk.

'—And so,' Binnings said flatly, 'you go back to your father. I told you that, before. There are good reasons for your going. Don't argue with me!'

'Reasons!' the woman broke in fiercely—in English as good as Binnings's own. 'I know there is a reason! That pretty daughter of the stupid store-keeper! I have seen you with her. Knowing your methods—and who should know more of them than I!—it needed but a glance to see what ran in your mind!'

'Now, now, don't be jealous. Don't make a scene,' Binnings said easily. He laughed. 'Be a good girl. Get your things together. Be ready to leave with Gonzales when I send him today.'

'I am not going! Until today, I have done everything you asked me to do. Unspeakable things, some of them! But I am not going back to Mexico, to be laughed at for the thing flung aside by you. You will better remember that I am no *peon* to be carried off at the saddle-bow, kept for a time, then flung aside, I warn you, Jack, that you will best reconsider. Best forget that you even tried to toss me off. It will be much safer for you!'

There was the sudden sound of hands clapping together, again and again. But Gavity knew that it was not clapping. He heard the thud of something falling heavily to the floor.

'Better for *you* to remember that none has ever threatened me and lived to tell of it,' Binnings's voice lifted furiously. 'You know me well enough to know that, if it were necessary, I would find means of dealing with you. Perhaps a knife across that pretty throat would not be needed. Perhaps no more is necessary than to put you in the hands of one of my faithful dogs, those of whom you know, who jump when I whistle! How if I sent you down in Little Mexico, common property of Big Pedro's gang?'

'You would not dare! And you say you have always killed those who threatened you? It is a proverb that everything must have its beginning. I think you may have come both to the beginning and the end! This big, fierce man, whom I led to what seemed certain death in Little Mexico, *he* has threatened you! More! He tricked you as if you had been a child, that first day of his appearance in La Fe; and like a child, too, he carried you to the jail. He is not dead! Nor, I think, will he die. I think that you realize when you stand before him that you stand before the better man.'

'Better man!' Binnings snarled. 'That stupid, clumsy, ignorant—'

There was the sound, again, of his hand upon her face.

'Get out, now!' he ordered. 'The little door. I have affairs to settle. I have no more time for you. Get your things together as I have told you. And—if you open that pretty mouth again, between now and the time Gonzales comes for you, I promise Gonzales's knife across your throat. You know Gonzales!'

Gavity came soundlessly to his feet. He was grinning. So Carlotta had not told a lie, altogether, when she said that she had been cast off. Inside there was Binnings, and Gavity thought that a call upon the tall man would be the most interesting thing he could do, just now. He felt carefully for the latch of this door.

Then, abruptly, light showed somewhere behind him. That alley door through which he had entered was open. He turned and saw them plainly—two men framed in the doorway. Then the door closed again. The men came toward him, muttering. He slid to the side and crouched behind barrels that reeked of whisky. The door behind which Binnings and Carlotta had quarreled opened and Binnings showed in the yellow rectangle.

'Well!' he said irritably. 'I thought you were never coming. I've just had a sort of left-handed adventure. An amusing incident,

254

anyway, our good friend, the Watchdog of La Fe, searched my room in the Stockmen's awhile ago. I saw him slip into the place and had an idea of what he was after. When he came out, I went up to my room. He'd carefully replaced everything he moved, but I could still see the prints of his big feet. I wonder what he thought to find.'

'Doubtless, a gang of assorted bank-robbers!'

This was Prather's voice. The two went into the room and the door swung shut. Gavity stood again and listened at the door. But the three were talking in tones so low that he got only the mutter of their voices. He hesitated. But before he had made up his mind to knock boldly, the alley door opened again. Two more men came into the warehouse and closed the door. He went back to his post behind the barrels.

This time Binnings did not open the door until the men were almost at it. They seemed to do something that signaled their arrival, for when Binnings appeared he had a pistol in his hand and stared out into the darkness before he grunted and stepped back to let them enter.

Gavity had a slanting glimpse of the room. There was a cot, a washstand. He thought of the chambermaid's remark about two or more lodgings. Was this—he wondered—Binnings's real living quarters? If so, no wonder that he had found nothing in the room at the Stockmen's.

He had recognized the two newcomers at the door. One was Winst, owner of the Criterion dance-hall. The other was that Idell who was supposed to be out in the country buying mules.

'It has all the earmarks of a thieves' council!' he told himself. 'The question is, do I try to listen—and hear almost nothing—or do I just break in and take the chance of that buying me something?'

The door swung abruptly open and he had time only to flatten himself against the wall when Binnings, pistol in hand, stood within a yard of him, leaning a little forward and talking to those in the room behind him.

'The bell rang!' he said uneasily. 'But I don't see anybody. That's damn queer . . . Nobody could come up the warehouse without stepping on the plank . . . And that bell doesn't ring without a foot on it . . . But I don't hear anything . . .'

'Gonzales and Saltillo are coming, aren't they?' Prather asked. 'Could it have been a rat? Some of 'em are the size of dogs, in this place!'

Gavity, too, was puzzled. He had not seen the alley door open. He had heard nothing. Apparently, he had somehow traversed the length of the warehouse without tripping over the alarm plank. His course had not been the

256

same as that of the others. But he was hardly concerned with that now. He lunged forward.

His Colt was rammed into Binnings's side and he slapped downward with left hand, knocking the pistol from Binnings's hand. He caught the wrist of Binnings's gunhand and jerked him around to face the lighted room.

'All right!' he grunted. 'In you go. I don't want to see a move from any of you—except as you reach for your ears! And as you stand up.'

His pistol came out past Binnings and menaced Prather, Ben Miles, Winst, and Idell. They got stiffly to their feet with hands at ear-level.

'Over against the wall, all of you!' Gavity commanded. 'Don't entertain notions. You should know, by now, what kind of shooting I can do. You ought to know that I haven't a reason in the world to feel kindly toward any of you.'

'What do you think you're doing in here?' Binnings demanded. But there was strain in his voice. 'This happens to be my building. You nor anyone else has any right—'

'*Right?* That's a quaint word for you to use! But if you want to know why I'm here, it's to tell you that the jig's up. I've suspected you almost ever since I dropped my loop over you in the street, Binnings—and naturally I suspected these others because they ran with you. Now, everything clicks together. Won't the town be excited! Mr. Binnings, the educated gentleman with pocketfuls of money to in-vest, chief of our stage-robbers and bank-robbers and murderers! And Mr. Prather, the alderman, and Mr. Winst and Mr. Miles—and Mr. Idell who used to be agent at Harmony Station . . . Yes, sir! When the town hears all this, they'll probably be hard to hold!'

He took from Binnings's leather-lined hip pockets the matched double-actions which had killed Wheelen and Tyloe. From Binnings's fob pockets came two pearl-handled, gold-plated .41 derringers. When he had these in his own waistband and coat pockets, Gavity stepped back for a survey of the room.

It was hung with Indian blankets, comfortably furnished, partitioned off the warehouse. There was a bed, a cot, a washstand, a tall wardrobe, a big table.

'Go ahead!' Binnings invited him with a sort of forced evenness of tone. 'You have the drop—this time. But you're making a damned fool of yourself, and your time in La Fe is drawing to an end!'

He sat down on the cot with hands locked behind his head and watched Gavity stonily.

Gavity began his search, keeping part of his attention for that rigid line of prisoners. He left the door open for by so doing, he thought, he could hear anyone else coming in from the alley. Every detail of that room he went over and at the end of ten minutes he confessed that he was as empty-handed, as baffled, as he had been in the Stockmen's Hotel. The only explanation he could give was that incriminating evidence might be hidden outside, among those boxes and bales in the warehouse. But he would need a party to search it; need a warrant. And he had small hope of getting that warrant.

'Now, if you're done messing up the place, perhaps you'll admit that you've acted the damned fool,' Binnings said acidly. 'Oh, by the way—what is it you're hunting?'

'You know damn' well what I'm hunting— all of you know what I'm hunting! The loot from the robberies the bunch of you staged! You know that I know that right here in this room is the bigger part of the gang that's wanted for every important robbery and murder done in this neighborhood during the past year or more. You know, Binnings, that I know why you had to kill Wheelen and Tyloe. You know that I know about Huckafee coming to you, to warn you that Wheelen guessed you to be *jefe* of the gang!'

'And—suppose that all this were true, my dear Watchdog?' Binnings inquired lazily. 'Where is your proof? Do you think that La Fe would believe men of the importance of these to be connected with robberies and murders? You'll be laughed out of town—

kicked out of town! That is—if you live . . .
Which I doubt very much indeed . . .'

Gavity scowled at the sudden change in
Binnings's tone. There was a ring oddly
triumphant about it.

'I very much doubt your living—even to
leave this room!'

'*Yo, támbien!* I, also!' a guttural voice said
from the doorway. 'Do—not—move—*gringo!*'

It was a huge Mexican with a Colt in each
hand. His round, fierce, brown face was split
in a tigerish grin.

'Up with those hands! Hup! Hup!' he said
in English. 'But let the pistols fall. It will gain
you—oh, perhaps ten minutes, of life.'

24. 'What's that box?'

Gavity hesitated briefly. His late prisoners
were turning, their hands coming down. They
smiled at him, but not pleasantly. They made
themselves comfortable on bed and chair.

'Well, it looks as if the play were going the
other way,' Prather said cheerfully. 'The
Watchdog of La Fe . . .'

Gavity let his pistols fall, catching each
deftly on a foot and easing it to the floor.
Then he dropped his hands and shrugged,
facing Binnings's cruel, triumphant smile.

'What do we do with him, *capitán?*' the

260

Mexican inquired of Binnings, in Spanish. 'A home for him under the floor, out there, when I have finished with him?'

'I believe so, Gonzales,' Binnings drawled, watching Gavity with cat-like grin. 'That is very good—very good for any blundering fool who thrusts his stupid head into my affairs—and thinks to live afterward.'

'So I was right!' Gavity said, with smile to match Binnings's. 'This is the gang—except for Saltillo and the little rats. All the bigger rats are here . . .'

He looked around from face to face; from Binnings to Prather, Winst, Miles, Idell. Then he turned a little and faced Gonzales solicitously. The Mexican's fierce grin widened.

'But, when you shoot me, Gonzales,' Gavity said courteously, 'I must turn my back, no? To keep unbroken that record of yours. I fear that sight of a man's eyes, meeting yours as you pull the trigger, will be so strange that you will miss!'

He had no real chance. He knew it. But he was measuring the distance, ready for the leap he would make. Gonzales could not miss at this six feet of range. Too, there were the others, all armed. Even Binnings had his pistols again. But if he could take Gonzales's slugs in anything but a spot instantly fatal, he would twist the Mexican about and, when he died, there would be others dead in this room.

261

So he laughed in Gonzales's face while he shifted his feet slightly.

'The Young Hero!' Binnings snarled. 'He dies bravely! But—he dies! And then—'

From the doorway behind Gonzales came a heavy report. The Mexican fell forward. Gavity had one glimpse of him. He was faceless from the slug that had torn through the back of his skull. His hands laxed as he swayed and the pistols dropped. But young Manuel was in too great a hurry to wait for him to topple. He shoved Gonzales with a foot and stood snarling like a cub-wolf with a Colt in each hand, menacing the room.

Gavity squatted and scooped up his own pistols in a lightning grab. He was conscious of movement among the others. Binnings's hands came up as he straightened. There was something about the twist of those hands which brought back to Gavity memory of the man he had seen on the trail, as he rode into La Fe—the man who had fired mockingly into the reward notices on the cottonwood.

But that was a thought which in no way slowed his own action. He began to fire from the squatting position. He fired at Binnings, but before his own bullets tore into Binnings he had winced with the thud of a slug in his thick deltoid muscle.

Prather was down, with Manuel's first shot at the room. Ben Miles fell under Gavity's lead. Who killed Winst and that crooked stage company man, Idell, Gavity never knew. For both were fairly shot to pieces as Gavity and Manuel emptied their Colts across the room. Suddenly, there was heavy silence. Gavity stood and exhaled breath gustily. Manuel grinned vaguely.

'I saw you come into this place and I followed. I had seen how you opened that door. It was I who stumbled upon the alarm and rang the bell in the warehouse. Then came Gonzales, who did not see me. Well, *patron* . . . It is a good thing that I took the money you gave me and bought these beautiful pistols, *no es verdad?*'

'I owe you my life!' Gavity told him, looking around.

'And now, what do we? The robbers are dead. You will be one very tall in La Fe, *patron!*'

'I am more likely to find myself running from La Fe, to avoid being hanged,' Gavity disagreed. 'I know everything of importance about all these men. I know that here, lacking Saltillo, is the council of the leaders. But I have no shadow of proof. There will be enough of the Prather side, in the city council, to cry out that I have murdered tall ones of La Fe. Somewhere is that proof, but I have not found it . . .'

An Indian blanket flapped on the far wall of the room. Gavity whirled with an oath. The blanket moved inward and a door was shown in that wall. The tall, slender Carlotta was framed in the opening. She stepped into the room.

'I can help you, *El Grande*,' she said evenly. 'Help you to get the evidence you need. Because he struck me, I will be glad to put into your hands that which he would have died to keep from your hands. Pull the knob of that washstand, there. Then pull the stand itself and—see the things you have hunted!'

She was set-faced. She looked sideways and down at Binnings and her mouth twisted in a slow smile, cruel, unutterably triumphant. She crossed the room to the washstand.

'I told him that you would kill him,' she said, without turning. 'I was right! It was his beginning and his end.'

She pulled at the edge of the washstand and swung it into the room like a door. There was a large cavity in the wall behind it. She motioned:

'The money taken from the First National Bank. The bars of gold and much of the money taken at Harmony Station; more money from robberies of stores—before you came and made the robbery of a store sheer suicide. Jack Binnings, whose woman I was, *he* was the Pedro Grande whom I described to you. As you know, he did cast me off. He was the planner and the leader. These others, they helped in greater or less degree.'

Gavity stared at the pile of bars and bags in

the cavity.

'Gonzales was chief of the Mexicans,' she went on tonelessly. 'Those made the rank and file of the gang. But there were Americans, too—men who loafed about the saloons here in La Fe. You arrested two of these—the men Hurgan and Lippy.'

Manuel looked from face to face as he reloaded his Colts. Gavity translated swiftly for him and Manuel gasped.

'Now, I direct your particular attention to a box here—a box that has no lock. You will need to break it open, for only Binnings knew the trick of it. In that box is something more valuable to you, even, than—'

Manuel cried out and jumped forward with pistols lifting. Gavity turned and the woman whirled at the stand. A pistol roared from the floor and she dropped as if axe-struck. Binnings, grinning horribly, had raised on an elbow. Now he tried to turn his Colt upon Gavity. Manuel shot him twice, running across the room. Binnings fell flat upon his back again.

Gavity dropped beside Carlotta and lifted her head and shoulders. But she was dead, so he let her gently down. He stood, frowning, to stare at each of the others. Then he shook his head and crossed to Binnings's cache. A large canvas sack, stuffed with bills and gold, had a neat memorandum in it—to B. Miles, so much; to each of the others in the room, so much; to Saltillo, so much. In another sack of coins, that lay upon the pile of small gold bars, was a waybill of the Midwest Company. The penciled words *Harmony Station* would have been a noose for these necks here.

'It's a fortune! A small fortune!' Gavity breathed. 'Apparently, Binnings didn't take a chance; he didn't really divide the loot and let the thickheads of the gang flash too much money around the saloons.'

He stood and looked at Manuel.

'Let's get all this out and cache it in the warehouse. I have to get word to Mayor Zelman. Someone might slip in here while we are gone. Manuelito, you are now a deputy marshal of La Fe. You will watch the alley while I am gone and let none into the warehouse by that back door.'

So they emptied the compartment and hid sacks and bars under boxes in the dark warehouse. Gavity took the small rosewood box—it was no more than six by ten by two inches—under his arm. Manuel grunted to him as they pushed the washstand back into place and once more looked around.

'*Muy bien!*' Gavity said impatiently. 'But be quick. For there is much to do and a small hole like this is nothing.'

He stood while Manuel appropriated a towel from the washstand and bandaged his wound. Then they went through the warehouse and into the sunlit alley.

'You watch here, as I directed,' Gavity told the boy. 'I will take this box to the gunsmith next door to the Gleaming Gem and have him open it. *She* said it was most valuable. It must contain jewels, for it is very light. Here!'

From a pocket he took the deputy marshal badge he had jerked from Huckafee in the Criterion and pinned it upon Manuel's swelling chest. Then he went down the alley to its mouth on Mason Street. Standing there, looking up and down, he found it amazing how the town was going quietly about its affairs, undisturbed by the bloody tragedy, the complete triumph, which had occurred in that shabby 'dobe building behind him. Apparently the thick walls had smothered the reports of pistols.

He turned toward Bowie Street and the Gem Saloon. But he had taken only a step or two when Bryan Ross came around the corner and, with sight of him, stopped short. Then Ross came on, short, thick legs driving hard heels against the planks. He faced Gavity rather like a terrier blocking the path of a Great Dane. When he spoke, the terrier comparison was increased.

'I want to tell you something, Big Gavity!' he snapped. 'After that Little Mexico business with that Mexican girl, I don't care what Zelman thinks of you, or how much he sings your praises. You stay out of my store; away from my house. Don't you dare speak to

267

Betty. Not that she'd speak to you, now, anyway! She feels the same as I do. She—'

'How about Binnings?' Gavity inquired gently. 'Same for him? Is he barred from the store and the house and—Betty?'

'He—he—Binnings is none of your affair!'

But there was the oddest hesitation about the little man. And now Ross seemed to realize that Gavity was pale under his tan, his eyes bloodshot, his shoulders sagging.

'What—what have you been up to, now? You got a bandage on! You—'

'So Binnings is none of my business . . . You always said you had me figured. I wonder if you had Binnings figured, too. You must have had. You're so damn' infallible. You must have guessed that he was the Big Thief of this gang of stage- and bank- and store-robbers and sneaking killers that have been hunted so long. You must have known that—for he was.'

'Was? Was?' Bryan Ross cried. His red face paled. 'You mean he—'

'I mean I just killed him. He's dead. So are Prather and Ben Miles and Idell of the Midwest Company and Winst of the Criterion and a tough Mexican named Gonzales from Little Mexico—and one worth the bunch of them, the woman I went to Little Mexico with. I have recovered a lot of the loot in Binnings's place. Zelman wins his five hundred from you and Hook and Mullins and Prather.'

He shrugged. Now that it was over, he felt

no triumph at all. Instead, he was very tired, almost sick. A thought came: Why not saddle Nubbins this very day and ride out to get Lupe and, with Manuel beside them, head for a place where the reward he would receive could buy a little ranch? She was a pretty child, a nice child; and he had only to crook his finger . . .

It was not much of a life, in prospect, but Betty was gone. He knew that. Even Binnings's death would not change her. She was too much under Bryan Ross's thumb to do anything her father disapproved. He had only to look at the hard, unfriendly red face to know that Ross disliked him as much as ever. And Ross's sudden recovery was in character.

'Well!' he cried. 'If all this is true—about Binnings and the others—I suppose the council will have to congratulate you. But as far as I'm personally concerned—'

There was a queer note to his voice, Gavity thought absently, even under the hostility of it. Relief? Now, why would word of the gang's going relieve Bryan Ross? How could it?'

'What's that box?' Ross demanded. 'Some of the loot?'

Gavity looked down at it without much interest. Then he shrugged and twisted his big hands. After all, the box itself was of no value. He watched the lid buckle—fly back. Then he frowned. There was nothing in the box but a black book. He let the box drop and opened

269

the book. On the flyleaf in a neat, round hand, he read Binnings's name.

' "John Binnings, sometime resident of Binnings, Commonwealth of Virginia," ' he read aloud. ' "His Diary." Well!'

He turned the pages of neat writing—and gasped. Some twisted streak of egotism in Binnings had led him to set down a detailed record of his crimes, extending over a period of ten years. Here were the names of his associates and helpers and those with whom he had dealt. It was not a day-by-day record, but, none the less, a record that would have hanged Binnings twenty times—and stripped the mantle of respectability (Gavity thought) from many men all the way from Montana to the Rio Grande here.

He snarled impatiently at Bryan Ross, who was snapping a question at him and craning his head, trying to see. He riffled the pages until he came to that section of the book dealing with the Rio Grande country. He nodded in satisfaction.

Here was Harmony Station. Here was the name of Prather and beside it Winst's. Ben Miles and Huckafee . . . Carlotta . . . Winn Wheelen and his deputy Tyloe—who were to die . . . The record of their death . . . His own name . . . Zelman and Buchanan . . .

He went back past Harmony Station and stared at the record of Tim Free's loss of a mule herd. And then he stiffened and looked across at Bryan Ross.

'This little book,' he said slowly, 'has more dynamite in it than four barrels could hold! You wouldn't believe that a man could be so damned foolish as to keep a record like this!'

It seemed that Binnings had always kept a string on those who dealt with him. Tim Free would never take personal revenge on the thieves who had killed his herders and taken his mules. There was the name of the man who had bought the mules—and the names of the men to whom *he* had sold them.

'Ross,' he almost whispered, looking around, 'if Tim Free knew that you had bought his mules, knowing that they were stolen—you can't deny it, because you altered the brands a dozen different ways and Binnings had entered every change—I think he would just about cut your heart out and eat it, raw!'

'God!' Ross gasped. 'Did he—did he put *that* down?'

Gavity watched him wilt; watched the pompousness go out of him like air from a pricked balloon. His choleric little eyes were haggard; his clothes seemed to bag upon a suddenly shrunken body. He looked very old and pitiful.

25. 'Yes, sir! It's true love'

Ross looked miserably up at Gavity—pleadingly, yet with something like surprise, too; as if it were a stranger he saw before him.

'I've gone through hell for that crooked money! It was the only shady deal I ever made, in all my life. I *had* to have it, to keep from losing the Slash R and making a pauper out of Betty. If it hadn't been for that, I'd have had to go back to punching cows myself. I would have lost the outfit if I hadn't done what I did do—and I reckon I'd do it again, if the same thing was true. I dealt with Binnings after his gang had stolen the mules. I blotted the brands and I sold 'em and I paid on the mortgage. I always aimed to pay back Tim Free. But I was scared he'd backtrack the money and come at me.'

He made a futile, helpless little gesture of thick shoulders. He was somehow very childish.

'Now, Tim Free'll kill me, because he hates a thief worse than he hates anything in the world and he'll know that I'm a thief. Everything's shot, Gavity. Everything. I was going to run for alderman, the regular term. Then I was going to be mayor before I stopped; maybe a member of the legislature and a congressman and senator. I'm getting rich here; going to be richer. I had it planned how I'd be a big man, not just in La Fe, but all over Texas. Now—'

Gavity grinned at him twistedly and shook his head. He was still very tired.

'I—I never gave you credit for having brains,' Ross went stammering on. 'I—I reckon I'm just a damn' hypocrite, Gavity. You're so big you make me feel so little . . . Maybe that was the start of my not liking you. But I did want Betty to climb with me. Gavity—for Betty, would you—I know I ought to get it in the neck. But if you'll not tell about this—If there's any way—Betty—'

'Queer! Damn' queer!' Gavity said drawlingly. 'There was a time when, if I'd had in my hand what I'm holding. I'd have said: I want to marry Betty. Either you'll give the bride away when I say the word, or there'll be lead singing—Tim Free's lead singing around your ears. It would have been one of those *bullets or bells* affairs; bullets or wedding bells. Now—'

His face was stonily set; he looked straight ahead. His hands jerked and there was the sound of tearing paper. He looked down and his eyes widened.

'I'll be damned! That's funny—mightily funny! The book seems to be torn. There are two–three pages gone. Seems to be the ones about mules, too . . . Oh, well'—he handed the sheets to Bryan Ross, forcing them into the fat, shaking hand—'I think there's enough left to settle just a lot of things. I take it we'll have a small emigration when the word's made public that we are holding the names of everybody who dealt with Binnings, everybody who worked with him.'

'And—and Betty?' Bryan Ross asked hesitantly. 'She—'

'Oh, don't think about *that!*' Gavity cried, smiling. 'I explained things to her; about pride and not marrying into any family at the point of a six-shooter. She understands. I'll not be here longer than's necessary to clean up the odds and ends. As soon as I can hand over the badge to Zelman, I'll be emigrating myself. Think I'll buy a little cow outfit with my rewards and stay to hell out of towns, hereafter.'

'But—'

'There's no "but" to it!' Gavity stopped him airily. 'You go ahead, Ross. You've had your lesson. You run for alderman and make mayor and legislator and even senator! Betty'll climb with you. Marry her to some nice butcher or grocer who's going to make money. You'll all be happy, and there won't be any steer-horns in that coat-of-arms you're going to have. And don't bother about Tim Free. Get that money back to him some day; I'll give him a song and dance about Binnings stealing the mules—and nothing more than that.'

He whirled and went past the staring little

man. Drifting men on the sidewalks stared at him, but he pushed on by, and to those who spoke he only grunted reply. He went into the Gleaming Gem and asked the bar-tender for Zelman.

'Think he went over to the Midwest,' the man told him, staring. 'But—What happened to you, Marshal? You get shot?'

'Mosquito,' Gavity said briefly. 'Certainly do get big, down here in the *bosque*. I'll find Zelman—'

He recrossed Bowie and went down Mason again. Bryan Ross had disappeared. At the mouth of the alley Gavity looked down toward the door of the warehouse. He could not see Manuel.

'Probably inside, watching from there,' he thought. 'A good kid; a damn' good kid! I reckon that idea was a good idea; take Lupe and Manuel and head out . . .'

Then he shook his head.

'No, it's not! It's no good, at all. She's too nice a child to treat that way. If I ride on out, she'll forget she thought she liked me. She'll marry somebody here and they'll farm and raise kids and be happy. I'll saddle Nubbins and we'll hit for California, lone-wolfing it . . .'

He went into the office of the stage company and looked around. A clerk came from the back and, with sight of the haggard Gavity, swallowed.

'Good—Lord!' he began. 'You—you ain't

been shot at again, Marshal? Why—'

'Where's Zelman?' Gavity asked him. 'They said at the Gem he'd come over here.'

'He was here—about a shipment of liquor. But he's gone to the store now. They're all short of whisky. I think he'll stop to see Winst, at the Criterion, about borrowing some from the Gem till his load gets here. But—You never said how you got that hurt—'

'That's right, I didn't,' Gavity agreed. 'Remind me to tell you about it, some time. Criterion . . . Thanks!'

As he went down Midwest Street toward Fay, he found himself hurrying. He wanted to find Zelman and turn over to the shrewd, fat little man everything he had, including this torn book under his arm. He wondered how long it would take to investigate the several angles of the gang's activity; to settle the details. He was very anxious to get Nubbins and be gone.

At the corner of Midwest and Fay he stood looking across at the Criterion. But he looked grimly—he could not help it—at the front of the Jones & Ross store. He wondered if he would see Betty before he left La Fe. He thought that one glance—preferably when she did not know that he stared—would be all he wanted.

'All I can stand!' he told himself sardonically.

He stepped into the street and walked

toward the Criterion's door, once he was sure that no slim, chintz-clad figure stood before the Ross store.

'*Patron! Patron!*' Manuel called, from somewhere on his right, near the Zelman store. 'Saltillo! He came by the warehouse! I am sure that he had been in the front room—by that door which the woman used; that he came out by that door. For he almost ran past me, on Mason Street! He—'

Gavity was almost at the other sidewalk. He stood frowning, facing Manuel on the opposite side of the street. And Manuel yelled sudden shrill warning. Gavity turned, obeying the pointing finger. Saltillo fired from the Criterion's door and came tigerishly out, a pistol in each hand, as Gavity staggered under the impact of the bullet that struck him in the breast.

Gavity let the book fall and automatically drew both Colts from the Hardin vest. He swayed; that terrific shock had shaken him. He had never found it so hard to lift the Colts. And Saltillo was coming at that springy step across the sidewalk, teeth glinting under small mustache, very like a cat stalking a paralyzed bird. His pistol was lifting. He seemed unworried by the wavering Colts in Gavity's hands.

'I *said* that I would see you again!' he said evenly. 'I do see you again—and I will be the last thing you see in life!'

Gavity let the hammer of his left-hand gun drop. Saltillo flinched with the bellow of it, even though the slug went harmlessly past him. Then Gavity stumbled forward. Saltillo fired, and there was a searing pain in Gavity's side. But he rammed the muzzle of the right-hand Colt all but into the embroidered jacket and fired. Then he fell . . .

He fired again as he touched the sidewalk with limp left hand, but that shot was automatic, loosed at nothing. The bullet tore into the planks of the sidewalk. He twisted slightly and looked up with glazed eyes.

Saltillo had dropped his pistols. Both hands were clasped over his belly. As Gavity braced himself for an instant, Saltillo's knees gave way and he sat tailor-fashion on the sidewalk, within a yard of Gavity.

'You—you killed me!' Saltillo gasped. 'But—by the Heads of the Disciples! I have killed you, too! I—I will see you—in Hell, *gringo!*'

Gavity fell upon his face. It was queer, a part of his brain told him, but along the sidewalk now was rushing a thick, black wave, like a dirty flood filling a dry arroyo. Already it had blotted out Fay Brothers and the Criterion. He tried to get up and climb the arroyo wall to escape it. But he could not move; the wave was within a foot of him and his muscles refused to obey him. He was going to drown . . .

But through that wave a voice came. Hands grasped his shoulder—strong, light hands. He was being dragged up and up. He could see nothing, but he felt an arm slipped under his shoulder, holding him. He heard a thin, fierce voice somewhere above him crying out:

'Fools! You fools! Don't stand there gaping, like so many idiots! Get a doctor!'

Then the wave engulfed him again and it was ages—pain-filled ages—later, that he opened his eyes a slit with the taste of whisky in his mouth. His head lay on something soft. There was a murmuring of voices around him. One was vaguely familiar, but he could not place it:

'All right? Of course he'll be all right! You couldn't kill him with a poll-axe! I have had forty years' experience with these Tarrant County Gavitys. They die in bed at the age of two hundred, simply and only because they're tired of living! If they weren't tired, they wouldn't die; they'd just go back to Georgia like the old gray mules. Odd, that my first case in La Fe should be a baby I saw into the world in Tarrant! Fine people, the Gavitys. But bullheads, all. This one chucked over a hundred thousand dollars' worth of ranch, because he fell out with his family!'

'A fine boy! I always said That was Bryan Ross, but interrupted instantly by Gavity's pillow:

'Daddy! You never said any such thing! You

never did in all your life say such a thing!'

'Well, I do now!' Ross snapped. 'What more do you want? How about moving him, Doctor? Out to my house?'

'Too much Daddy! Too little Betty!' Gavity mumbled, as he had said once before.

'Arthur!' a voice breathed, at his very ear. 'You can hear! And you're all right! You're going to be all right—for me? You're going to the house—'

'Arthur?' the doctor cried. 'Arthur? He *must* love her! He must—else Big Gavity would never let her call him that. It was a fighting word. Yes, sir! It's true love . . . Come along, Ross. Let's see about a wagon to carry him—a big wagon.'

'Of course it's true love—Arthur!' Betty whispered in Gavity's ear. 'It never was anything else, except—Well, jealousy, maybe. And that's supposed to be a part of love.'

Gavity thought hazily of Binnings; of that rosebud.

'Then I suppose that's what I've got, too,' he muttered. 'True love—so bad a case I'll probably never get over it. Oh, well! I don't—really care!'